I0599455

Henry Wilkinson Williams

The Life of the Rev. Joseph Wood

With Extracts from his Diary

Henry Wilkinson Williams

The Life of the Rev. Joseph Wood
With Extracts from his Diary

ISBN/EAN: 9783744665209

Printed in Europe, USA, Canada, Australia, Japan

Cover: Foto ©Raphael Reischuk / pixelio.de

More available books at **www.hansebooks.com**

LIFE OF THE

REV. JOSEPH WOOD,

BY THE

REV. H. W. WILLIAMS.

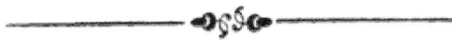

Yours affectionately

THE LIFE

OF THE

REV. JOSEPH WOOD,

WITH

EXTRACTS FROM HIS DIARY.

BY THE

REV. HENRY W. WILLIAMS,

AUTHOR OF "AN EXPOSITION OF ST. PAUL'S EPISTLE TO THE ROMANS," ETC.

LONDON:

WESLEYAN CONFERENCE OFFICE,
2, CASTLE-ST., CITY-ROAD;
SOLD AT 66, PATERNOSTER-ROW.

1871.

PRINTED BY HAYMAN BROTHERS AND LILLY,

19, CROSS ST., HATTON GARDEN, E.C.

PREFACE.

—oo:o:oo—

FROM the time of the decease of my beloved
friend, the Rev. Joseph Wood, I felt, in common
with many others, that it was a duty which *some one*
owed to the Church of God, to place on permanent
record the leading facts of his honourable and useful
career. So strong was this impression, that I was
about to write to his only surviving son, to express
my hope that a Memoir of his father was in course of
preparation, when I received from him and his
esteemed mother a request that I would undertake it,
accompanied with the offer to place in my hands his
interesting Diary. Such a request I could not but
regard as a call from Divine Providence to attempt a
work which, by exhibiting the riches of the Saviour's
grace, and presenting a beautiful example of sustained and untiring zeal, might prove a blessing to
multitudes.

When Mr. Wood was entirely laid aside from his
beloved work of preaching Christ, and when a
tremulous movement of his right hand had made
writing difficult, he commenced gathering together
the leading incidents of his course, thinking, probably,
that they would interest his family and some of his
friends. In these papers he has given extracts from
his early Diary, connecting them by means of expla-
natory statements. These papers, however, close

with his ministry in the Newport (Monmouthshire) Circuit, the first to which he was appointed. The opening statement will, I doubt not, interest many :—

"My great and glorious Master having seen good to bid me stand aside for the present, I propose, by the aid of the Holy One, to gather a few early recollections, that I might set them up as remembrancers of the amazing mercy, and infinite condescension, and long forbearance, of my Heavenly Father towards the most unworthy of all His children. Having had, since the failure in my health, a paralytic shake in my right hand and arm, and an inability to apply my mind closely to any subject long together without injury, it might seem to be an unpropitious season for commencing such a work : but I should, perhaps, gain nothing by delay, while I might lose all. I will, therefore, endeavour to proceed as far as the Lord shall enable me ; and I trust, by His grace, to seek in this, as in every other thing, the glory and praise of His excellent Name."

Mr. Wood's labours in the Kingswood Circuit, in Cornwall, in Exeter, in the Bristol South Circuit, during his first appointment to it, and in Birmingham West, are sketched in a condensed Diary, in which he was accustomed to write about once a month, selecting any incidents from his daily memoranda which he thought it desirable to preserve. These daily memoranda he appears afterwards to have destroyed. Between September 2nd, 1847, and November 17th, 1851, only one entry occurs in this Book, that entry containing a brief notice of his ministry in the Bristol North Circuit between the Conference of 1847 and that of 1850. From the commencement of 1852 until his right hand could no longer trace his thoughts, we have the leading events of each day, recorded by himself in two thick volumes, with occasional notices of the exercises of his own mind, and the spiritual consolation and support with which he was favoured.

The materials for a biography of this devoted Minister are thus most ample and authentic; and I trust that I may have been enabled to trace his course so as to interest and edify the thoughtful reader. My own acquaintance with several of the spheres of labour which Mr. Wood occupied has enabled me to speak of them with a degree of confidence which I could not otherwise have felt. I deem it a privilege and honour to have been called, in the order of Divine Providence, to endeavour to perpetuate the memory of one whom I so profoundly esteemed, and in doing so to honour HIM who is the Head and Lord of the universal Church, and from Whom all the gifts and graces of His servants are derived.

H. W. W.

EXETER,
December 9th, 1870.

CONTENTS.

LIFE OF THE

REV. JOSEPH WOOD.

THE LIFE

OF THE

REV. JOSEPH WOOD.

CHAPTER I.

INTRODUCTORY THOUGHTS AND RECOLLECTIONS.

" AND they glorified GOD in me." In the spirit of this declaration of the Apostle Paul, we propose to trace the history of one of the most devoted and successful Ministers whom the Lord Jesus ever "gave" to His Church.

The name of JOSEPH WOOD is affectionately cherished by multitudes in the several Circuits in which he laboured, and the influence of his spirit and example still remains. To many who will read these pages he was personally known; and they will readily remember his form and his whole bearing and manner. But if, through the blessing of God, this work should live, and should afford encouragement and stimulus to young Ministers in future years, many whom it will reach will be dependent upon it for a vivid conception of him. For the sake of such

B

persons it may not be improper for me to recall, in the very opening of the work, the image of my beloved friend, as it rises to my own mind.

From my first introduction to Mr. Wood, until my last interview with him when his day of active service to the Church had closed, I was deeply impressed with the conviction that he was *a man of God.* There was a hallowed influence connected with his whole deportment and conversation, which could only result from the rich anointing of the Spirit of Christ constantly resting upon him. The simplicity and earnestness of his personal piety,—the pure benevolence which made him anxious for the happiness of all,—the holy zeal for the honour of his Master which caused him ever to look reprovingly on sin,—and his constant readiness to put forth efforts to lead those around him to Christ,—powerfully affected me. Among the varied recollections of a somewhat lengthened ministry, few things stand forth more prominently to my mind than my happy intercourse with Mr. Wood in some of the earlier years of that ministry, and the advantage which I derived from observing his spirit and character. I can never think of him without a grateful acknowledgment of the abundant grace of our Saviour Christ vouchsafed to His servant, or without a vivid impression of the commingling dignity, and loveliness, and power, which sustained consecration to God imparts to the human mind. In Mr. Wood, more, perhaps, than in any other man whom I have ever known,—and I love to recall the Christian excellencies of many of my friends and fellow-labourers who have passed to their heavenly rest,— the beautiful lines of Cowper were exemplified,

" When one that holds communion with the skies,
    Has filled his urn where these pure waters rise,
    And once more mingles with us meaner things,
    'Tis even as if an angel shook his wings:
    Immortal fragrance fills the circle wide,
    That tells us whence his treasures are supplied."

It is probable, that the impression now referred to would be that produced on every one possessed of spiritual affections and sympathies, who was brought into personal intercourse with Mr. Wood; while the first feeling of all who listened to his public ministrations would be, that he lived habitually under a profound conviction of the realities of which he spoke, and that his whole soul was intent on the salvation of those whom he addressed. Everything else, indeed, was cast into the shade by the transcendent importance of the truths which he had to announce, and the greatness of the interests which he had to secure. But it was impossible to converse long with Mr. Wood without perceiving that he was also a man of *cultivated intellect.* The following narrative will show the passionate desire which he cherished in youth for the acquisition of knowledge, and the earnestness with which he applied himself to classical and mathematical studies. He possessed, too, very considerable powers of thought. His mind was vigorous and active; and his judgment eminently sound. Had he indulged his taste for literary and scientific pursuits, he would probably have excelled in some departments of general knowledge; but, after his entrance upon the ministry, he kept this taste in check, that he might give himself up entirely to the great work to which the Lord Jesus had called him. The love of the souls of men became with him an absorbing passion, only less strong than his love to the Saviour. To that sacred passion he surrendered his whole being; and he cared not what labours he undertook, or into what dangers he rushed, if he could but lead men to the Lord Jesus.

It is not intended, however, in these introductory remarks, to delineate the character of Mr. Wood, but only to indicate what manner of man he was, in order to awaken the interest of those who did not personally know him in the narrative about to be given. And here, perhaps, some reference ought to be made to his form and general appearance. He was of the middle height, and well-proportioned. Being of the sanguineous temperament, he possessed and manifested a robust energy, regulated, however, and softened, by his deep religious feeling and high-toned benevolence. His countenance expressed the decision and earnestness of his character, while it was often lighted up with benignity, and reflected the purity and love that dwelt within him. He looked like a man who had a great work to do for Christ, and who felt that no opportunity of accomplishing it must be lost. But this expression of earnestness in his Master's work was blended with the kindliness of friendship and sympathy; and you felt that you could always turn to him with confidence for counsel and help.

The record of the earthly career of such a man may, under the blessing of God, be useful to many. Happily, the materials for such a record are not scanty; and they disclose to us, in particular, the workings of that inner life, derived from the Spirit of Christ, the outward development of which was so striking and so lovely. To *young Ministers* this

Memoir is more especially commended. It illustrates the blessedness of entire consecration to God,—the importance of a simple purpose to do Christ's work, and accomplish Christ's will, in every effort in the Church,—and the power of fervent, believing prayer. The ministry of Joseph Wood was instrumental in bringing hundreds—I might even say thousands—of men to a saving knowledge of the Lord Jesus. And the great secret of his success was his holy walk with God, and the singleness of aim which marked all his public labours, and all his pastoral intercourse with his people. He stands before us as a beautiful example of the fulfilment of the Saviour's promise, "IF ANY MAN SERVE ME, HIM WILL MY FATHER HONOUR."

CHAPTER II.

—◦○○◦—

JOSEPH WOOD was the eldest son of Mr. Charles Wood, and was born on February 23rd, 1797. His father was a man of considerable mental culture, and kept a school at Banwell, a village in Somersetshire, about sixteen miles from Bristol. He was, also, an eminently pious man, and for many years laboured zealously and successfully as a Local Preacher in the Wesleyan-Methodist Communion. Long after he had passed to his heavenly rest, he was spoken of in terms of strong affection and high esteem, by those who had known him, and to whom he had often ministered the Word of Life. His son records with deep interest two remarks made to him, as he pursued his own career of service to Christ, illustrative of the character of his father. A gentleman once said to him, "It always did me good to see your father come into my house: there was something so good and holy about him that it was felt by all." Another person observed, "I never met your father to speak with him on any subject, but before we parted he said something to me on spiritual matters, generally inquiring for my soul's prosperity." His mother was equally devoted and spiritual; and their anxious desire was, that all their children should be led to a personal closure with Christ, and stand as witnesses for Him.

When Joseph was in his ninth year, his excellent father was removed by death. In returning from the important village of Wrington, on the evening of one Lord's day, after preaching to a crowded congregation, Mr. Charles Wood took a severe cold, which was followed by inflammation of the lungs, and within a fortnight he entered into rest. His dying experience illustrated the blessedness of the religion which he had long enjoyed, and evinced the unfailing faithfulness of the Lord Jesus. It was a death of holy triumph; and his emphatic declaration, "I am going to God," showed the fulness of heavenly hope that sustained his soul. His son records two affecting incidents, as the closing scene drew near. Observing his wife weeping at his bed-side, he endeavoured to comfort her by saying, "I have always believed in the doctrine of the ministry of angels; and, if it shall so please God, I will be a ministering spirit to you and the children." The other fact shows how strong was his solicitude for the salvation of his neighbours. There were several persons around him whom he had often endeavoured to benefit; and he had them called into his room, and, bolstered up in bed, he gave them his last invitation and warning. He then fell back exhausted; and soon afterwards departed to be with Christ, on December 27th, 1805, having just completed his forty-eighth year.

Mrs. Wood was left a widow, moderately provided for, with five children,—Joseph, the eldest, being nearly nine years of age, and the youngest being a little infant. But He in whom "the father-

less findeth mercy," and who cares for the widow
in her solitude, watched over that family for good.
The pious mother was accustomed to say, "If the
Lord should ask me, as He did Solomon, 'What
shall I give thee?' I would say, 'The conversion of
all my children.'" This desire was granted. When
her honoured son had finished his career of public
service, and in languor and feebleness retraced the
scenes of his childhood, he gratefully records, "We
all in youth began to serve God; all became, early
in life, members of the Wesleyan Church; and I
believe that we are all, at this day, walking in the
fear and love of God."

In reviewing the lives of eminent Christians, it is
not often that we have the means of tracing the
gracious operations of the Holy Spirit upon their
minds during the years of childhood. In the case of
Joseph Wood, we *are* enabled to do this; and his
history may well serve as a stimulus and an encouragement to parents to seek *the early conversion of
their children*,—to lead them onward, as soon as they
are capable of a thoughtful and believing appro-
priation of the Redeemer's sacrifice, to lay hold on
Him, that they may rejoice in the sweet consciousness of the favour and love of God. "As early as I
can remember," Mr. Wood says, "I was visited with
convictions of sin; and these greatly increased about
the time of my father's removal. In my feelings of
penitential distress, I have looked at the lambs in
their frisky gambols, and wept that, while they were
innocent and happy, I was guilty and under the
displeasure of the Almighty. In corners unseen,
and unheard by human ears, I used to pour out my
supplications to God, and He heard me. He set me

free from condemnation, and gave me to rejoice in my redeeming Lord. Unknown to any one, I soon began to write my experience in a little book, and went on with a glad heart."

The "little book" here referred to was soon afterwards torn up; but his mother who, through a singular circumstance, met with some of the leaves, and thus became acquainted with the inner workings of her boy's heart, encouraged him to cleave to the Saviour, and to resume his writing. He did so, and minutely recorded several of his temptations, together with the fluctuations of his religious feelings. Some of the entries, preserved by himself in later life, show how rich and deep a joy often filled his heart when he was a child, and with what jealousy he watched over his feelings, and words, and actions. We insert a few, written when he was in his twelfth year :—" August 14th, 1808. I have had no particular besetment this week. Sometimes the Lord has shone upon my soul, so that I have been all in a rapture, and when I have been alone, I could spend most of the day in praising the Lord.—August 21st. I have been living to God this week. My chief delight has been in praying to Him and praising His name.— August 28th. I have been beset by many vain thoughts and words this week ; but by the grace of God I have withstood them.—September 4th. At times my thoughts have not been for the glory of God ; but, on recollecting myself I have turned my thoughts to Him.— September 11th. Sometimes this week I have been happy in the Lord : at others my mind has been drawn away.—September 18th. I have been very happy in God this week. Praise the Lord.—September 25th. I have been tempted to vain thoughts this week, so that my mind has been drawn away: but by the grace of God, I have been delivered.—October 24th. The Lord has been abundantly present with me this week, although I have had temptations from Satan.— November 7th. I sin before I am aware, and I pray unto the Lord to give me a quick, discerning eye.— December 26th. I strive to keep 'a conscience void of offence,' by thinking in the day time of something good that I have heard or read.—December 30th. This day, glory be unto the Lord, He hath given me power over sin. I can say, at the conclusion of this day, that I have not knowingly sinned against the Lord.—December 31st. Glory be unto the Lord, He hath given me power this day also, to overcome sin : and when the tempter cometh, he goeth out empty.— January 1st, 1809. Glory be unto the Lord. I have this day been filled with His fulness, and this my earthen vessel with heavenly treasure.—January 2nd. This day my cup has run over with God's love, so that I have been enabled to say, 'My soul doth magnify the Lord, and my spirit doth rejoice in God my Saviour.'—January 3rd. Glory be unto the Lord : He hath kept me this day so that I can say, 'Walking in all His ways, I find my heaven on earth begun.' "

This season of holy comfort and abounding joy was followed by a period of harassing conflict. It is impossible to read the simple record of his inward struggles without a vivid impression of the great fact which the Scriptures disclose,—that an unseen spiritual agency is often permitted to assail our Christian principles, though that agency is held under restraint by our adorable Lord. Thoughts which were most distressing to this pious youth, from which, indeed, he recoiled with horror, were again and again suggested to his mind: but the grace of Christ upheld him in the fiery trial, and enabled him to conquer. In after-life he was accustomed to regard this period of his religious history as one of preparation for the work to which he was called as a Christian Pastor.

The tenderness of conscience by which Joseph was happily distinguished made him bitterly regret any deviation, in word or feeling, from the Divine law. Such deviations he records, and sorrowfully acknowledges the loss of conscious peace with God which followed them. Speaking of the close of the year 1810, and the beginning of 1811, when he was about fourteen years of age, he says, "My experience about this time was very various. When not at school, I was chiefly engaged on my uncle's farm, and being frequently amongst persons who were foolish, worldly, and wicked, I often suffered much loss. Still the fear of God was so deeply rooted in my heart, that every deviation from the right way was followed by sorrow, shame, and remorse. While in this unsatisfactory state, I was invited by a kind friend to become a member of the Methodist Society. My dear mother often talked to me on religious subjects; but I had never told her the conflicts of my spirit. But the kind friend referred to addressed me in winning words of love and power; and I resolved, by God's help, to comply, which I did on the Sunday following. Mrs. Horner, the wife of the Rev. W. Horner, the Superintendent of the Banwell Circuit, met a class after the preaching on Sundays. With them I wished to unite. But I had not told any one of my intention; and, not wishing the retiring congregation to see me remain for the first time, I with-

drew with them. Now, however, I found it more
difficult than I had anticipated to return to the chapel.
Of this the enemy did not fail to take advantage,
and I was almost induced to go away. But the Lord
had compassion on me: His Spirit strove with me
mightily, and constrained me to re-enter the house
of prayer, and seek the benefit of Christian fellowship. Glory and praise to my God for bringing me
to this decision! At the renewal of the quarterly
tokens of membership, Mr. Horner gave me my first
Society-ticket, dated March, 1811, containing Prov.
i. 23, which I am glad to have preserved. Previous
to this, I had been living without the enjoyment of
peace with God: but the week I became decided to
confess Christ in the world, my forfeited peace was
restored; the love of God was again shed abroad
in my heart, and I rejoiced greatly in the Lord my
Redeemer. O that from this time I had been
faithful!"

In the beginning of the last extract, Mr. Wood
alludes to his early education. After the decease of
his father, he had been adopted by an uncle, Mr.
Edward Wood, a highly respectable farmer in Banwell, and a truly pious man,—one who, like his own
father, laboured cheerfully and actively as a Local
Preacher. He was sent by his uncle, in the first
instance, to the village-school: but his thirst for
knowledge made him long for some higher teaching.
His own record on this subject is deeply interesting.
"I found little," he says, "in the village-school to
satisfy my mental cravings. My desire for information and improvement was intense. I had always a
book with me, and had acquired such a habit of
reading while walking, that neither was the reading

nor the walking much interfered with by the other. To read and study was my rest and refreshment after exertion; and I never desired or needed any other amusement. My uncle acceded to my particular request to be permitted to walk to Axbridge, four miles from Banwell, two evenings in the week, to obtain instruction from a gentleman who was considered a clever tutor, with whom I stayed from six to about eight o'clock each time. This was of great advantage to me while it continued; but before I had been with him half a year, my instructer died, and I had again to go in quest of some one who could and would guide my pursuit of knowledge. I had heard of able men in Bristol; but my means did not allow me to become a pupil in one of their establishments. By the good providence of God I was led to consult that profound scholar and eminently pious man, Mr. Thomas Exley, M.A., and to choose him as my teacher."

It was on November 5th, 1813, that Joseph Wood, not quite seventeen years of age, came to Bristol, to avail himself of the tuition of Mr. Exley. He appears to have enjoyed this great advantage for about a year, and then to have returned to Banwell, to pursue his studies alone, but with untiring assiduity and vigour. His mode of life while in Bristol is thus recorded by himself:—"I rise in the morning about five o'clock, and go to bed about ten at night. My order of proceeding is this. Before I begin my other studies, I take the word of God, and, after reading a chapter, I pray to God to bless my endeavours. I do the same after dinner. On Tuesday, Thursday, and Saturday mornings, when I return from taking my lessons at Mr. Exley's, I seldom apply myself to that which has to be committed to memory. For

this I generally find the morning most favourable.
I have also found it of advantage in the evening to
relieve the mind of more severe studies by the lighter
reading of history, etc.; and I read Mr. Wesley's
History of England with this view." On the 23rd of
February, 1814, when he completed his seventeenth
year, we find him recording that he had just finished
spherical geometry, and that, on expressing his wish
to commence another branch of study, his accomplished tutor told him that he thought he had too
much to do already. "I, however, persevered," he
adds, "with more eagerness for learning than care
for my health."

The public and social means of grace which
Joseph Wood enjoyed in the city of Bristol, where
Methodism was fully developed, and where not only
the Ministers, but many of the leading office-bearers,
were men of eminent piety and large experience in
Divine things, were very profitable to him : but the
richest communications of grace appear to have been
realised by him in secret fellowship with God.
Under the date of December 13th, 1813, he makes
the following entry in his Diary :—" For some little
time past I have been greatly stirred up to seek
purity of heart. I have desired it, and have found
that desires alone will never bring the blessing.
Sometimes, indeed, I have been much in earnest, but
have not persevered. A short time since I was
quickened under a sermon which I heard in Ebenezer
Chapel, King Street. On returning to my lodgings,
I immediately went to my room, without waiting to
get a light; but the God of light and grace manifested Himself as my portion. I was enabled to
exercise faith in His word, and to say, ' O Lord, I come

to Thee for a fulfilment of Thy promises! I am vile and sinful, unworthy of the least of Thy favours; but Thou, of Thy free grace, hast promised, and declared Thyself willing to perform all Thy faithful word. Why, then, do I not receive? I believe and know that Thou hast pardoned all my past sins, and I believe that Thou art able and willing to keep me from sin. Lord, I believe Thy every word. I believe the blessing into my soul.' I then felt such an invigoration of my faith, and such an outpouring of the love of God, as I never did before. The enemy is active with his temptations; but by the grace of God I am enabled to resist and overcome."

In the year 1814 the Conference was held in Bristol, and Joseph Wood was present at some of the public religious services connected with it. These were attended with great spiritual blessing to him; but he speaks with peculiar gratitude of one occasion of secret prayer, when God imparted to him the richest communications of peace, and love, and strength. "The best season," he says, "I have lately had was on Tuesday evening, August 16th, while engaged with God in fervent prayer for a clean heart. The fire of Divine love glowed in my soul, and the evils of my nature fled before the brightness of His appearing."

The next entry in his early Diary which he has preserved, shows how this gracious visitation from on high was followed by a season of conflict; but it illustrates also the establishment in grace which this youthful Christian had now attained. It is dated October 30th, 1814:—"I lament that I do not enjoy that measure of Divine love overflowing my soul that I did in the latter part of August last. For a few

weeks I enjoyed the presence of God almost continually: but it was powerfully suggested to my
mind that I had not attained that state of grace
which I thought I had. My mind was assailed by
wandering thoughts, and I concluded that I should
have higher enjoyments if I possessed the blessing of
entire holiness, and that I should repel with greater
decision and power every evil thing that Satan presented to my mind. Instead of holding fast the
beginning of my confidence, and earnestly pursuing
after the things before, I lost much through the want
of spiritual discernment and through unbelief. Still
I have not felt so much of the evil nature, nor have
trivial things had power to draw away my mind,
since the gracious manifestation of God's love vouchsafed to me on Tuesday, the 16th of August last. I
also still endeavour to grow in grace. I see and
feel the necessity of being entirely the Lord's; and
I hunger and thirst after holiness."

After his return to Banwell, in the autumn of 1814,
Mr. Wood, as we shall henceforth call him, assisted
his uncle, and in the evenings pursued his studies
with diligence and earnestness. " To avoid desultory
efforts," he writes, " I arrange for every evening to
have its proper work. If any time remains, after
attending to the assigned work of the evening, I
take some book that I may have in reading, and
generally continue until midnight. I also divide the
day into parts, allowing one part for meditating on
the Scriptures, another on Science, etc., whenever
my duties will allow me freely to exercise my
thoughts." A few weeks after this entry was made,
we find him prolonging these midnight studies. He
states that he had often found it to be advantageous

to make extracts from the works which he was
reading, or even abridgments of them; and that in
this employment he sat up until one o'clock in the
morning, and sometimes until after two. All this
shows the intense desire of knowledge which he
cherished, and the perseverance with which he
applied himself to its acquisition; but the youthful
student should be affectionately warned against midnight studies, as tending gradually to undermine the
health, to detract from the freshness and vigour of
the intellect, and to shorten the period of active
service in the Church or in the world.

The religious experience of Mr. Wood, at this time,
was marked by that lively apprehension of spiritual
realities, that intimate communion with God, and that
intense longing after entire holiness, which we have
already observed. One paper which he preserved
records his solemn covenant-engagement with God to
be His in time and in eternity. The circumstances
under which it was written were peculiarly solemn;
and as he reviewed his life when his public labours
were over, he recalls these circumstances, and adds
the reflection which a thoughtful and earnest Christian, remembering the defects of his service to God,
would naturally make. "I have found a document,"
he writes, "that fills one side of a folio sheet of paper,
dated January 15th, 1815. It was written by me, and
signed and sealed by my hand, and is an extract from
the covenant-service, in which I most solemnly devote
all I have and all I am to the service and glory of
the Triune Jehovah, Father, Son, and Holy Ghost, to
do and to suffer all His will in time and eternity. It
was a solemn and impressive occasion. My mother
and the family had, as usual, retired to rest, leaving

me to my studies. Here in the still night, and alone
with God, in deep humiliation of soul, I was enabled,
by the power of the Holy Spirit, to lay hold of Christ
as my only, all-sufficient, and everlasting Saviour,
and to claim the Almighty as my reconciled Father
and covenant-Friend; while the Holy One, in grace
and love Divine, sealed God's acceptance of me and
my offering upon my heart. I praise the Lord that,
through His abounding grace and mercy, I have
never ceased to rejoice that I entered into this
covenant. But, alas, how imperfectly I have kept
it! Had I been faithful in the covenant, and in its
many occasions of renewal, my 'peace would have
flowed like a river.' But this I am compelled to
leave to my covenant High-Priest, 'whose blood for
me did once atone,' and who 'still loves and keeps
His own.'"

CHAPTER III.

FIRST LABOURS AS A LOCAL PREACHER.—ENGAGEMENT AS

A SCHOOLMASTER AT BANWELL.

1815—1818.

WE have now to contemplate Mr. Wood entering upon a course of public service to Christ. The intensity of his religious convictions, the warmth of his spiritual affections, and his deep solicitude for the salvation of his fellow-men, marked him out as one whom the Head of the Church was preparing for extensive usefulness; while his profound interest in the truth of Christ, the habits of study which he had formed, and the readiness of utterance with which he was endowed, seemed to point to the public declaration of the Gospel as the sphere in which he should labour. When he was in his nineteenth year, he had a distinct conviction of duty in reference to this work; and the providence of God soon opened his way to engage in it, while the inward comfort that followed his early efforts, and the success that attended them, assured him that he was obeying a Divine call.

His own record of his first attempts at exhortation and preaching will be read with interest. Under the date of August 18th, 1815, he writes, "At present I hunger and thirst after righteousness, and long for the destruction of everything opposed to the Divine will. I feel a love to the souls of my fellow men, and zeal for the glory of God. I often feel a conviction that it is my duty to warn sinners 'to flee from the wrath to come:' and at Woodburrow, a village about two miles from Banwell, on two occasions, in the prayer-meeting, when there was not a sufficient number of prayer-leaders present to conduct the service, I gave an address with much liberty. For some time I resisted this impression, thinking it might not be from above: but, on obeying the call, my mind, which had been in gloom, was filled with light and joy in God, and *fruits* bearing the Redeemer's sanction accompanied the word." The record proceeds :—"September 19th. On Sunday last I accompanied my uncle to Rooksbridge and Berrow, he being appointed to preach there. On arriving at Rooksbridge, I found that there was a call for help at South Brent, and I preached there in the afternoon. This was the first time that I conducted the entire service. On the Sunday following I preached at Allerton. On October 1st, at Lympsham, and on the 8th at Loxton. Since I began to speak publicly in the name of the Lord, I have been greatly encouraged and blessed ; and am determined, in His strength, to speak for Him whenever He may call me to do so."

The Banwell Circuit, to which Mr. Wood's labours as a Local Preacher were devoted, was very extensive. The village of Banwell was selected as the residence of the Ministers, on account of its central situation : but several places in the Circuit exceeded it in population and in general interest. The town of Weston-super-mare, then in its infancy, but which has since become an attractive watering-place, and has been constituted the head of a Wesleyan-Methodist Circuit, was comprehended in it. Wrington, also, the birth-place of John Locke, and near which the late Mrs. Hannah More resided for many years,— Nailsea, rendered important by its works for the manufacture of glass,—and the little town of Axbridge, belonged to this Circuit. It comprised nearly thirty places where preaching was established, being bounded by the Bristol Circuit on the north, the Taunton Circuit on the south, and the Midsomer-Norton and Shepton-Mallet Circuits on the east, while it reached to the Bristol Channel on the west. In the extracts from Mr. Wood's early Diary which have been preserved, we meet not only with the names of the places just referred to, and those mentioned in the account of his first attempts at preaching, but also with those of Burnham, East Brent, Highbridge, Huntspill, Mark, Wedmore, Cheddar, Cross, Worle, Barton, Compton-Martin, Churchill, Blagdon, Yatton, Congresbury, North Weston, Oldmixton, Langford, Puxton, Sandford and Bleadon. In all these places he preached the word of life with great fervour; and in all, or nearly all, he was the instrument of leading men to the knowledge of Christ and the enjoyment of His salvation.

A few extracts from his Diary will illustrate the character of his labours, and the blessing of God which rested upon them, while they disclose the sacred jealousy with which he watched over the life of God in his own soul.

"Sunday, November 12th, 1815.—A good and profitable day. I was blessed under the word preached by Mr. Wheelhouse in the morning; and the Lord gave me much enlargement while speaking to a large company at Woodburrow in the evening, some of whom appeared to be much affected."

"Sunday, November 26th.—I felt liberty in speaking at Rooksbridge and Berrow; and I feel thankful that the friends appear to receive me with affection, no doubt chiefly in recollection of my sainted father. I feel my soul alive to God, and I long to increase in faith, love, humility, and every other grace of the Spirit."

"Sunday, December 3rd.—My soul is happy. In the evening I went to Cross, according to my appointment on the new plan, and found liberty to speak for God, and a greater desire than ever to spend and be spent in His service."

"Tuesday, December 19th.—I have not experienced this week so much peace and joy in believing as I sometimes do; yet I know that I am in God's favour, and I endeavour to keep a single eye to His glory in all I do. Last Sunday I preached at South Brent at ten o'clock, at East Brent at two, and at Lympsham at six o'clock, and returned home after preaching. This is the hardest Sunday's labour I have yet performed, having walked all the way,—more than twenty miles,—and the weather in the morning being very rough."

"Tuesday, December 26th.—Last Sunday I preached at Weston-super-mare in the evening; and, the day following being Christmas-day, I remained and preached there again at two o'clock, p.m. I was thankful to God that the word was with power to some sinners' hearts."

"Thursday, January 4th, 1816.—On Sunday evening last I preached to a crowded congregation at Mark, and found it a good time. Not being often at home on Sundays, except early in the morning, I last Sunday met in my uncle's class at seven o'clock, a.m. These are precious times which I greatly prize."

"Sunday, January 21st.—I preached at Nailsea and Backwell. On Wednesday the 24th, I assisted at a watch-night at Allerton, and on Friday, the 26th, at Mark. There were crowded congregations; and I believe such meetings held annually, and closed about 9 o'clock, p.m., are attended by a general quickening, and are productive of much good."

"Sunday, January 28th.—I preached at Burnham, where there has been preaching but a few times. The congregation was large and respectable, and the prospect is encouraging. Yesterday a friend told me that he had encouragement for me; that a woman who heard me preach at Lympsham, on December 17th, felt the word come with power to her heart; that she went home weeping exceedingly, and although she had before been prejudiced against class-meetings, and was not willing that her husband should meet, she had now herself begun to meet. To God be all the glory."

"Sunday, February 4th.—I preached at Allerton in the morning, and at Wedmore in the afternoon and evening. I was greatly harassed by the enemy on the way. It was a long and unpleasant walk on a wet morning; and Satan suggested that, although I was going to preach to others that they should love God, I did not love Him myself. I at once examined carefully my motives, and found that I was not going in quest of wealth or honour; and I was sure I was not seeking a walk of pleasure that dirty, winterly morning. I felt that I was going because I loved God, and loved redeemed but perishing souls. Immediately the tempter fled. I went on my way glad of heart, and was much aided in speaking in the name of the Lord to large congregations."

"Sunday, March 10th.—The preacher appointed not arriving, I preached in the morning at Banwell, in the afternoon at Sandford, and, as I had promised to supply Burnham, more than ten miles distant, in the evening, I borrowed a horse, and went and found a large congregation. I had a sore throat, and did not expect more than barely to be carried through; but my blessed Master gave me great liberty while endeavouring to speak in His name. I praise the Lord, I feel that I am, in a measure, growing in grace. I am nothing and have nothing: but Christ is all, and, coming to 'the Father of mercies' through Him, my need is supplied, and my soul filled with Divine love. O may I ever walk humbly before my God, relying upon Him for time and for eternity!"

These extracts relate to his earliest labours in preaching Christ; and the Diary from which they are taken shows that, even when he was yet on trial as a Local Preacher, he was employed almost every Lord's day, and that on the week evenings he frequently availed himself of opportunities of engaging in the work which he loved. But he did not confine himself to this mode of usefulness. He formed a class at Woodburrow, the village already mentioned, about two miles from Banwell, over which he watched with great interest and affection. Under the date of Wednesday, February 14th, 1816, he writes, "After preaching at Woodburrow, I invited any who might have a desire to give their hearts to God, and to become members of the Society, to remain. Twelve did so, two or three of whom had previously met in other classes; and forthwith I met the new class for the first time." Soon afterwards he says, "I met the class at Woodburrow. Their number is thirteen; and I believe that they all have a sincere desire to become devoted to God. Four or five are earnestly seeking salvation in distress of soul." Notices of a similar character repeatedly occur, and show the solicitude with which Mr. Wood cared for the spiritual welfare of every one who met with him, the distress which he felt when any occasion of offence arose, and his holy joy when the number of sincere inquirers was augmented. After a year or two, he became the Leader of a class, consisting chiefly of young men, in Banwell, which he met at seven o'clock in the morning of the Lord's day, before going to his appointments to preach. He shrank from no labour, and no expenditure of time, in the cause of the Redeemer. This second class afforded him, as, indeed, did that at Woodburrow, great encouragement; and he felt that, in endeavouring to establish *young men* in the faith of Christ, and to lead them onward in the path of piety, he was engaged in a work the importance of which could scarcely be over-estimated. Nor was this all. At the request of the Ministers, he acted as the Secretary of a body of prayer-leaders in Banwell, and took the general oversight of their arrangements. At the first, Woodburrow was the only village which they visited; but in about a year from the formation of the new organization, the prayer-leaders' "plan" comprehended six places.

We have seen that, on returning to Banwell, after availing himself of the tuition of Mr. Exley, Mr. Wood assisted his uncle, and devoted himself, whenever opportunity was afforded, to the improvement of his own mind. In the spring of 1816 he was advised to commence a day-school in the room which his revered father so long occupied for that purpose. After much thought and prayer, he complied with the wishes of his friends, and opened his school on July 16th of that year. The brief record of this event in his Diary shows his solicitude to be properly qualified for the duties which thus devolved upon him. "With much assiduity," he says, "I am endeavouring to pursue my studies, relating both to general information and to public duties." Throughout life Mr. Wood was a man of high principle; and when he engaged in tuition, as the sphere of action which Divine Providence seemed to open to him, he felt that he was bound to acquire and maintain every possible qualification for it. He distributed his leisure hours between the various subjects of study which required his attention; and few moments, as he himself remarks, "lingered unemployed." About eight months after the opening of his school, he writes in his Diary, "I generally begin my evening's reading about nine o'clock, when I also prepare for public labours. This requires some time, as, besides being employed every Sunday on the Local-Preachers' Plan, I preach once a month at each of the following villages, viz., Woodburrow, Puxton, Churchill, Old-mixton, and sometimes at Congresbury; and I praise my God that these engagements, which I believe to be my duty, are also my delight. It must, however, be obvious that my evening's arrangement for study is often interrupted; but, when this is the case, I endeavour to press forward with greater diligence, that no department may get into arrear." As the

result of his assiduous attention to the improvement
of his pupils, his school prospered greatly; and he
thankfully records the fact, that on March 31st, 1817,
he had nine new scholars, adding, "O that I may
have grace to perform my duty by them!" Nine
months afterwards he says, "I have lately enlarged
my school-room, but it is now very full."

Some interesting incidents in his personal history,
which happened about this time, are recorded in his
Journal. Under the date of August 29th, 1816, he
writes, "This evening I took a walk in Banwell
Wood, where, meditating on the goodness of God, I
felt my mind brought under a gracious influence.
Passing on I came to a bush thickly-wooded both at
the top and the sides, except at one small opening,
where it looked as if a sheep had sometimes entered
and lain down. The place being curious, I stooped
down, and, entering this natural arbour, sat on a stone
I found there. Although when I entered I had no
intention to remain there a minute, yet when I sat
down I began to contemplate my past life and
my present state. I considered how unfaithful I had
been to the grace vouchsafed to me; how often I
had grieved my heavenly Father, and not regarded
with sufficient tenderness the feelings of my beloved
earthly parent. My mind was immediately with-
drawn from the pleasant objects and delightful
scenery by which I was surrounded; and my
soul was plunged in the depth of self-abasement.
I believe I never saw so much of my vileness, and
unworthiness to look towards heaven, or to take
the name of God into my lips, as at this time.
I cast myself and my burden at the footstool of
Divine mercy, and pleaded the precious blood of

Christ. Bowing my knees before God, I felt in that place the Spirit of prayer come upon me. I had not continued long in supplication before all darkness was dispersed by my Redeemer's appearing, like a bright and cloudless morning after a night of storm. My soul was filled with Divine love, and I went home rejoicing in the God of my salvation."

Another entry gives an account of an interview which he sought with the Rev. Dr. Randolph, at that time Vicar of Banwell; and of the encouragement afforded to him in his work of preaching by an eminent Minister of the Baptist denomination, the Rev. Dr. Ryland, of Bristol.—" Sunday, June 15th, 1817. Having a desire to obtain an acquaintance with the Hebrew language, but no means of instruction, I last evening applied to Dr. Randolph, Vicar of Banwell, to solicit the favour of his giving me some advice. He at once told me that he would give me a book or two, but inquired what was my object in desiring to learn it. I told him that I wished to become acquainted with the original languages of the Scriptures. On this he intimated a supposition that I intended to become a teacher or preacher. Mrs. Randolph, who was sitting in the room, now said, 'But, Mr. Wood, you do preach occasionally; do you not?' Upon this the Doctor began to express his disapprobation, saying that he considered it wrong to leave the Church. I gave him to understand that I had never left the Church, having been brought up in separation therefrom; which he thought was very wrong. He also thought that I should have obtained a better knowledge of Latin and Greek before I began to preach. I said I should gladly have acquired more information, if I had been favoured with the opportunity. He

thought that many who went about to preach did so
from pure motives, but were never called, and only
supposed themselves to be: he also thought me too
young for the work. I told him that, through Divine
mercy, I had experienced the power of godliness,
and was well satisfied that I had a call from God to
preach the Gospel to others; that I had long resisted
this conviction of duty until constrained to yield. He
then began to speak of the importance of the work.
I told him I saw and felt it to be so. Meantime the Hebrew seemed lost in the preaching. When I was about
to depart, Mrs. Randolph reminded him of his promise
about the books. He replied that the books were in
Bristol, and that when he went there he would bring
me one. I should have said more, but thought he
appeared not quite easy as our conversation proceeded. To-day I had an opportunity of shaking
hands with another D.D., whose spirit was more
genial. I preached in the evening at Weston-super-
mare from Phil. iv. 19. Dr. Ryland, of the Baptist
College, Bristol, was present. In a kind and fatherly
manner he gave me his hand when I came from the
pulpit, inquired for my name, and wished me 'God
speed.' "

On several occasions, during these early years,
Mr. Wood visited the neighbouring city of Bristol, to
enjoy opportunities of religious improvement, as well
as to confer with his revered instructer, Mr. Exley.
Soon after he had begun to preach, he was invited by
the late Mr. James Wood, of that city, to spend a
Sabbath there, that he might witness the gracious
revival of religion with which the Methodist Societies
and congregations were then favoured. He went
accordingly on the Saturday afternoon; and grate-

fully records the animating and profitable services of
the following day. "In the morning," he says, "I
heard the Rev. William Martin preach in Guinea
Street Chapel. In the afternoon I attended the love-
feast in the same chapel, which was crowded ; and
we were favoured with a blessed season. In the
evening I heard the Rev. Joseph Taylor, at King
Street ; after which there was a prayer-meeting, to
which most of the congregation stayed, and a second
prayer-meeting followed, when about two hundred
remained. Then it was that the Lord poured out
abundantly of His Spirit, and six or seven entered
into the liberty of the children of God. The next day
I returned to Banwell, greatly blessed by my visit. I
went expecting to receive blessings from God, and I
was not disappointed. More especially on leaving
the Guinea Street love-feast, panting after the fulness
of the Spirit, just as I came to the pavement on
Redcliff Hill, my soul was instantaneously filled with
the Holy One, so that I felt as if I had as much as I
could sustain without falling to the ground. Praise
the Lord, O my soul!" On occasions of great
public interest, as the District Missionary Anniversary,
or the opening of a new chapel, Mr. Wood endeavoured to be present in the city in which he had
resided for a short time, and to which he ever continued attached. He was one of the collectors at the
opening of the St. Philip's Chapel, in August, 1817,
and heard the sermons of the Revs. Richard Watson,
Jabez Bunting, and Robert Newton, who all took part
in the services of that memorable day. The sermon
which Mr. Bunting, afterwards Dr. Bunting, preached
on that occasion is given as the first in his published
Discourses, and is a beautiful specimen of his instruc-

tive and eminently powerful ministrations. To all three of these eminent ministers Mr. Wood listened with great interest and satisfaction, and doubtless derived from their expositions enlarged views of Christian truth. It was scarcely possible, indeed, as the writer can gratefully testify, for any thoughtful and devout person to listen to the profound discourses of Richard Watson, in particular, without having new trains of thought opened to his mind, and receiving a deeper impression of the glory of Christ and the grandeur of the mediatorial scheme. About nine months afterwards, Mr. Wood again went to Bristol, to attend some of the services of the District Missionary Anniversary. "On Wednesday, May 14th, 1818," he writes, "I had the privilege of hearing Richard Watson in Ebenezer Chapel, King Street, from 2 Cor. x. 13, 14. On the day following the Missionary Meeting was held. These were mighty occasions, calculated powerfully to arouse the Church to the claims of the world. Introduced by my former tutor, Mr. Exley, I had a short conversation with Dr. Adam Clarke in the evening."

During these years of early evangelical toil, Mr. Wood was repeatedly gladdened by instances of success; but, while his heart was cheered and strengthened by the manifest blessing of God upon his labours, he never forgot that all spiritual life is from the Holy Ghost, and that the glory of all that is really good belongs to the Triune Jehovah. Two brief extracts from his Diary, bearing on this subject, may properly close this chapter.—"Wednesday, March 19th, 1817. I preached at Woodburrow from 2 Cor. vi. 17, 18. One who had been going back became decided to begin anew."—"Sunday,

December 6th, 1818. I preached at Weston and
Worle; and after the evening service held a prayer-
meeting. Some obtained forgiving mercy, and
others, conscience-stricken, cried aloud for pardon. We repeatedly concluded the meeting, but
in vain; for we could not induce them to rise
from their knees and depart, until our strength was
exhausted."

CHAPTER IV.

———◦⋅◦⋅◦⋅◦◦———

1818-1826.

NO one can have followed the career of Mr. Wood, as we have endeavoured to trace it, without an impression that he was designed by the Lord Jesus to be separated to the work of the ministry. While he took an interest in general knowledge, and diligently cultivated his mind that he might faithfully discharge the duties of his profession as a school-master, his absorbing desire was to preach Christ to men, and actually to lead them to Him for salvation. When he had completed his twenty-first year, he had strong convictions of duty in reference to the Christian ministry as his proper vocation. These convictions never left him; and although, for several years, obstacles were thrown in his path, and he sought to find satisfaction of spirit by doing all the good he could in his more limited sphere as a Local Preacher, yet his heart was never truly at rest until he was set free from secular avocations, and the announcement of the riches of the Saviour's grace, and the care of the souls of men, became the one business of his life.

It was on the occasion of his visit to Bristol at

the Missionary Anniversary in May 1818, that this subject was first named to him by others. The Rev. James M. Byron, who was acquainted with his parents when he was born, and who had baptized him when an infant, was now in Bristol, and sent requesting him to call on him. He did so, and Mr. Byron inquired whether his thoughts were at all directed to the Christian Ministry. Mr. Wood frankly told him the impression that rested on his mind; and Mr. Byron encouraged him to come forward as a candidate for the sacred office. A correspondence ensued between them. Under the date of November 9th, 1818, Mr. Wood says, "I have to-day a letter from Mr. Byron in reply to one from me, in which he advises me to offer myself for a Missionary. I am in a strait. O my God, direct me! I feel that the Lord is my portion, and that I am, through grace, willing to do what He would have me do, and to do it when and wheresoever He would have it done." At the commencement of the following year, Mr. Wood visited Bristol, and was introduced to the Rev. Walter Griffith, the Superintendent of the Bristol Circuit and Chairman of the District, who was favourably impressed with his piety, intelligence and zeal. The way into the ministry seemed now to be opening to him; but the opposition of his uncle, whom he highly esteemed, and who was most anxious to retain him in the Banwell Circuit, presented, for several years, a formidable obstacle.

His own record of the various incidents connected with his first offer of himself for Missionary service, and of the conflicting emotions of his own heart, is so interesting that it may well be given at length. "On Saturday, January 2nd, 1819," he says, "I went to

Bristol, and on the following day I attended the covenant-service in the afternoon, and preached for Mr. Exley in the Limekiln Lane Chapel in the evening. I breakfasted with the Rev. Walter Griffith, the following morning, who advised me to converse with our Circuit Ministers respecting giving myself wholly to the work. Our Superintendent, the Rev. F. Wrigley, advises me to proceed. I mentioned it to my uncle on Saturday, January 30th, who is very much against it, and came to me on Tuesday, February 2nd, when I stated to him my persuasion that I should offer myself as a Missionary to the heathen. He strongly opposed it, and urged his conviction that I should fall a victim to the climate, if I went to India, as I wished to do. It was suggested that, if set apart to the work, I should not preach much more than I am now in the habit of doing, and that at present I am rendering important service to my native Circuit. He was much grieved and left me. As he would not tarry, I wrote to him, frankly and affectionately stating my thoughts. Since this he has appeared as affectionate as usual; but I lament that it has so troubled him that he often gets but little sleep. To grieve him grieves me. But what can I do? I feel I can sacrifice all worldly prospects to the will of my God. To go or to stay, Lord, I am willing. Deign to make known Thy good pleasure; and here am I, by this grace made willing. I am all unworthiness, but Thou art all love." "On Friday evening, March 26th, 1819, I rode to Bristol, and conversed with the Rev. Walter Griffith, and next morning breakfasted at the Rev. Thomas Wood's. All advised me to proceed, and that Mr. Wrigley should propose me as a Missionary candidate. For at this period I had no desire to come out in the home-work, but I longed to preach Christ where He had not been known. When riding to Bristol, as above named, I thought what my feelings would be were I then riding from Banwell for the last time. I earnestly wished for a friend, both able and faithful, who, unbiassed, would give me some advice. There passed in review my mother and the family, with my uncle and other friends. O how my heart was bound! But it was powerfully applied to my mind, as if One spoke, telling me that He was the Friend to whom I might unbosom all my care; and immediately these words were applied, 'He that loveth father or mother more than Me is not worthy of Me,' and an inquiry followed, Cannot the Lord supply to my mother all my lack of service, and will He not, if He calls for my service elsewhere? My heart replied, He can,—He will, and I submit without reservation." —" April 3rd, 1819. As Mr. Wrigley intends to propose me at the Quarterly Meeting on Tuesday next, as a Missionary candidate, I wrote as follows to my uncle :—

'Dear Uncle,

Extremely reluctant to disoblige you, but still constrained to perform a duty, I take up my pen to inform you that Mr. Wrigley intends to bring forawrd the subject of my going out as a Missionary at the Quarterly Meeting. I have weighed the matter again and again; and I feel that the powerful influence of natural affection would constrain me to remain at home; but the superior power of a certain indescribable authority in my heart impels me to go. This authority I believe to be the will of God. My prayer has been, that God would either open or shut up the

way, just as He sees fit, without regard to *my* will, or
to that of any creature; that He would send me where
and about what He may determine, doing all according to the counsel of His own will, and I engaging
with Him that, by His grace, whatever He may show
me to be His pleasure, that shall also be mine. I am
satisfied with having discharged a duty in speaking
to Mr. Wrigley, as I before informed you. I now
leave this matter in the hands of God. If He shuts up
the way, I am satisfied; if He calls me to go forth, I
obey: but if I am prevented by earthly considerations
from doing what I believe to be the will of God, I am
a miserable man. If you wish to see me before the
meeting, I will wait on you whenever you may appoint.
Meantime, praying that God's will may be done, I
remain,

Your very affectionate nephew,
JOSEPH WOOD.'"

Mr. Wood continues:—" One of our very respectable friends, a valued Local Preacher, was at my
uncle's when my letter came to hand, and he came
from my uncle to me, not, he said, to offer any opinion,
but to propose some thoughts for my consideration.
They were briefly as follows. He remarked, that I
am continually engaged in preaching on Sundays,
and often on week-evenings;—that I meet a class on
Sunday mornings in Banwell, and have the care of
the flock at Woodburrow, and am engaged in other
public duties;—that I have a prospect of comfort in
temporal things;—that I have a dear mother, an
uncle whom I greatly love, and a brother and three
sisters younger than myself;—also that the Lord has
been graciously pleased to own my labours at home,

and that I have the prospect of being still useful. He urged further, that I should also consider that, by leaving home, I might expect to forego all temporal comforts, and to have hardships, crosses, and difficulties among a strange people with strange manners and a strange language, with no kind mother or sisters to soothe and cheer me in affliction and dying: for, if I went, he believed he should soon hear of my death. These were my friend's reasonings; to which I replied that, if it be God's will that I should go, and I refuse, He might blight my prospects of comfort and usefulness at home by various forms of disappointment and affliction;—that if He calls me to go abroad, He will open my way, support me in the work, and enable me to publish among thousands of perishing heathen 'the unsearchable riches of Christ.'" —After narrating this conversation, Mr. Wood adds, in his Diary, the prayer:—" O Thou God of Abraham, Isaac, and Jacob, Thou Father of our Lord Jesus Christ, the vineyard is Thine, and Thine the right to appoint the labourers. If Thou seest fit that I should stay and labour as at present, I readily acquiesce. But if it seemeth good in Thy sight that I should labour in some other part of Thy vineyard, lead me forth, and by Thy grace I will cheerfully follow: but let all be done as Thou, O my Father, my God, my All, even as Thou *only* shalt approve. Hear and answer all my requests through the blood of atonement, once shed for me!"

The Quarterly Meeting came; and, at the proper time, the Superintendent of the Circuit proposed Mr. Wood as a candidate for the ministry, stating that he offered himself specially for Missionary work. His uncle warmly opposed the nomination, chiefly on the ground that his constitution and manner of preaching were such that in a hot climate, and especially in India, to which his thoughts were directed, he must, humanly speaking, soon be laid aside. Of his spiritual qualifications for the work of the ministry there was but one opinion; nor was the Superintendent Minister disposed to yield to the objection alleged. But the earnestness and determination of his uncle succeeded so far, that the matter was allowed to drop, and no vote was taken. At the District Meeting, however, the Rev. Walter Griffith conversed with the Superintendent, the Rev. F. Wrigley, on the circumstances. of the case; and they both strongly advised Mr. Wood to allow himself to be proposed at the next Quarterly Meeting, intimating that, if he passed that Meeting, he might be examined—the case being an exceptional one—by three Superintendents instead of the full District Committee. When informed of this, he replied that he wished to be passive in the matter, and not to do anything by way of proposing himself; and, recording this circumstance in his Diary, he adds, "I leave it, O my God, to Thee, and to the servants of Thy Church: do with me, I beseech Thee, as seemeth good in Thy sight." The June Quarterly Meeting arrived; and then, for the second time, Mr. Wood was proposed as a Missionary candidate. The record in his Journal is, in substance,—"The Stewards opposed the proposal on the ground of my being wanted at home, and went on so to speak of me that the Rev. Joseph Bowes, the second Minister, told them they would only induce the Conference to take me. My uncle also strongly objected. They were, however, unanimous in their vote, that I should not leave the Circuit."

It is almost unnecessary to point out that, in coming to such a decision, the Banwell Quarterly Meeting abused the power entrusted to it. The provision, that every candidate for the ministry among us shall be approved by the Quarterly Meeting of the Circuit in which he resides, is designed to give to our people an opportunity of attesting, or refusing to attest, the intellectual and spiritual qualifications of the candidates in question, and not of deciding whether they shall be retained at home, to render important service to that particular Circuit, or go forth, separated to the work of Christ, to devote all their energies to Him. The opposition of Mr. Wood's uncle was prompted chiefly by his deep solicitude for the preservation of his nephew's life. He had a settled conviction that he would soon fall a prey to the climate of India. His mode of preaching, at this time, was such as greatly to try his strength. He spoke very loudly and rapidly; and often, at the close of the labours of the Lord's day, he was utterly exhausted. There can be no doubt that his uncle sincerely and strongly loved him, and that he had cherished the hope that, when he should be called away, his nephew would remain on his estate, and devote his energies to the advancement of religion in the neighbourhood. But his uncle's opposition was unquestionably carried too far, and did not sufficiently respect the sacredness of a conviction so deep and abiding as that which filled the heart of Mr. Wood, that the separated ministry was the sphere for which the Lord Jesus Christ designed him. That opposition, however, was ultimately overruled for good. It is not improbable that, had he gone to India, the result might have been that which his uncle feared; and it may be questioned whether his special gifts adapted him so much to Missionary service among the population of India, as to those evangelistic efforts at home to which he was at length set apart, and which God crowned with such abundant success.

But the decision of the Banwell Quarterly Meeting did not at once close all overtures on the subject. That decision was taken on a false issue; and it cannot, therefore, be wondered at, that not only the Ministers of the Circuit, but several of those in Bristol, including the Chairman of the District, to whom his case was fully known, were dissatisfied with the result. Accordingly they took steps still to keep the subject before him. The Conference of 1819 was held in Bristol, and Mr. Wood attended some of its public services. He was introduced to the Rev. Jabez Bunting, who wished him to have an interview with the Missionary Secretary, the Rev. Joseph Taylor, and with the Rev. Richard Watson. He accordingly met these honoured men; and Mr. Taylor promised to write to his uncle, to remonstrate with him on his opposition. This promise he lost no time in fulfilling; for on August 14th of that year Mr. Wood received a letter from him, telling him that his uncle then made but little objection to his going forth as a Missionary except on the ground of his health, and that, in Mr. Taylor's opinion, he would, at some time, obtain his full consent.

While this important matter still occupied his attention, he applied himself diligently to the duties which immediately pressed upon him, and took a lively interest in everything that affected the prosperity of the cause of God around him. A few extracts from his Diary, during the later months of the year 1819, will show how he was engaged, and will illustrate the workings of his heart.

"Monday, August 30th.—I proposed a plan in our last Trustee Meeting for reducing the Chapel-debts in the Circuit, which was cordially received."

"October 2nd.—I went to Bleadon, to seek for a place in which to hold Divine worship. Through God's blessing my success exceeded my expectations. Two families who resided in the first house I entered, readily and thankfully consented. I have been examining myself, and I mourn in secret before God on account of my unfaithfulness and the remaining corruptions of my heart."

"Sunday, November 14th.—This day I met my class at seven o'clock, a.m., as usual, and have since preached at Sandford once, and at Banwell twice with liberty. I praise the Lord, but I feel the danger of my position. Crowded congregations attend my preaching, and my heart is prone to pride : and how shall I be preserved from 'falling into the condemnation of the devil?' But how should *I* dare to be proud,—I, who have nothing that is wise, or good, or strong, but what God has freely given ? Shall I boast as if I had not received it? I, who have so many humiliating recollections? No, O my God! Every thing I do which merits censure I take to myself, for I know it is all my own : but everything praiseworthy comes of Thy free and sovereign grace, and I place all at Thy footstool, where I would always be found myself, offering the sacrifice of continual thanksgiving and zealous obedience."

"December 2nd.—I preached to a full and very attentive congregation at Hutton, for the first time of a week-evening, and have made arrangements for Hutton and Bleadon to have fortnightly service. O Lord, prosper Thou Thy work! I have lately been urged to enlarge my School; but this I could not do without getting settled, which a powerfully restraining influence forbids. Until the Missionary question is settled, I must remain as I am, trusting in God that He will not suffer me to err, while earnestly desiring to know, and sincerely endeavouring to do, His good pleasure."

In the early part of the year 1820, Mr. Wood spent a short time from home; but, during this period of comparative relaxation, he was ever ready to engage in preaching the Gospel, and he endeavoured to maintain everywhere the spirit and deportment of the Christian. He remarks in his Journal, "As I generally sit very close to study, it seems strange to be so much from home as I have lately been; but I find that my health has improved thereby. I endeavour, by Divine grace, to spread 'the savour of the knowledge of Christ' wherever I go, although I feel it difficult to preserve the spirit of devotion while continually changing from one house and company to another. I cannot but praise the Lord for His goodness, in that I everywhere find friends exceedingly kind, conscious as I am of my unworthiness of the affection and respect so freely bestowed." In the entries which follow, several interesting incidents are narrated, illustrative of the power of Divine grace, and of the success with which God crowned the unostentatious labours of His servant :—

"Monday, January 31st, 1820.—I was at Mark

watchnight on Tuesday, at Sandford on Thursday, and preached yesterday at Highbridge and Berrow. I felt encouragement at Berrow by being informed that, when I was last there, a hardened servant of Satan, who had been arraigned at the bar three times, was 'pricked in the heart,' and for several days and nights he had very little rest, but is now a member of the Society. May the Lord keep him steadfast, and receive all the glory! I felt great satisfaction last evening, arising from a consciousness of having, by Divine help, cleared my soul in the sight of God in regard of lukewarm professors of religion. May the Lord cause the arrow to pierce deep, but deliver them from going down into eternal death!"

"February 10th, 1820.—After preaching at Hutton, I explained the system of Methodism, and the nature and design of our Class-meetings; and desired those who earnestly desired salvation to remain. We reckon that about eight have a genuine work of grace begun in their hearts. Returning home after the service, my soul was filled with Divine consolation in seeing the Master's work prosper. All glory to God alone!"

"Wednesday, February 23rd, 1820.—The twenty-three years of my life have been crowded with mercies and with causes of humiliation. I feel abased in the dust, and know that it is of mercy and long forbearance that I am not cast out of the vineyard. Still my soul follows hard after the Lord; and my supreme desire and earnest endeavour is, to do all His will."

It does not appear that at the March Quarterly Meeting of this year anything was said about Mr. Wood's engaging in the Missionary work. The people among whom he now laboured were very unwilling to part with him; and he himself calmly and prayerfully waiting the openings of Divine Providence. He was solicited by many persons to remove from Banwell, and establish a school in some larger and more influential place. He records this circumstance under the date of June 19th, 1820, and adds, "I seek to know and to do all the will of God. O my God, make Thou me to walk in 'the path of the just!'"

During the Midsummer vacation of this year, Mr. Wood, for the first time, visited London. He naturally went to view the places of chief historical interest in the metropolis; and, going one evening to the House of Commons, he had the pleasure of hearing Lord Castlereagh, Mr. Tierney, and Mr. Canning, besides other speakers. He availed himself also of opportunities of religious improvement. He went to a Missionary Meeting held in the Spitalfields Chapel; and, on the Lord's-day, he heard the Rev. Richard Watson preach twice, in the forenoon at Great Queen Street Chapel, and in the evening at City Road. He visited also the Mission House in Hatton Garden, and had a conversation with the Secretary, the Rev. Joseph Taylor, though the substance of that conversation is not recorded.

In the month of September, 1820, Mr. Wood began seriously to entertain the thought of removing to Weston-super-mare, as being a more suitable place for a boarding school than Banwell. After much careful deliberation and prayer, he decided on taking this step, and began to make preparation for it; but it was not until April 16th, 1821 that he actually changed his residence. The interval was marked by two interesting events,—the one connected with the Church, and showing the high esteem in which he was held in the Banwell Circuit, and the other intimately affecting his domestic happiness, and shedding its influence over all the subsequent years of his life.

On his return from a visit to some friends at the beginning of the year 1821, he found that, at the December Quarterly Meeting, he had been appointed one of the Circuit Stewards of the Banwell Circuit, in connection with one who is still remembered by many, and among them by the writer, with affectionate respect,—Mr. John Carrington. With a degree of hesitation he undertook this office, humbly resolving to discharge its duties, by Divine help, faithfully and affectionately. His notice of the first Quarterly Meeting which he attended in his new official character shows the energy, and the love of propriety and order, which always distinguished him. Under the date of April 12th, 1821, he says, "Our Quarterly Meeting was held to-day. We began by resolving to take minutes of our proceedings, and to conform to the rules observed in well-regulated assemblies. In this way we got through our business in less time and with greater order than we have for a long period been accustomed to." His impression of the proceedings of District Committees, when first he attended one in the capacity of Circuit Steward, will be read by some with interest. To explain the entry in his Diary, it should be mentioned that Bath was then comprehended in the Bristol District.—"Monday, May 28th, 1821. Last Tuesday I went to Bristol, and the next morning rode over to Bath, and attended the District Meeting. I was quite satisfied with everything, except the heavy pressure upon poor preachers in needy Circuits."

The other event alluded to was the formation of a matrimonial engagement with the lady whose gentle spirit and placid manners, as well as her deep and consistent piety, rendered her a most suitable companion for him during his many years of ceaseless activity, and who, after soothing the few years of feebleness and languor that followed, still survives to cherish the remembrance of his Christian excellencies. Being at the head of a boarding-school, he felt the need of a wife who could share his anxieties, and promote the comfort of his pupils; and, after much prayer for Divine guidance, he made an offer of marriage to Miss Mary Ann Hellier Collings, of Nempnett, which was accepted. This was in February, 1821, when Mr. Wood had nearly completed his twenty-fourth year; and on July 2nd, of the same year, they were married in Nempnett Church. On the 10th of that month, he gratefully records, "Last evening we returned to Weston; and to-day my school re-opens. Everything seems more fully to wear the character of *home*. Indeed, the word seems to possess a more interesting and impressive significance than I ever before apprehended."

Mr. Wood's residence in Weston-super-mare was marked by efforts to introduce the Gospel to places which seemed to be in utter spiritual darkness. His entry in his Diary on Sunday, September 30th, 1821, is, "I preached at Weston this evening. In the afternoon I went to Kew-Stoke, where the people appear to be sitting in darkness that might be felt. I distributed some tracts, which were well received: and I promised to call again." On Sunday, October 14th,

1821, he writes, "In the forenoon I again visited Kew-Stoke, changed their tracts which they had read, and which they had lent about to one another. I hope soon to restore to them a Sabbath-school. I have also visited Uphill, and endeavoured to get a room for commencing Divine worship, and obtained a conditional promise. This is the first Sunday in which I have not preached at all since I began. All glory to God alone!"

But his stay in Weston was brief. It soon appeared, to use his own words, that his removal to that town was "not favourable to the establishment of a boarding school for *boys*." "Many parents," he adds, "have a dread of their sons getting into danger, especially as I cannot be always with them." At the same time an opening presented itself in the populous village of Yatton; and on November 6th, 1821, Mr. Wood removed his establishment to that place. Here his school prospered greatly; and, before twelve months had elapsed, he found the accommodation which his house afforded to be quite insufficient. His landlord was unwilling to enlarge it, and no other could be procured; and at length he was compelled again to change his residence. A very commodious house, every way eligible for a boarding school, was vacant at Langford, near Wrington; and to this place, which was far more central for his public labours, he removed at the beginning of October, 1822. Here he remained, increasingly respected and beloved, and enjoying great temporal prosperity, until a constraining conviction of duty led him to sacrifice these bright prospects, and to go forth to the proper business of his life,—the announcement of the Christian message, and the manifold labours of the Christian pastorate.

Mr. Wood's residence at Yatton, though it scarcely extended over one year, was made the means of abundant spiritual good to that place and its neighbourhood. Immediately upon coming to it, he applied himself diligently to evangelistic labours. He visited the poor-house for reading, exhortation, and prayer; and he sought out sick persons, many of whom he found in a state of lamentable spiritual ignorance. He introduced Methodist preaching, also, into Kingston, a small village about three miles from Yatton,— going there, in the first instance, with a friend, who knew it well, to make arrangements for a public service, and to invite the people to come, and then visiting them, according to his appointment, and preaching to them from the words, "Men and brethren, children of the stock of Abraham, and whosoever among you feareth God, to you is the word of this salvation sent." (Acts xiii. 26.) The house which he first obtained for preaching was soon closed against him, through the influence of the landlord: but another person at once offered his house, and sent a message to that effect to Mr. Wood. Again and again he visited Kingston, and rejoiced in the saving impressions which were produced on some minds. He succeeded also in obtaining a much more commodious room for preaching in Yatton, than the one previously occupied, and in securing for that place a regular supply of preachers on every Lord's day. Upon his removal to Langford, he visited the poor-house at Wrington, to read the Scriptures to the inmates, adding brief and earnest exhortations, and then engaging in prayer, just as he had done at Yatton; and, as his visits were favourably received, he established a weekly meeting of this kind. He devoted his best energies, also, to the advancement of the cause of Christ in Langford itself, continuing, all the while, his extensive labours, as a Local Preacher, in the Banwell Circuit generally.

It must not be supposed, however, that while Mr. Wood was thus zealously pursuing his evangelistic labours, his own religious experience was, at all times, joyous and exultant. There were some seasons, in his history, of protracted spiritual conflict. Such a season occurred just after his removal to Langford; and it may, perhaps, encourage some who are greatly harassed in the Christian warfare, to read a few of the records which this man of God has left of the peculiar exercises of mind through which he then passed. "Monday, October 14th, 1822.—My mind is cold and lifeless. It is my sorrow, but I scarcely know the cause. I have cried earnestly to God for deliverance; but, although holpen, I am yet cold and dry."—"Monday, October 21st. I preached last evening at Weston with great liberty, but I have been greatly tried and powerfully tempted during the week. Still the Lord has been my Helper; and to His restraining grace I render glory and praise for ever."—"Monday, November 25th. In the course of last week I have been very powerfully and almost incessantly assailed by Satan. Even while pouring out my soul in ejaculatory prayer for help and deliverance, sinful imaginations have been suddenly presented to my mind with such force that I have sometimes been almost ready to despair of ultimately obtaining the victory. But, glory to God's infinite compassion, He doth not suffer us to be always so severely exercised, or our 'spirits would fail before Him.' He appears in due time with mitigation or deliverance, and brings a blessing with Him."

Mr. Wood had now also experience of the anxieties, and joys, and griefs, of married life. He records with grateful feelings the birth of a son in May 1822, and the merciful preservation of his beloved wife. About six months afterwards he speaks of his deep emotions when his "dear little boy" was very ill, and acknowledges the abounding goodness of God in answering prayer for his restoration. In July, 1824, a second child was born to him; but, when eleven months had passed, he was called to experience, for the first time, the deep sorrow which fills the heart of an affectionate parent on the death of a beloved infant. His second son was called *Charles*, after his grandfather; and Mr. Wood speaks of him as an extraordinary child, and refers to his decease as the heaviest trial that had yet befallen him. But God graciously sustained the bereaved parents; and as they knelt together in prayer, after their heavy loss, they were enabled to say, "The Lord gave, and the Lord hath taken away: blessed be the Name of the Lord." This was a form of sorrow which, in subsequent years, Mr. Wood had several times to endure. Of all his children, his eldest son only, who bears his own honoured name, survives: the rest passed in infancy or early childhood to the presence of Him who bought them with His blood.

It is pleasing to think of the strength and tenderness of Mr. Wood's domestic affections. They who observed him only from a distance would be impressed chiefly with his intense zeal for the salvation of men, and the untiring energy with which he applied himself

to his great work for Christ : but while these were
the prominent features of his character, he was also a
man of fine and tender sensibilities. In the several
relations of a son, a husband, and a father, these
sensibilities were called forth; and we may point to
him as one who combined an absorbing devotion to
the Redeemer and His cause with the *pure human love*
that gladdens the domestic circle. He cultivated, also,
a sacred regard to *duty*, and a high sense of *honour*.
Amidst all his engagements in preaching, he continued
to apply himself to study, that he might be ready to
meet all the claims of his profession; and in his
business-transactions he thought of others, and manifested a sterling integrity and real nobleness of character. One entry in his Journal, illustrative of his filial
dutifulness, and of his affectionate solicitude for his
brother and his sisters, may be here inserted. If it
should seem to involve a disclosure of family arrangements, that may well be excused, since it shows how
truly kind and noble Mr. Wood was, through the
abounding grace of God, and how rich a satisfaction
results from acts of filial piety and fraternal kindness.
Under the date of November 29th, 1824, he writes,
"My late revered father, Charles Wood, having died
intestate, nearly the whole of his property devolved to
me as his heir-at-law. My widowed mother took the
rents of this property, and with frugality and God's
blessing managed to provide for the family. But
being about to renew the copyhold, I thought it a
fitting opportunity to make such provision for my
mother, and my brother and three sisters, as I believe
my father would have done, had he not been unex-
pectedly removed. I therefore settled on my mother
an annuity and a house to live in during her life; and

I conveyed the whole to the use of the family, without taking any advantage to myself. I signed the deed of settlement last Wednesday, and gave praise and glory to God for a heart to do that which I believe to be just and kind."

But we turn again to the evangelistic labours of Mr. Wood while resident in Langford. His great delight was "to declare the testimony of God" respecting His Son; and he loved to proclaim it to those who were sitting in darkness. He breathed the true Home-Missionary spirit. Wherever his lot was cast, he looked around to see what places were destitute of the light of evangelical truth, and then took measures to convey it to them. His Journal contains an interesting account of an effort which he made, about twelve months after he came to Langford, to benefit the inhabitants of a small village on the Mendip hills; and, coming in between his notices of his visits to this place, is an incident which we gladly preserve, as illustrating the kind and catholic feeling of a venerable clergyman of the Established Church. —"Friday, October 17th, 1823. Last Wednesday evening, for the first time, I preached at *Charter-House*, a detached village near the summit of the Mendip range of hills, their parish church being many miles distant. It is but about four miles from Langford; but the road, when dark, is unpleasant and dangerous. Black Down, over which it lies, is uncultivated, and the correct path is intersected by many others. The way, in some places, is steep and rugged: in others it runs near swamps in which horses are said to have perished. Persons acquainted with the Down sometimes get out of their way by night, as there are no enclosures or high objects to

guide the traveller. I preached to a little room-full
of attentive hearers with satisfaction. My revered
father spent amongst this people a portion of his
evangelistic labours; and my beloved mother informs
me that my father told her how, on one occasion,
when they expected him, they came out on the hill to
meet him and sang, 'How beautiful upon the moun-
tains are the feet of him that bringeth good tidings,
that publisheth peace; that bringeth good tidings of
good, that publisheth salvation; that saith unto Zion,
Thy God reigneth.'—October 23rd. I again preached
at Charter-House, and took down five names of
persons willing to unite in Christian fellowship. May
the God of Israel erect even here a Church which
shall stand until the end of time!—Monday, November
3rd. I was visited by the Rev. Mr. Jones, the pious
and venerable incumbent of this parish, who has
preached at Churchill Church fifty years, and continues
his labours both here and at Shipham. He was
acquainted with the Wesleys and Fletcher. He
thanked me for visiting the sick.—Monday, November
10th. I preached yesterday afternoon at Charter-
House. I met the little Society afterwards, and find
a good work begun among them. Their expressions
are not the same, but they describe similar feelings to
those of persons who have heard details of religious
experience a thousand times. I rejoice and praise
God that the standard of the Cross is planted among
these cottagers, and that a few are gathered around
it. May the Lord grant it stability and success!"

Another attempt of his to introduce Christian
worship into a destitute neighbourhood is recorded in
the following interesting passage.—"Monday, July
5th, 1824. It being the vacation, I rode over from

Nempnett to Nailsea; and, on crossing the turnpike road near the New Inn, in the locality commonly called *Downside*, it occurred to me to inquire if they had a place of worship near. Seeing a man who appeared to be a farmer working in his field, I rode up to the hedge and hailed him. On telling him for what I was making inquiry, he said that they had no place of worship near, and added, 'I'll tell you what was in my mind, Sir, when you rode up and called me. I was thinking that I am sixty-three years old, and that it is time for me to think about my soul. I have a tenant in a house adjoining my own, who keeps bad company and makes a noise on Sundays, and I was thinking I would warn him out, and if any one would come and preach there he should be welcome.' He then said, 'I don't know you, but I suppose you are a preacher; and if you think our kitchen would do for a time, you shall have that.' I, of course, gladly accepted the offer, and preached there on Sunday morning, July 11th. The room was quite filled with attentive hearers, who expressed their earnest desire that I would come again. Accordingly, on Sunday, August 1, 1824, I preached again at farmer W——'s, at Downside, where many appeared to feel the word."

The sphere of Christian labour in which Mr. Wood now moved was an important and extensive one: but the conviction still pressed on his mind, that he ought to be separated to the work of the Christian ministry. Many things, indeed, tended to induce him to remain in his present position. He was at the head of a flourishing boarding-school, and had the prospect of becoming moderately rich; he had acquired considerable influence in the neighbourhood in which he lived; and he had now a delicate wife and a son, for whom it was both his duty and his happiness to care. The financial economy of the Wesleyan Methodist Connexion would require that, if admitted to the ministry, he should maintain his family for four years on the income of a single Minister, receiving, probably, in the Circuit to which he might be appointed, not more than £60 or £70 a year, and having himself either to provide a house, or secure furnished apartments; and that he should forego all claim on the Connexional Funds for his son, and for any other children who might be born to him during his probation. But he was willing to sacrifice his worldly advantages, and to submit to temporary inconvenience and suffering, in obedience to the call which summoned him to leave all secular avocations, and to give himself wholly to the work of saving souls. He felt that it was, at least, his duty to offer himself to the Methodist Conference, as a candidate for the ministry. Under the date of August 15, 1825, we have the following record:—"Having always had a conviction that I ought to be wholly given to the work of the ministry, in order to be satisfied on this important point, I offered to go into the regular work as a single man, *i.e.*, to maintain my wife and child, and any other child that I might have during my four years of probation, at my own expense. The Rev. Richard Reece and some other leading Ministers advocated my cause: but a great number of candidates offering who are single men, the Conference determined to take these first. No doubt a wise and just decision, which left nothing unpleasant in my mind, but, on the contrary, it seemed to relieve me of the responsibility of being found at home." Happily this decision was not accepted by Mr. Wood as final. His deep conviction of duty to Christ led him to renew his offer in the following year, though he was then more than twenty-nine years of age. Writing on May 11th, 1826, he says, " Respecting my being wholly given to the work of the ministry, the door seems to be opened by the Lord of the vineyard. I was duly brought forward at the last Quarterly Meeting of the Circuit, and have to-day passed the examination of the Bristol District Meeting. I had endeavoured to consider well the doctrines of the Gospel, but had made no special and anxious preparation. I implored Divine aid, that, if the Lord saw fit to call me more fully into the work of preaching the word, I might be at no loss for a suitable reply to any question that might be proposed. I felt no trepidation, but was quite calm; and my answers were deemed satisfactory. Yesterday was the day of the Anniversary Meeting of the Missionary Society for the Bristol District. I was glad to have an invitation to dine at Mr. Hall's, as it gave me an opportunity of being in the company of Richard Watson and other esteemed Ministers." The Conference of this year accepted his offer, and appointed him to the Newport (Monmouthshire) Circuit, as the colleague of the Rev. Humphrey Parsons. His closing service in the Banwell Circuit was at Langford, on Friday evening, August 25th; and on the following day, amidst the tears and prayers of the people whom he loved, and for whose souls he had laboured, he went forth to a yet wider sphere of sacred service, to which, from that hour, he devoted, by God's grace, his undivided energies.

CHAPTER V.

ENTRANCE UPON THE MINISTRY.—THE NEWPORT (MONMOUTH-
SHIRE) CIRCUIT.

1826—1829.

MR. WOOD was now introduced to that ministry to which the Lord Jesus Christ had called
him, and for which his history, up to this time, had
been a course of preparation. His character was
already formed. He was in his thirtieth year; he
had had considerable experience of the world, and
had taken a prominent part in the activities of the
Church; his principles were fixed and established,
and his aims definite and constant. In the full vigour
of manhood, though occasionally the subject of pain
and suffering, he went forth as one of Christ's commissioned servants, to accomplish *one* work,—even to
lead sinful men to Him, and then to build them up in
faith and holiness.

The Newport (Monmouthshire) Circuit, to which
he was now appointed, was a wide and, in several
respects, an important one. In the town itself, there
was, at that time, only one Chapel occupied by the
English Wesleyan-Methodists, capable of seating
about four hundred persons. As a general rule, each
of the two Ministers preached in the town on two
successive Sundays out of every four, occasionally
taking some neighbouring country place in the after-

noon. One Lord's day in every month was given by
each of the Ministers to Earlswood, which lay in the
direction of Chepstow, and to the interesting little
town of Usk,—a small Society, which met for worship
in a private house, at a place called Pen-y-cae-mawr,
being visited in the forenoon. The old-fashioned
chapel at Earlswood stood in a romantic situation,
far away from any village; but to it, on a fine Sabbath afternoon, the people flocked for several miles
around, and listened with eagerness to the word of
life. The writer well remembers the first occasion
on which he himself, about six years afterwards,
visited these places. It was a lovely Sabbath morning in August; and after riding some six miles on
the high road from Newport to Chepstow, he had to
go by a bridle-path through a beautiful wood about
four miles further, to reach the cottage in which the
forenoon service was conducted. A frugal repast
followed, the poor people making the preacher
heartily welcome to their humble fare; and then
there was a ride of four miles to Earlswood, and,
after the service, another ride of eight miles brought
him to Usk, where, after preaching, he remained for
the night. The labours of the fourth Sabbath in
every month were, for the most part, given either to
the ancient town of Caerleon, about three miles
distant from Newport, or to Risca, Blackwood, and
other places to the west of Newport. During the
"in" fortnight, the week-day services were mostly in
the town, and one or two places comparatively near
to it; but during the "out" fortnight several distant
country places were visited, the preachers remaining
from home several nights.

At the time when Mr. Parsons and Mr. Wood

entered upon their joint pastorate in Newport, the cause of Methodism was comparatively low. There were only 260 members of the Society in the whole Circuit; and the spiritual state of the congregations was such as to awaken considerable solicitude. But the Ministers met with a very cordial reception; and the people evinced a disposition to do everything to promote their comfort.

Mr. Wood commenced his ministry in the town of Newport itself, on the day after his arrival. Strange thoughts and feelings came into his mind, as he rose on that Sabbath morning, having left his wife and child behind him in Somersetshire, until he could make arrangements for their reception. It was suggested to him that he had gone out of his Providential path, and that in Newport he would never be blessed or happy. But, after recording this, he adds, "I cried to the Lord, and He delivered me: He gave me encouragement and a blessing. I preached in the morning and evening in Newport, and in the afternoon at Bassaleg. The Lord gave the word with power, and, on the following evening, one young person came to the class which I met, seeking salvation, who was the fruit of last Sunday evening's labour." This was only an earnest of the abundant spiritual success which was to follow his labours in this town and Circuit.

No time was lost by him in entering upon a course of systematic pastoral visitation. Not only did he find out the members of the Society, and the seat-holders, in the town of Newport; but in every part of the Circuit he visited from house to house, inducing many who had neglected religion to attend the worship of God, and speaking to them directly on the subject of their personal salvation. In one or two instances, he made arrangements to remain after preaching, for the night, in country places in which it had not been customary to do so, that he might spend part of the following day in these Home-Missionary efforts. A few extracts from his Diary will show the earnestness with which he gave himself up to the work of the Lord, and the blessing which rested upon his labours. After speaking of the first Sabbath which he spent at Pen-y-cae-mawr, Earlswood, and Usk, and referring to the lovely prospects which now and then met the eye in riding through Wentwood, in places where the wood opened, he thus describes the work of the following week.—"Monday, September 11th, 1826. This was the monthly market-day at Usk. Riding into the town from Mr. W.——'s, of the Rhyader, I observed a considerable number of persons on the bank of the river, near the bridge, engaged in their sports, and I felt it my duty to go to them; but in going on such an errand I never felt a greater cross. However, after putting up my horse, and calling upon a few friends, I went to the roughs, and found they had just finished a battle which they had been fighting. I went into the midst of them, and told them that I had a message from God unto them, and requested their attention while I delivered it. While addressing them they acknowledged the truth of what I spoke, and when I prayed many of them took off their hats. They treated me not only with civility,—which I hardly expected from a number of ruffian-looking fellows,—but with respect, and I believe they all dispersed when I left them. In the evening I preached at Gwahalog to a large company of very poor people. On *Tuesday,* at Corn Hill, where we lodge with deep poverty and a hearty welcome. *Wednesday* I was at Earlswood, and on *Thursday* at Shirenewton, about four miles from Chepstow. My time has been chiefly occupied in visiting the members of the Society and the hearers, and, in many cases, those who do not hear. In small neighbourhoods I have gone from house to house, without respect of persons, talking, reading, and praying with them until I have been exhausted : but, blessed be God, He has given me an entrance among the people, and I am persuaded that He has made these little visits of spiritual good to some. I have lately been strongly tempted to vain and evil thoughts, but by looking to the Lord I obtain succour and deliverance." Two months afterwards he writes, " We have had a blessed week. The Divine presence has been with us in every ordinance and good has been done. We have taken another week-evening preaching appointment in connection with Usk.—According to my usual plan, I visited from house to house, and stopped and talked with those I met on the road. In some cases I went to persons who were at work in their fields, raising their potatoes, and in one instance of this kind, while addressing a little company, a woman present cried out aloud, bursting into a flood of tears.—Glory to God, my own soul is blessed and in prosperity. It is truly my meat and drink to do the will of Him who hath sent me." In the beginning of December he writes, " I have been very much encouraged in this week's labour. We had upwards of one hundred at the Monday evening preaching at Usk, a greater number, the friends say, than they ever had before on a week-evening. On Wednesday evening I preached as usual at Llantrissaint, when many assembled. At the time before last of my appointment there, I was told of a gentleman who is reputed to be the second in point of wealth in the parish, but who is famed for his boisterous and resolute spirit, and who often swears in a terrible manner. I never felt a heavier cross to visit at any other place. But duty urged me, and I ascended the hill on the side of which stood his house. I had never seen him, nor had he seen me, before: but I found him a tall, portly, elderly man, and very intelligent. I conversed with him, read and expounded a portion of God's word, and prayed. After prayer he manifested a degree of inward agitation, but treated me with great civility and respect. Last Wednesday I went there again. He appeared glad to see me, and invited me to take tea at his house on my next visit to the neighbourhood. O may our good Lord pluck this brand from the burning! I preached at Earlswood on Thursday, and desired those to stay after the first service who were determined to follow Christ,—the subject on which I had been preaching. The chapel was more than half filled, and not one left. Our great Master was eminently present."

Towards the commencement of the following year, 1827, we meet with several entries bearing on his own religious experience, as well as on his pastoral work. Two of these may be here given.— "Sunday, January 21st. To-day, both morning and evening, I have found the Lord present in His house. I have been earnestly seeking to become more powerfully impressed with the love of souls, and to guard against any tendency to lukewarmness of spirit or formality in my duties."—"Saturday, February 24th. A short time ago I feared that the fre-

quency of my pastoral visits would lead to their being
but little heeded, and that, on my part, I should get to
attend to them as a matter of course, without feeling.
But, blessed be my God, I have this week been much
encouraged. Some have been brought under conviction; many feel in a degree the quickening power
of the word; and a few are added to our numbers.
I feel my own soul blessed in the work of the Lord,
and I pant for closer fellowship with Him. Yesterday
I completed my thirtieth year. O how can I worthily
magnify my heavenly Father for the mercies of one
day, how much less for thirty years of uninterrupted
blessing!"

It was an established custom to hold a love-feast
at Earlswood in the afternoon of Easter Monday, to
be followed by a sermon in the same place in the
evening. It fell to Mr. Wood's lot to conduct these
services during each of the three years which he spent
in the Circuit. The first of these occasions is thus
referred to in his Diary:—"April 21st, 1827. On
Monday last we held a love-feast at Earlswood, where
our friends have been accustomed to admit almost
any one who might choose to attend. To this I
objected, and would consent to the admission of none
without a ticket or a note. The chapel was filled,
both in the galleries and below, and we were favoured
with a gracious season. More than forty spoke their
experience, of whom the greater number gave sub-
stantial testimonies to the truth as it is in Jesus. Five
engaged in prayer, and a Divine unction was felt.
The love-feast, which began a little before two o'clock,
we closed at five, not being able to continue longer
on account of the evening preaching. This I did
reluctantly, as the longer we continued the more

lively the meeting became. The evening service continued until a late hour, as many were deeply distressed in soul, while others went home rejoicing in a sin-forgiving God and Saviour." Mr. Wood adds, "I have lately felt much blessed in preaching the word. The Holy One conveys it with power to the hearts of many. My own soul has been refreshed and encouraged, inasmuch as the Lord is making me instrumental in promoting the salvation of souls. But I feel very anxious that all who are benefited should render all the praise to the Triune Jehovah. I dread the thought of their attributing to me that which belongs to God only. But I know that the Lord heareth prayer, and will save souls. Glory be to His holy and glorious Name for ever and ever! Amen!"

In connection with Mr. Wood's labours on the north-eastern side of the Circuit, it is right to mention another incident, illustrative of the sacred boldness with which his love to Christ and to the souls of men inspired him, and illustrative also of the power which God gave him over some of the roughest and most thoughtless of our race. He was at Usk in the month of June, 1827, on the day of their pleasure-fair; and he writes, "After preaching I saw a great crowd moving in the direction of a field in the vicinity; and, as it appeared to me that a pitched battle was about to be fought, I could not remain where I was, but going towards the spot where the multitude was assembled, I found one man with his shirt off, and another nearly ready to begin the fight. I requested their attention for two minutes: and then, raising my voice so as to be heard above their uproar and swearing, I addressed them on the illegality, the danger, the wickedness, and the

F

disgrace of their proceedings, and advised them to lead a new life. I expected some insult; but, on the contrary, they treated me with great respect. Those who had placed themselves in advantageous positions to see the fight were the first to retire, as if ashamed of the prominent stations they occupied. The men put on their clothes; and all gradually but peaceably withdrew, except a few who continued about me as if desirous of hearing all I had to say. Praise to our Jehovah Jesus, 'the Prince of peace.'"

It must not be supposed, however, that Mr. Wood's energies were devoted chiefly to the country parts of the Circuit, and that he put forth less effort in the town of Newport itself. Here he preached with great zeal and earnestness, often, during the summer, conducting a service in the open air, immediately after the evening service in the chapel. Here, too, he carried out assiduously his plan of pastoral visitation; and, as he made it a rule not only to utter words of affectionate interest in those on whom he called, but to address them pointedly on the subject of personal religion, his visits were, under the Divine blessing, productive of great spiritual good. About the middle of the period that he spent in this Circuit, he records, "Yesterday I began again my visiting round from house to house under strong temptation to discouragement, thinking I should be regarded by the people as one bringing old tales. But I was never so much encouraged in this department of my work. *I went to every house, not excepting the Inns;* and I found many under good impressions. One of the members had become negligent. I first wrestled with God, and then conversed with the backsliding member. The Lord was pleased to soften her heart; she wept, and determined in the strength of grace to begin again. God greatly blessed my own soul while teaching and preaching from one house to another."

While Mr. Wood was thus assiduously engaged in the active labours of the ministry, he was called to endure domestic anxiety and suffering. The health of his beloved wife was several times seriously affected; and twice, during his three years' residence in Newport, she gave birth to children who were still-born. It was necessary, on several occasions, for her to have change of air; and, in the hope of recruiting her strength, she spent many months in Somersetshire, amidst the scenes of his labours as a Local Preacher. His affectionate heart was touched with her sufferings, but he had again and aagin to rejoice in the interposition of God on her behalf. In connection with one of his visits to Nempnett, where Mrs. Wood's relatives lived, to bring her and his son back with him to Newport, a serious accident befell them all, which threatened to be fatal to Mr. Wood, and the effects of which he retained, in a measure, to the end of life. As they were proceeding to Bristol in an open conveyance, in descending a hill, the horse suddenly began to plunge; and when the driver pulled up strongly the reins to check him, one of them broke. The driver instantly attempted to alight, to seize the head of the horse; but he was violently thrown forward, and Mr. and Mrs. Wood and their son were left in the conveyance, while the horse continued furiously to gallop forward. Ultimately the vehicle was brought into collision with the hedge, at the side of the road, and all three were thrown out, Mr. Wood, in particular, falling upon his face which was severely bruised and injured. On the following morning Mrs. Wood was seized with convulsions, as the result of the fearful shock which her nervous system had sustained. These recurred, at intervals of about an hour, until her medical attendants considered her case hopeless. But, in answer to his fervent prayer, she was mercifully restored. "When human help failed," he writes, "the Lord appeared in power and compassion. I cried mightily to Him, and He gave me a promise, 'Call upon Me in the day of trouble: I will deliver thee, and thou shalt glorify Me.' I felt I had a grain of faith: the 'mountain' was removed. From that moment she had no fit. She slept, and on the following morning reason began to exercise its functions, and her progress since that time astonishes all. Blessed, blessed be the Lord!"

It was during Mr. Wood's residence in Newport, that his esteemed uncle, Mr. Edward Wood, of Banwell, who had so strongly opposed his going out as a Missionary to India, was removed by death. On receiving the tidings of his uncle's dangerous illness, Mr. Wood hastened to Banwell to visit him; but before he arrived the mortal scene had closed. The record in his Diary shows the high esteem in which he held his uncle, and the affection with which he cherished his memory. "After my father's decease," he says, "I was much at my uncle's for several years. He had no family of his own, and he was very dear to me, as I believe I also was to him. He was a man of strict integrity, of inflexible adherence to what he believed to be right, and was always ready to render any kind office in his power to his neighbours. For more than thirty years he

was a Local Preacher in the Banwell Circuit, and
often went to his appointments when, from an
affliction, he had to ride in pain all the way. He
preached his last sermon at Wrington, the Sunday
before he was taken for death;—the same place at
which my beloved and revered father preached *his* last
sermon twenty-two years ago. O may I be found
more earnestly 'pressing toward the mark, for the
prize of my high calling,' that I may, at every moment,
be prepared to obey the call which yet lingers!"

The decease of his uncle became the occasion of
a beautiful and impressive development of Mr. Wood's
nobleness of character and delicate sense of honour
In consequence of a defect in his uncle's will, all his
leasehold property legally became his, as being his
heir-at-law. But, although Mr. Wood had, at this
time, to maintain himself, and his wife and son, on
the trifling allowances of an unmarried Minister, together with the little private property that he possessed,
he did not avail himself of the additional property
which thus accrued to him, nor did he even propose
to share it with his aunt. He assigned the whole of
it to her during her life, and did not reserve any
advantage to himself, after her decease, over his
younger brother and his sisters. Under the date of
Saturday, March 22nd, 1828, we find the following
entry in his Diary:—"Through an omission, my
uncle's will, as far as it related to his leasehold
property, was inefficient, and that property devolved
to me as his heir-at-law. By a deed of settlement, I
have settled the dwelling-house which he occupied,
and his leasehold property, on his widow during her
life, and, after her decease that it shall be divided
equally among the family, as I settled my late

father's property in 1824. I know it was my uncle's intention to alter his will, and to leave a larger bequest to me, as being his heir, and as a proof of his attachment and approval: but, as this was not done, I could not, in honour and the fear of God, take more than an equal share with my brother and three sisters; and I praise the Lord who inclined me so to do." Mr. Wood adds the following remarkable incident. " A singular circumstance occurred in connection with this event. Soon after my uncle's decease, before I knew that his will was ineffectual, or had the least idea of it, I dreamed that I was in Banwell churchyard, by his grave; and, while standing there, I saw him come forth. He stood by the side of a table upon which there lay some folio writing paper, as if partially written upon. I went towards him; and, on my doing so, he cast his eyes upon his will, as if inviting my attention, and, looking with an air of dissatisfaction, he said, ' That is not the thing that I intended: but thou needest not be governed by it, for it is not binding, and thou dost know how to manage.' " His uncle, it is added, in explanation, was always accustomed to address him by the singular pronoun " thou."

It is pleasing to reflect on the high honour, and the utter absence of selfishness, which marked this transaction. The zealous evangelist and pastor rose far above the love of money, and acted with scrupulous fidelity on the charge, " Look not every man on his own things, but every man also on the things of others." Thus his spirit was kept happily free from the distractions of a worldly state of feeling, and was enabled to apply itself with freshness and vigour to the work of the Lord.

The preaching of Mr. Wood in the Newport Circuit was often attended with remarkable power, and the people seemed riveted to the spot as they listened to his faithful appeals. One singular instance of this, at a week-evening service, may be given. Under the date of December 7th, 1828, he writes, "On Tuesday last I went to Alltaryn. They had not heard of my coming, but in a few minutes they collected a congregation, to whom I preached; and, as usual, after the conclusion of the service, I sat down for the assembly to disperse. They, however, both young and old, resumed their seats, or continued standing, as they were before I concluded, and declined either to move or speak, but fixed their attention on me. After waiting some time, I saw that I must begin again. I did so, and, after addressing them in a sitting posture, for some time, we again sang and prayed, and they separated. The Lord is doing a great work in that neighbourhood. Blessed be His holy Name!"

Mr. Wood's residence in Newport was marked by active co-operation with Christians of other denominations. Immediately after his arrival, Admiral Pearson visited the town, to promote the erection of a Seamen's Chapel, for the special benefit of the numerous sailors belonging to, or visiting, that flourishing port. Mr. Wood consented to act on the Committee appointed to carry out the design, and rendered important aid to the project. His counsels were especially valuable when the preparation of a suitable Trust Deed engaged the attention of the Committee; and that Deed, securing permanently the evangelical character of the teaching to be given in "the Mariners' Church," as the building was termed, was prepared very much according to his advice. The pulpit of that church was occupied, in turn, by the Ministers of various Christian denominations; and Mr. Wood cheerfully undertook the services which were assigned to him.

Another service which he rendered to the cause of our common Christianity, during his residence in this town, was the resuscitation of the Newport and West Monmouthshire Auxiliary of the British and Foreign Bible Society. He exerted himself unweariedly to bring about this result; and, being appointed one of the secretaries, he threw all his energies into the work, endeavouring to form Branch Associations throughout the neighbourhood, calling on persons of influence to enlist their sympathy in favour of the movement, and ultimately engaging in a personal canvass of the town of Newport, to secure a supply of the Scriptures to every family. He records with pleasure an interview which he had with Major Mackworth, an officer of sincere and deep piety, who had fixed his residence between Caerleon and Usk; and afterwards mentions their combined efforts to form a Ladies' Association in that neighbourhood. But the most remarkable of his efforts in this cause was the personal canvass before referred to, the account of which shall be given in his own words. Under the date of January 11th, 1829, he writes, "At a Meeting of our Bible Committee held October 17th last, it was resolved to canvass the town in order to ascertain who were without the Holy Scriptures. Some of the members of the Committee thought that this work would be better done by the Ministers of the town. I happened to be the only Minister present, and of course could not answer for those who were absent;

but I engaged, as to a supply of the Bible, to lay the state of the town before an ensuing meeting of the Committee. I the more readily engaged in this work because I wished to bear my testimony for God to all the accessible inhabitants of Newport before leaving them, and this errand furnished me with a good reason for calling at their houses. I set about the work accordingly; and on Friday last I had the gratification, by God's blessing, to state to the Committee, that I had visited upwards of *seven hundred families in Newport and Pillgwenlly.* To nearly all of these I have spoken on the subject of their present and eternal salvation. May the Lord command abundantly of His blessing, even life for evermore! The Bible Society occupies much attention: but it circulates *the word of 'the living God;'* and if I may be instrumental of sending abroad an increased number of copies in this town and neighbourhood, I will praise God, count it an honour which He has deigned to put upon me, and endeavour by rising earlier in the morning to get up my time. The immediate result of the canvass was the sale of nearly two hundred copies of the Scriptures, to be paid for by weekly contributions, to gather which collectors have been appointed."

Thus did this devoted servant of the Lord Jesus toil to save the souls of men. His three years' labour in the Newport Circuit yielded, through the Divine blessing, much precious fruit. The number of members in the Society returned to the Conference of 1829 was 340, being an increase of 80 on the number reported in 1826. Many, in this his first Circuit, as well as in other spheres of his hallowed labour, will form his "joy and crown of rejoicing in the day of the Lord Jesus." His association with his Superintendent,

the Rev. Humphrey Parsons, was eminently agreeable and happy.   The closing record in that part of
his Diary which relates to his ministry in Newport, is
a grateful acknowledgment of the uniform kindness
of Mr. Parsons, and his readiness to encourage him in
every effort to extend the kingdom of the Redeemer.

CHAPTER VI.

1829—1832.

TOWARDS the close of August, 1829, Mr. Wood removed to the Kingswood Circuit. He entered upon his ministry there by preaching on the forenoon of the Lord's day in the Kingswood Chapel, in the afternoon at Hanham, and in the evening at Redfield. The first of these services he had anticipated with much solicitude. The congregation that he was, for the first time, to address, included the sons of Ministers who were being trained at the old Kingswood School, together with their masters and the family of the Governor; and the thought of preaching to so many who were accustomed to listen to accomplished Ministers, and to some who were themselves preachers, as well as the thought that he was to stand in the pulpit which Mr. Wesley had so often occupied, considerably affected him. But when he reached the chapel, his depression ceased, and the consciousness of Divine help, and of the presence of the Spirit to apply the word with power, filled him with sacred joy. The experience of that day gave the promise of abundant blessing from God on his labours in his new sphere.

The zeal which Mr. Wood had manifested in his former Circuit still characterised him. It was a zeal enkindled by the Holy Spirit, and sustained by habitual communion with God; while the deep and solemn conviction which he cherished of the sinfulness and danger of unconverted men, of the efficacy of the sacrifice of Jesus, and of the preciousness of the salvation which is realised *in* HIM, made him "instant in season, out of season," in endeavouring to win souls. He had recourse to the measures which he had adopted in Newport and its neighbourhood, and which had there been made so useful. He made arrangements, for instance, to preach in private houses, and was greatly encouraged by the eagerness of the people around to attend these services, and by the instances of genuine conversion which came under his notice. He frequently preached in the open air, both on the Lord's day and on week-days. And he was indefatigable in pastoral visitation, seeking to rouse careless and lukewarm professors, as well as to build up and comfort those who were truly devoted to God, and availing himself of every opportunity of appealing to the unconverted members of the families on which he called. He knew how to blend fidelity with tenderness. To the poor and sorrowful, who knew and loved the Saviour, he was a son of consolation; but the directness of his appeals to the conscience was, at times, even terrible to the insincere professor and to those who were trifling with the mercy of God in Christ. The extent of his labours in this department was astonishing. It was no uncommon thing for him to pay 150 "spiritual visits," as he appropriately terms them in his Journal, in the course of a month, and sometimes the number rose as high as 190 or even 200. Nor was he appalled by the presence of disease, and the consciousness of danger. At one time, during his residence at Kingswood, typhus fever was prevalent in the neighbourhood; but he visited those who suffered from it without hesitation and without fear. Under the date of July 21st, 1830, he writes, "There being many sick in different parts of the Circuit, I borrowed a horse, and rode through nearly all the Circuit, and visited many. Several are ill of typhus fever." This was not the only occasion on which he availed himself of the readiness of his friends to furnish him with a horse, to enable him to carry out his system of pastoral visitation further than he could otherwise have done. A gentleman still resident at Kingswood, who well remembers his ministry in that Circuit,—Mr. George Dix,—writes to me, "I have known him worn down with walking; but, wishing to visit more persons, he would borrow a horse to enable him to do so. He carried it to such an extent that I feared he would materially injure himself. I tried, therefore, to restrain him, pointing out to him what I thought the consequences would be; but he would say, 'Souls are perishing: if you saw a house on fire would you not do all you could to rescue the inmates? Must I not, therefore, do all I can for the salvation of souls?'"

In the words now quoted we have a disclosure of the convictions and feelings that prompted Mr. Wood to these indefatigable labours, and sustained him in them. To us who are yet spared in the holy ministry he stands forth a beautiful pattern of quenchless love to the souls of men, and self-renouncing devotion to the cause of our blessed Lord. He "watched for the souls" of the people of his charge, as one "that must give account," caring for them, as the Apostle's language implies, with *sleepless vigilance*, and never losing sight of their eternal interests. But his example can scarcely be urged as one to be copied by *all* Ministers, in regard to the *extent* to which he gave himself up to pastoral visitation. Reviewing his career, so abundantly owned of God, we cannot wish that it had been at all different: but it may be questioned whether, in some of the important spheres of labour which he was called to occupy, his pulpit ministrations, intelligent and valuable as they were, might not have been even richer and more effective, had he kept a larger portion of every forenoon for study. As a *general* rule, it may, perhaps, be affirmed, that the forenoon of every day should be spent by a Minister in his own house, in the studies appropriate to his sacred calling, and the afternoon be given to systematic pastoral visitation. But if the solemn sense of personal responsibility, and the intense longing for the salvation of men, which Mr. Wood cherished, influenced us all, who can estimate the blessing that would come down upon the Churches, and the power that would be exerted upon the world around?

It was not long before he was cheered by witnessing a gracious awakening. He moved amidst scenes of revival which filled him with sacred joy; but he sought to conduct all the meetings of which he took charge, so as to guard the spirituality of the work. Under the date of November 25th, 1829, he writes in his Journal, "Since my former entry I have been engaged almost every night, and the Lord has made bare His holy arm in turning sinners from darkness to light in almost every meeting. Last Sunday evening, I believe upwards of forty were earnestly seeking the salvation of God; and lately I have almost had to use force to get the people from the chapel. To dis-

courage every appearance of mere excitement of the
animal feelings, I always have those who faint taken
out of the meeting; since, if they are never so
sincere, we can do them no good until they are
recovered, for which the air is very useful, or if it
should be through mere sympathy, through seeing
others in distress, it is desirable to suppress whatever
is not from the Holy One. My own soul is much
blessed with the Divine power. I feel that I am the
Lord's, I trust altogether, body, soul, and spirit: but
O for a fulness! I want a constant plenitude of the
Spirit of God, and I groan for a brighter manifestation
of my Redeemer in my soul." A little later, December 14th, 1829, we find him thus recording the work of
one Lord's day:—"Yesterday I preached in the
morning at Redfield. In the afternoon, before
preaching, I met some young members and gave
several notes of admission; and after preaching I met
two classes. Both afternoon and evening the chapel
was crowded to excess. After the evening preaching
we continued in exhortation and prayer, and some
who came careless and thoughtless were powerfully
convinced. After ten o'clock, with great difficulty we
induced them to leave the chapel, and some went
home weeping aloud through the street."

Several of the colliery-villages in the neighbourhood of Kingswood were in a dark and low condition;
and there was one place which Mr. Wood speaks of
as "*cold* Clay Hill," the people of which seemed
utterly unmoved by the evangelistic efforts that had
been put forth, so that it was in contemplation, when
he entered upon the Circuit, to abandon our cause
there. But even in this place the power of God was
manifested. Several were convinced of sin, and new

vigour was infused into the little Society. In another place, termed "The Fish Ponds," Mr. Wood took a special interest, and was the means of again introducing Methodism into it. His efforts to benefit this place were crowned by God with signal success. Under the date of Tuesday, January, 5th, 1830, he writes, "For some time I had felt a wish to preach at the Fish Ponds, although I was not acquainted with the place. Having heard of a man who would be glad to have preaching in his house, I went over yesterday, and preached from Isaiah lv. 6, 7. The word of the Lord was with power. Many felt. I explained to some who remained the nature of Church-communion as it exists among us, and desired any to give me their names who were willing to unite for assisting each other to work out their salvation. Nine did so, among whom were a man and his wife who have been in the way twenty-five years." The work thus auspiciously commenced continued to prosper. A chapel was erected; and when Mr. Wood was about to close his three years' labour in the Circuit, he thus gratefully acknowledges the work which the Lord had wrought there. "I met," he says, "the Trustees of the Fish Ponds Chapel. Now that the accounts of the chapel are settled, after the enlargement, the Trustees have a debt of £50, and the seats are let to the amount of £14 per annum. Praise the Lord for the prosperity with which He has been pleased to visit that village. About two years and a half since we had no cause there. Now we have a chapel that will seat three hundred persons well filled, and the seats well let. We have also sixty members in four classes, and more than two hundred children in the Sunday School. To

God, who alone hath wrought the work, be all the glory!"

Some idea may be formed of the amount of hallowed toil which Mr. Wood was accustomed, at this period, to crowd into the Lord's day, from one or two entries in his Diary.—"Sunday, June 20th, 1830. I preached at Redfield, at 10½ o'clock; without doors at Lawrence Hill at 12¼, and without doors at Rose Green at 2. There was a large company, some of whom got under a shed where I stood, but many could not come near it. I renewed tickets afterwards. At 6 o'clock I preached at Redfield again, addressed the Society, and then held another meeting. Some were in distress."—"Sunday, June 27th, 1830. I preached at the Fish Ponds at 8 o'clock, and renewed tickets, at Redfield at 10½, at Kingswood at 2½, and met the Society and renewed tickets, and on the Hill at 6 o'clock, without doors, to about 1,000 people. Afterwards we had a meeting in the chapel for those who were desiring salvation. A day of good. Glory to God!" Such an amount of labour on the Lord's day is certainly far too much for ordinary men. But Mr. Wood undertook it with delight. Though occasionally the subject of pain and weakness, his constitution was naturally robust, and his temperament ardent; and he cheerfully devoted his untiring energy to the work of the Master whom he loved. In some degree he could adopt the words prophetically uttered of the Lord Jesus Himself, and which *His* career so beautifully exemplified, "The zeal of Thine house hath eaten Me up."

In the youths who were being trained at Kingswood School, he took an affectionate interest. The pastoral charge of that establishment devolved, of

G

course, chiefly upon the Governor; but Mr. Wood
gladly availed himself of opportunities of meeting the
boys for religious conversation and prayer. Under
the date of Sunday, January 24th, 1830, he writes, "I
met the boys before afternoon preaching, and was
greatly rejoiced to find several who were happy in
God. When I met them a few days before, not one
of them enjoyed an evidence of pardon." On February 7th, he says, "I met the boys at Kingswood, and
was truly thankful to find several who could rejoice
in a sense of God's forgiving love, and others are
earnestly seeking the same blessing." But these
modest entries in his Journal convey but a faint idea
of his efforts to promote the spiritual welfare of these
youths. The Rev. Dr. James, now the Secretary of
the Wesleyan-Methodist Conference, has favoured me
with a brief notice of his personal recollections of this
period of Mr. Wood's labours. "My remembrances
of the late Rev. Joseph Wood," he writes, "are all
hallowed and happy. This is particularly the case
as to the time of his sojourn in the Kingswood Circuit. I was among the senior scholars when he was
appointed, and shall never forget the intense and
overwhelming earnestness of his preaching. It made
an indelible impression on my mind. Many of the
boys, under his powerful sermons, were convinced of
sin, and a remarkable outpouring of the Holy Spirit
was vouchsafed to the School at large. Nor was he
satisfied with pulpit efforts to do us good. It was his
practice to invite a few boys at a time to take tea
with him on a Saturday afternoon, and the time was
occupied with efforts to lead us to Christ, and
affectionate and most powerful prayers on our
behalf. I well remember several of those Saturday

evening meetings. On the last occasion of the kind he gave me my first ticket of admission into the Methodist Society."

The relief of the poor, who abounded in Kingswood and its neighbourhood, and especially the relief of those who were sick as well as poor, engaged a large share of Mr. Wood's attention. He took a leading part in the operations of the Benevolent Society, and was one of its most assiduous visitors. At an early period of his residence in Kingswood he records, "I attended the general Committee of the Benevolent Society at 11 o'clock, and the Visitors' Meeting in the evening. I have been much engaged lately in visiting cases of distress, to find out proper objects of charity in order to relieve them from the Benevolent Society. The sight of so much distress is exceedingly painful ; but how exquisite the pleasure of being able to administer relief!" In addition to the resources which the Benevolent Society afforded, Mr. Wood frequently had considerable sums placed at his disposal, to be distributed among the necessitous and deserving. Among the friends who thus assisted him in his labours of Christian love, the name of the late Robert Lewis, Esq., of Downend, stands prominent. Again and again he handed Mr. Wood £10 or even £20 for the relief of cases of distress, and thus gladdened the heart of the faithful pastor. After recording, on one occasion, the receipt of a cheque for £20 from this gentleman, Mr. Wood exclaims, "Praise the Lord for this! Another supply for the poor! O, how shall I sufficiently magnify His compassion! May my God very abundantly and continually bless His servant, Robert Lewis, and crown him with everlasting blessedness!" It was Mr.

Wood's practice to send to Mr. Lewis, from time to time, an account of the manner in which the money so entrusted to him had been expended; and during one period of three months he found that he had visited 201 cases, containing 750 persons in family. "Of these," he adds, "59 were cases of affliction; 56 were poor widows; and 43 fatherless children; and of the widows 23 were from 70 to 90 years of age." But he did not glory in himself as he reflected upon these services to the poor and desolate. "I feel," he says, "that God has greatly honoured me in permitting and strengthening me to do this. I almost shudder lest I should think anything of my efforts in this matter as involving merit. No; *far, far, far* from it. I am truly—and, I trust, I deeply feel it—'an unprofitable servant;' and I can look on nothing I have said or done but I feel that it needs the sprinkling of the blood of the atonement, and must be thus sprinkled before it can be accepted of God."

At the conclusion of his first year in the Kingswood Circuit, Mr. Wood was received into full connection with the Conference, as a Minister of Jesus Christ, set apart entirely to His work. The Conference of 1830, the first which Mr. Wood attended, was held in Leeds, and its proceedings and public services called forth deep interest in his mind. The following year the Conference assembled in Bristol, and another opportunity was thus afforded to him of being present at its deliberations, and enjoying the pulpit ministrations of some of the most distinguished Ministers of that day. From these assemblies of his brethren he came back to his Circuit with renewed zeal, and with simple devotedness to the work of his Master, Christ.

On several occasions Mr. Wood was earnestly solicited to visit the scenes of his former labours, both in the Circuit in which he had so long resided as a Local Preacher, and in the Newport Circuit which he had recently left. With some of these requests he complied, always taking care to limit these visits, so that his own Circuit should not suffer from them. The expressions of attachment with which he was everywhere greeted, more especially in the Newport Circuit, deeply affected him ; and his spirit was again and again gladdened by witnessing his spiritual children still "walking in the truth." During his residence in Kingswood, also, he laboured to remedy some evils which had existed in the state of the chapel-trusts in the Banwell Circuit, to reduce the heavy debts upon them, and to obtain for several of them a new appointment of Trustees.

But, amidst all his public labours, he cultivated assiduously his personal piety. The records in his Diary of spiritual blessings received, of holy peace and joy filling his soul, of constant strivings after higher attainments in holiness, are very instructive and edifying; while the notices of temptations endured—temptations which, in one place, he speaks of as "abundant, fierce, and foul"—shows that he was no stranger to the inward conflicts of the Christian life, and to the fierce assaults of the powers of darkness. After the statement just cited he exclaims, "Lord, every moment sustain me. I am as an infant : teach, nourish, and hold me up. O may I abide every trial, and prove as gold thoroughly purified!" But these seasons of spiritual conflict, though frequently recurring, were far outnumbered by seasons of holy tranquillity and intense aspirations after more intimate communion with God; and some yet living who knew him in Kingswood speak of him as an eminently holy man, one whose whole bearing and conduct were in accordance with the doctrines which he preached.

In these exercises of sacred toil and cheerful service to Christ and to mankind, his three years in Kingswood passed rapidly away. During this period the number of members in the Society had increased from 650 to 900, and every interest was now, by the blessing of God, in a flourishing condition. Mr. Wood's heart was filled with humble gratitude to God, as he reflected on the goodness which had been shown to him, and the manifold proofs that "the hand of the Lord" had indeed been with him. In the spirit of entire self-dedication to the Lord Jesus, he made preparations to enter upon a new sphere of labour. Several Circuits, and among them Camborne and Derby, requested his ministerial labours, when his term at Kingswood should expire. He accepted the invitation of the former of these Circuits, and was appointed to it by the Conference of 1832: and in August of that year he had to tear himself from the embraces of multitudes who loved him, and to whom he had been the messenger of God for good. One poor woman, who was powerfully convinced of sin under a sermon which he preached in the open air, only a few days before he left, being ignorant of the Methodist economy which requires a change of Ministers after three years, came to him among the rest, and with sobs and cries entreated him not to go away. "I felt," he says, after recording the fact, "a keen pang in parting from this infant just struggling into spiritual life." But the separation was inevitable:

and, after spending a little time with his own and
Mrs. Wood's relatives in the neighbourhood of Banwell and Nempnett, he reached Camborne on the
24th of August, with Mrs. Wood and his son, and
received a cordial welcome to his new home.

CHAPTER VII.

———∘∘⦂⦁⦂∘∘———

THE CAMBORNE CIRCUIT.

1832—1835.

THE county of Cornwall, in which the next six years of Mr. Wood's life were spent, presents a beautiful and impressive illustration of the elevating influence of a living Christianity on the mass of a population. The cordial reception of the truth of Christ has softened and refined the character of multitudes who would otherwise have been rough and defiant; it has given a right direction to their natural impetuosity; it has made them thoughtful and discriminating, and created a taste for intellectual pleasures; and it has rendered the cottages of the poor the abodes of peace, contentment, and domestic happiness.

In no part of our country has God more signally honoured the instrumentality of Wesleyan Methodism. The self-denying labours of Mr. Wesley himself, and of those who shared his privations and toils, were rewarded with a rich harvest of souls; and a similar blessing has attended the efforts of successive generations of Methodist Ministers, and of the noble men who, as Local Preachers or Class-Leaders, have sought to extend Christ's spiritual kingdom. In towns comparatively small spacious sanctuaries have been erected, many of which are filled with devout and

earnest hearers; and almost every little village and
hamlet has its chapel, its Sunday-school, and its
class-meetings. There is a love, too, among the
Cornish Methodists, for a rich and deep exposition of
the word of God; and that feeling extends even to
the village congregations. The writer turns affectionately to a county in which some of the best years
of his own early ministry were spent, and in which
he was permitted to witness some of the most remarkable displays of the power of the Holy Ghost in
leading men to Christ that have occurred in the
history of the Church.

The Camborne Circuit, to which Mr. Wood was
now appointed, embraced a large mining population.
The principal places, besides Camborne, were
Tuckingmill and Pool, which lie between it and
Redruth; but there were several country places,
some of which were at a considerable distance
from the Circuit-town, and to which the Ministers
rode,—a good horse being then an indispensable
requisite in every Cornish Circuit. As often as the
Sabbath came round, the beautiful chapel in Camborne presented an impressive sight. It was the
privilege of the writer to spend two or three Sabbaths
there a few years later; and he can never lose the
impression of the thoughtful, earnest countenances of
the working men who filled the whole space under
the gallery on one side of the chapel, sitting very
closely together, and apparently devouring the word
of life. The congregation was a large and intelligent one; and the devotional habits of hundreds who
were present, and their profound sympathy with the
truth, were a great help to the servants of Christ who
had to unfold to them His message. The Societies

in many parts of the Circuit were large. At the Conference of 1832 the number of members was 2,356, bearing, probably, a larger proportion to the number of inhabitants than could be found in any other part of the kingdom.

During the first two years of Mr. Wood's residence in Camborne, he was the second Minister, being associated with the late Rev. John Davis: in the third year, he took the superintendency of the Circuit, having as his colleague the late Rev. Thomas Jewell. About three months after his entrance upon his work, he makes this entry in his Journal:—"In commencing my labours in this Circuit, I had to meet a great number of classes to renew their quarterly tickets, and was exceedingly blessed in hearing the deep, sound, clear experience of many. About eighteen months since there was an extraordinary ingathering in this Circuit, about 1,400 having joined the Society. These have stood remarkably well; and although I foresaw that it was likely we should have much up-hill work with them, yet I have seen reason to be encouraged. In the public means the Lord has been present, and several very promising young persons have joined the Society, particularly at Camborne and Tuckingmill. Some backsliders have been powerfully wrought upon, and are returning to God with broken hearts. But while there is very much that is encouraging in the neighbourhood of Camborne, the more distant parts of the Circuit appear to be less in earnest, and in many minds there is much apathy. O may the Lord greatly quicken them! Some at Camborne have lately been clearly brought into full salvation, and many others are hungering and thirsting after that great blessing. We began, a few weeks since, a prayer-meeting at half past five o'clock on Wednesday mornings. This has proved a blessing: the presence of the Lord has been felt by us in an extraordinary degree, and the number attending is increasing."

It was not long before Mr. Wood's attention was directed to the sufferings of the poor in Camborne and its neighbourhood, and the adoption of suitable measures for their relief. The feelings which had prompted and sustained him in his arduous labours in connection with the Kingswood Benevolent Society, would not allow him to look with indifference on poverty and destitution, wherever he might reside. But the account of his proceedings shall be given in his own words. "In this large and populous parish, containing about 8,000 souls, there exists often much distress, arising partly from a redundancy of hands for the work, partly from the injurious operation of the present mode of paying the miners, and partly from the very small number of those who are able to afford assistance to the poor by whom they are surrounded. Another lamentable consideration is, the great number of accidents which happen in the mines, by which men are disabled and frequently killed; which, combined with the pernicious character of the occupation of mining, as the men have frequently to work in bad air, inducing consumptions and abridging their lives, throws upon charity a great number of widows and fatherless children. Still in this parish there existed no Benevolent Society. A small sick fund, raised in our own Society, and which was in a languishing state, was the only thing of the kind. My spirit was much stirred for the poor, and I named it to a few. Having some encouragement, I printed proposals for forming a Benevolent Society, dated December 3rd, 1832, and calling a meeting for the 7th. A few attended, when I explained the nature and operations of the proposed Society, and it was determined to commence on the plan proposed. I, at first, had, of necessity, to fill the office of Secretary, and have been much engaged since that time in endeavouring to get it into working order. In order to do this, I have drawn a rough map of the parish, and divided it into seventeen districts, for most of which I have obtained visitors, and am filling up the remainder. In connection with this, it will be necessary to form a working society of Ladies for making up such articles of dress as we may want to give away. I find a general willingness among them to enter into this design, and expect they will have a meeting in a few days. May the Lord prosper these efforts to alleviate the distresses of the suffering poor, and accept all the glory of whatever good may be accomplished; for all the praise is due to Him alone!"

It is almost needless to say, that Mr. Wood applied himself in Camborne, as in his former Circuits, to the pastoral visitation of his people, making his calls really "spiritual visits," and pointedly addressing the unconverted members of families on their guilt and danger, and inviting them to Christ for salvation. In the month of October, 1832, we find him engaging in a personal canvass of the town for subscriptions to our Foreign Missions, and making this subordinate to his great work. After mentioning that he had undertaken such a canvass, he adds, "This I do the more readily, and prefer doing *alone*, that I might the more freely talk to all on whom I call respecting their everlasting salvation." Such a statement needs no comment. O that the same spirit of holy zeal for Christ, and for the souls of men, rested upon us all!

Among the incidents which marked his life of continuous pastoral labour, and the notices of his personal history and experience, supplied by his Diary, the following may be selected:—

"January 27th, 1833.—In visiting I found a young person who, when I was in the neighbourhood before, got away and would not be seen by me. I, however, prayed for her in my heart. She was now pleased to be talked with, and I found that conviction had seized her when she ran away, and had not left her from that time."

"February 10th.—A good day, on which I felt much of God. At the Lord's Supper in the evening, Miss —— was set at liberty. She had long been holding something, not willing to part with all. She had also desired to obtain pardon in her closet, quite alone: but this evening she gave up all, and cast her soul on Christ, willing that He should do anything with her. Then the Lord broke into her soul in such power that, in spite of all her previous wishes to the contrary, she burst aloud into praise and thanksgiving. So will the Lord humble our pride, softening or casting out every thing unyielding, before he forms the clay into a vessel of honour; and well He does, or the work would be marred, and unlike a vessel of God's workmanship."

"February 24th.—I had a high day. It was a time of power in the morning at Forest Gate, and at the Lord's Supper which followed the public service. In the afternoon I preached and administered the sacrament at Porkellis; and in the evening preached and held a love-feast at Crelly. It was, I think, upon the whole, the best I ever attended. They spoke briefly and to the point, not a minute being lost between the speakers, with an unusual degree of Divine unction. It was with difficulty that I persuaded them to give over speaking about ten o'clock, telling them that it was time for them and for myself to go to our homes."

"March 3rd.—Glory to my good Lord, I have had a blessed day, after a sharp trial yesterday! Well, I would always have trials, if I might not otherwise have strong consolations."

"April 14th.—In the love-feast at Camborne, several bore a most clear testimony to the cleansing power of the Holy Ghost, who had received the blessing within the last few months. This I feel to be a cause of gratitude and encouragement."

"May 5th.—I was greatly exhausted this evening at Tuckingmill, having gone a long visiting round in the afternoon, and prayed with eight families. I have a desire to fill up every moment on the Lord's day, when not engaged in public duties, in visiting, etc., but perhaps I have sometimes gone beyond the mark, and by too much exertion in the course of the day have suffered, and the congregation has suffered, in the evening. The Lord teach me wisdom!"

"May 18th.—I preached at Penzance, and made a collection for their Tract Society. On Monday, the 19th, I went to the Land's End, and sat on the point of the cliff. The scenery here is so majestic and awful as to be almost overwhelming. I went there-

from to the Logan Rock, and by the help of a man of
the neighbourhood, putting his hands against the
side of the rock for my feet to rest on, I got to the
top of it. The man then set it in motion. The
feeling is peculiar, and not a little trying to the
nervous system, while rocking on a rock of more
than seventy tons weight on the verge of a towering
precipice. Although quite wearied when I returned,
yet it was long before I could sufficiently compose
myself to obtain sleep, so deeply impressed and
almost overpowered was my mind with the scenery,
and with the situations in which I had been."

In the month of June, 1833, Mr. Wood, with his
wife and son, visited Banwell, and then spent a few
days at Kingswood, amidst the scenes of his recent
happy and successful labours. He was deeply affected by the proofs of warm affection which met him
on every hand, and especially by the crowds that
came again to hear from his lips the word of life.
" The kindness of the friends," he writes, "was
without measure; but the excitement was too great,
and for some days I suffered greatly therefrom. I
am sure they think too highly of me, and make far
too much of me. O let the Lord accept the honour!
for, if I have been useful to them, it was only because
He chose to employ me."

Soon after his return to Camborne, he was
visited by his esteemed friends, the late Samuel
Budgett, Esq., of Kingswood, with Mrs. Budgett,
and his sister, Miss Sarah Budgett. He greatly
enjoyed their society, and, as far as his public and
pastoral duties permitted, accompanied them to some
of the most interesting spots in Cornwall, which

naturally attract the attention of visitors. In his varied labours he was greatly encouraged by the manifest proofs of the presence of the Lord, and by the numerous instances of conversion and spiritual quickening with which he was favoured. His own religious experience was marked by firm trust in Christ and conscious self-dedication to Him ; and he enjoyed many seasons of most blessed and intimate fellowship with God, intermingled with others of severe mental conflict. Two extracts from his Diary will illustrate this. Under the date of August 11th, 1833, he writes, "In the prayer-meeting last evening after preaching, I felt an extraordinary measure of the Divine influence. I have seldom felt such power with God. Glory, glory to His Name! I have had, for some time past, such views of my unworthiness, and remembrance of past sin, that my spirit has been well nigh overwhelmed, and but for the cross of Christ my Saviour I could not look up. The powers of darkness, endeavouring to induce discouragement and apathy, have mightily wrought with fiery trial; but I magnify my God that I find Him lifting up my head, so that I can rejoice in His salvation. O how good, how unspeakably gracious, is my God to His poor servant!" And under the date of October 6th, we find these cheering words :— "I have lately enjoyed sweet and gracious manifestations of the presence and power of God. There have been a sinking into nothing, and feeling Him to be my God and my all, a peace in God and continual resting in the atonement of Jesus Christ, a more intimate communion and fellowship, and eternity more desirable and glorious, a holding all as from God, and a directing all to Him as my end. Glory be to the Father, the Son, and the Holy Ghost. Amen."

The energy of Mr. Wood developed itself in every form of benevolent effort which lay within his power. Towards the commencement of the year 1834 we find him attending a meeting called to consider the best means of providing education for the poor of Camborne. At that meeting he proposed a series of resolutions, all of which were carried, and he accepted the office of Minute Secretary. "This," he observes, "I should have declined, having my hands full already; but I thought that perhaps it would not be easy to find one vigorously to carry out the plan proposed." He conducted a correspondence with the Lords Commissioners of the Treasury, and obtained from them a portion of the Parliamentary Grant towards building School-rooms for Charity Schools; and he had the great satisfaction of seeing such a building erected in Camborne, and well-appointed Day-Schools in active operation.

It is a long-established custom, in connection with Cornish Methodism, that a sermon should be preached on Whit-Monday in Gwennap Pit,—a large natural amphitheatre in which Mr. Wesley, and several of the early Methodist Preachers, often declared the message of salvation. In the year 1834 Mr. Wood was requested to undertake this service; and his account of the day deserves to be placed on record :— "On Monday, May 19th, I preached at Gwennap Pit. This vast amphitheatre was crowded, presenting one unbroken cloud of human beings from the bottom to the utmost verge of the enclosure, and by some who were there I was informed that there were many hundreds outside who could not gain admittance. Considering that the voice ascends, I stood lower on one side of the pit than preachers generally have been accustomed to do. I also stood so as to have the wind at my back, which was a help in carrying forward my voice, and those who stood farthest off on the opposite side said they could distinctly hear while I published 'the grace of God which bringeth salvation unto all men,' etc. The sight of such a concourse is awfully impressive ; and, while standing among the collected thousands, the whole of whom rising on the terraced interior of the Pit are visible, one is powerfully impressed with a sense of one's own individual insignificance. Having put forth all my strength in order to be heard, I felt somewhat exhausted ; but, after we got to the Pit, a note was received from the Preacher who was, according to custom, to occupy the pulpit in the evening at the chapel ; and I could not withstand the importunity of the friends and the Preacher to preach again at Karharrack. There I felt much power from God, and a refreshing shower fell which made us all greatly to rejoice. Glory to my great King!"

A singular incident, which occurred about this time, is recorded by Mr. Wood. In one of the smaller country places of his Circuit, the people were accustomed to carry the pulpit-Bible after the service to a private house, and to take it back to the chapel when again wanted for Divine worship. The Bible was of the 8vo. size ; and on a week-evening, when Mr. Wood was just about to preach, he took up the book before him to find his text, but on opening it found it to be a volume of the *Methodist Magazine* for 1804. On the page at which he opened it, there stood prominently the words, "My grace is sufficient for thee." His mind was arrested by this passage, and, as there was not time to have the Bible fetched, he resolved to give an address to the people upon it. Two months afterwards he learned, that a woman, a member of a neighbouring Society, who had just lost her husband under circumstances peculiarly distressing, and who was labouring under great depression of mind, being even tempted by Satan to self-destruction, was at that service; and under that address the snare was broken, and her soul was filled with abundant comfort.

Peculiar circumstances deferred Mr. Wood's visit, this year, to Somersetshire, until August. At that time Mrs. Wood's mother was dangerously ill; but they arrived in time to see her and minister to her comfort. Mr. Wood preached on the Lord's day in three places in the Banwell Circuit, making in each a collection for the chapel; and then devoted two days to the Kingswood Circuit, preaching in the evenings at Hanham Street and Redfield. He left Mrs. Wood and their son with her mother to remain until the mortal scene should close; and he himself hastened back to Camborne, the chief pastoral charge of which now devolved on him. Mrs. Collings lingered until September 23rd, 1834, when she departed, happy in that Saviour whom she had long known and loved.

Soon after Mr. Wood had entered upon the superintendency of the Camborne Circuit, many parts of the Cornwall District were disturbed by the agitation which then affected the Connexion, the occasion, or pretext, of which was the establishment of the Theological Institution for accepted candidates for the ministry. Happily his own Circuit was preserved in peace; but the influences that were at work around tended to hinder spiritual prosperity. The Missionary income of the Camborne Circuit in the year 1834 exceeded the amount raised in any preceding year, and in this Mr. Wood greatly rejoiced. But his own soul was often the seat of severe and harassing conflicts. Towards the beginning of 1835 he writes, "About two months since I had, for a long period, to encounter the most violent and repeated temptations. I could often merely cry for help, and cast my soul on Christ who graciously sustained me. After that period a season of dryness came on, that tried me exceedingly, and I was led, in the latter case as in the former, to see my utter weakness and worthlessness, and to wonder at God's condescending goodness in deigning in any way to employ me. But I feel at present, blessed be God, more spiritual refreshing. O for the full baptism of the Holy One!"

In April, 1835, he experienced a merciful preservation from the attempt of a wicked man seriously to injure him. While he was preaching, on a week-evening, at Kehelland, in his own Circuit, a large stone was thrown through the window of the chapel opposite to the pulpit with great violence. This stone was evidently aimed at him; but it was diverted from its course by the bar of the window, and struck the pulpit only. A small fragment of the broken glass struck Mr. Wood on one temple, but produced no material injury. The congregation was greatly alarmed; but Mr. Wood, after requesting one or two to find, if possible, the offender, calmly proceeded with his discourse, rejoicing in the gracious interposition of Divine Providence on his behalf.

In the spring of this year he visited the Scilly

Islands, in company with the late Rev. John Baker, then of Truro, on a Missionary deputation ; and his narrative of that visit is full of interest. "We left Penzance," he says, "on May 15th, soon after 10 o'clock, a.m. ; and, after a rough passage, we arrived at St. Mary's a little before 7 o'clock the following morning. These Islands form a truly picturesque and interesting group. They are very numerous, although only about six are inhabited. Lying near to each other, the sail from one to another would be very inviting, but for the stormy character of the sea in these parts, and the rapidity of the currents. This is so much the case that, on the finest day, if a visit be paid to another island, say Tresco, which is the next in importance to St. Mary's, there is no calculating with any confidence on being able to get back, even if you stay there but an hour ; and the distance is but three miles. Persons are sometimes detained in this way several days before they can return to their homes. The number of accidents, too, is considerable. The Islands are greatly over-populated, and the poverty in the off-islands, *i.e.*, all but St. Mary's, is very great. Still the people cling to their rocks as the limpets on their shores, and would almost prefer starving together to being removed. Their manners are very gentle, more so, indeed, than those of any class of people among whom I have ever been. St. Mary's contains about 1,400 inhabitants, nearly half of the whole population of the Islands. The town is neat and pleasantly situated. They have no robberies, and never put up the shutters of their shop-windows but once in the week, on Saturday evening. Our chapel in the town will contain 500 persons, and there are two in the country. On

Sunday morning and afternoon I preached, and Mr. Baker on Sunday evening. On Monday evening we held our Missionary Meeting. The Rev. W——, a young clergyman lately come to the Islands, who is simple-hearted and truly devoted to God, was at our chapel on Sunday afternoon, and assisted at the public meeting by moving one of the resolutions. May the Lord keep him and make him abundantly useful ! On Tuesday, there being no wind for sailing homeward, we went to Tresco. I rambled among the cottagers, and saw their mode of living, and inquired into their state. We informed them that we intended to hold service in the chapel at one o'clock. The building will hold two hundred; and it was nearly filled. I preached, and Mr. Baker exhorted. They drank in the word, as the thirsty ground doth the rain. Their simplicity and fervent affection was such as I can never forget. One of the deputation has been accustomed to visit them on the Sunday afternoon when the weather would permit; but this was impossible on the present occasion, as on Sunday it was blowing a gale, and I was truly thankful for an opportunity of visiting them on Tuesday. Mr. Baker preached at St. Mary's on Tuesday morning, and I engaged in the same work, after returning from Tresco, on Tuesday evening. A gracious sense of the Divine presence and blessing pervaded all the services. We left by the packet on Wednesday morning, highly gratified, much profited, and truly thankful. We got to Penzance on Thursday morning between four and five o'clock, returned to Camborne by a van, and I went to my place at Crelly, and preached in the evening. The geological formation of the Islands resembles that of the Land's End, from which it is probable they were at some time disrupted; but they have no mine."

Shortly after his return to Camborne, Mr. Wood met with an accident which laid him aside, for more than three weeks, from active service, and put to a severe test his Christian resignation. But the grace of God sustained him, and made even this season of trial one of permanent spiritual blessing. "On Tuesday, June 2nd," he writes, "I went to Porkellis. In my way from seeing one of our dying members, the horse fell with me and upon my left leg. This caused a contusion of the small bone, and my ankle-joint was much injured. I got some who came to the spot to lift me on the horse, and I rode to the chapel, determined, if possible, to preach; but, on being lifted from the horse, I was in such excruciating pain that I found it impossible. I was again lifted up, and in great misery rode home. The surgeon considers the case likely to give more pain, and to be more tedious, than if the bone had been broken. This is to me a new kind of discipline. I have felt no difficulty, according to my ability, to exercise the active graces; but the Lord would now teach me more of the passive. The most trying part of the exercise is, my being unable to engage in my usual work, although I know the Lord can do well without me. I am poor sinful dust and ashes, richly deserving chastisement. O may He sanctify every stroke, and if He shall see good further to employ me, may I ever hereafter be the better for this visitation! Amen, for Christ's sake, Amen."

On Tuesday, June 30th, he thus comments on his affliction, and records his first efforts to resume his beloved work of preaching Christ. "This evening

four weeks the accident happened by which I am
still confined. I have felt, I trust, a perfect willingness
to suffer all God's will; but I have experienced spiritual
conflicts peculiarly distressing. Satan has been let
loose, in some degree, as if to sift me as wheat; all
my foundations have seemed to tremble; and while I
have felt that I would rather be crushed to atoms than
yield to the enemy, I have also been deeply conscious
that without God's grace I could do nothing but sin.
Sometimes I have felt as if I could be glad to get into
some retired spot, in which to mourn my past offences,
and, if God should so far condescend to employ me, that I
may there search out, in order to do good to, any forsaken
ones of the human family whom I might be permitted
to serve. Heaven has never appeared so exceedingly
desirable, not as a refuge from sorrow, but as a refuge
from sin, to partake of purity unalloyed and uninterrupted. In the midst of all I have been enabled to
cast my worthless soul on the Redeemer, and He has
deigned to refresh me. Last Thursday I for the first
time, got into the chapel on my crutches; and, sitting
in a chair under the pulpit, with my foot on a pillow
in another chair, I preached. The exertion occasioned
increased swelling in my foot, as did also meeting the
British School Committee and the Benevolent Visitors
at our house on the following day. Still I was encouraged to try again on Sunday evening; and,
holding the rails, I hopped up backwards, and so got
to the pulpit. Sitting on a high seat, and with my
foot bolstered up, I conducted the service with a
degree of comfort and liberty that surprised myself.
I went overwhelmed with a sense of my unworthiness;
and the Lord, in infinite condescension, showed me
that He had not cast me off utterly. I gave tickets

afterwards. On the Sunday previous I began to do a little by giving tickets in our house, when we had very gracious seasons; and in the evening two backsliders recovered a sense of forgiveness of sins through faith in the atoning blood. This afternoon, for the first time, I have got on my crutches to the road. I cannot yet use my foot, but 'the will of the Lord be done.' It is all unspeakable mercy."

While Mr. Wood was slowly recovering from the effects of this accident, the Rev. J. H. James, now Dr. James, visited Camborne, and from him I have received the following interesting statement, following upon that quoted in the preceding chapter respecting Mr. Wood's efforts to benefit the youths at Kingswood. "I left Kingswood in 1830, and the next time I saw Mr. Wood was at Camborne in the year 1835. I had just been recommended by the District Meeting as a candidate for our Ministry, and was employed as a supply in the Camelford Circuit, then in a state of fearful agitation and confusion. An opportunity occurred to me of visiting the West of Cornwall, and I spent a Sunday and three following days at Camborne. Mr. Wood was then laid by from his full work by an accident: but he found plenty for me to do. I shall never forget the Sunday evening service in the Camborne chapel. The place was densely crowded; and, being then under twenty years of age, I was absolutely terrified at the sight of such a mass of people. But God poured out His Spirit upon us at the very commencement of the service, and more than thirty persons professed to find peace with God. Mr. Wood, lame as he was, took a most active part in the work, and cheered me on and helped me in a way that won my lasting gratitude. Some scores of persons were converted during the first four days of that memorable week." Dr. James adds, "I have seen Mr. Wood often subsequently in various Circuits, and once was his guest for more than three weeks. What a holy, busy, happy life of Christian service and enjoyment he lived! He was, in his own house, one of the most genial friends I ever had; and his great and repeated kindnesses to me live in fond remembrance."

Mr. Wood was not able to attend the Conference of 1835; but, on the day of its assembling, he held special prayer-meetings to implore the Divine blessing on its deliberations and arrangements. In August he was sufficiently restored to be able to pay a short visit to his beloved mother at Banwell, and to minister again to his old friends at Kingswood. He then returned by the steamer from Bristol to Cornwall; and on Friday, the 28th of that month, he left Camborne, amidst many tokens of sincere affection, for the beautiful town of Truro.

CHAPTER VIII.

THE TRURO CIRCUIT.

1835—1838.

THE sphere of labour upon which Mr. Wood now entered was different, in some respects, from that which he had just left. The population of Truro is not a mining population, though there are mines within two or three miles to the west and south. The town is remarkable, among Cornish towns, for its regularity and neatness; and some parts of it are very beautiful. It may, perhaps, be regarded as the principal town of Cornwall, though Penzance and Falmouth are nearly equal to it in importance. At the time of Mr. Wood's appointment there was one large and handsome Wesleyan-Methodist chapel in it, and a smaller one in which services were occasionally held. In Truro the influence of the Established Church was far greater, relatively, than in most other parts of Cornwall; and there was one Congregational and one Baptist Church. Very recently also a chapel had been erected for the Methodist New Connexion, in consequence of a division which had taken place among the members of our own Communion.

The Circuit of which Truro was the head was an extensive one; but each Minister was provided with a horse for his own use. On the eastern side of the town there were several agricultural villages, in which there were commodious chapels; and the congregations in these listened to the word of God with a quiet and earnest thoughtfulness which was very impressive. It is pleasing to recall, in particular, the large village of Probus, about five miles from Truro, with its spacious chapel, and to remember "the Leaders' pew," just below the pulpit, with the intelligent faces of the pious and well-informed men who then occupied it. On the western side of the town, and towards the south, the Circuit included a mining district, the congregations in which were more excitable, but were prepared to appreciate the deeper truths of the Gospel. Some interesting villages at a distance of five, seven, and eight miles, were comprehended in the Circuit; and among these was Mitchell, or St. Michael, which, previously to the passing of the Reform Bill in 1832, sent two members to the British Parliament. The congregation in the town of Truro was a quiet and genteel one; and among the leading members of our Society there were some men of considerable refinement and culture.

At the time of Mr. Wood's entrance upon the Circuit, it was suffering from the effects of two divisions that had recently taken place. His appointment, at that juncture, as the Superintendent Minister, was eminently suitable. His firm but conciliatory bearing, his solicitude for the recovery of those who had been led astray, and his intense zeal for the salvation of men, enabled him to exert a very beneficial influence. He sought to promote, in all the Societies, a vivid apprehension of unseen and eternal things,—to concentrate the attention of believers on the duty and privilege of entire consecration to God,

—and to engage his people in earnest efforts to lead others to the Saviour. Nor were his labours in vain. In answer to fervent prayer, the Holy Spirit was poured out; the number of members in Society largely increased; and, when he left the Circuit, there was a far healthier tone of feeling, and an expectation of yet richer blessing.

In the earlier part of Mr. Wood's residence in Truro, he was still suffering from the effects of the accident of which we have spoken. He was unable to ride on horse-back, or to walk without the aid of a crutch and stick; but he attended to all his appointments, being driven to the several country places, and he moved about, as well as he could, among his people. But he was troubled that he could not more fully carry out his plan of pastoral visitation. "I am greatly fettered," he writes, "in visiting the people. O may the Lord, if He sees good, soon set me free again!"

He had not long to wait for the spiritual prosperity for which he prayed and laboured. His own efforts, and those of his esteemed and affectionate colleague, the Rev. Samuel Timms, were greatly blessed, even during the first quarter of their associated ministry. Under the date of January 5th, 1836, Mr. Wood writes in his Journal, "Glory to God, the Father, Son, and Spirit, for the innumerable mercies of another year. I feel more than ever His boundless lovingkindness to a poor vile worm. I have made no entry for some months, not for want of incidents that I should have been glad to mark, but my time has been taken up in the service of the Church beyond any precedent. God, in his abundant grace, has been reviving us this quarter, and

we gave more than 220 notes of admission on trial
at the last renewal of tickets. At our last Local
Preachers' Meeting we devoted some time to spiritual
conversation, and parted under a blessed uniting and
quickening influence. At our Quarterly Meeting
last Monday, we devoted a part of the time to a
similar purpose. A most hallowing and melting
feeling pervaded the meeting. The power of God
was mightily felt. One who has many years, at
different periods, been Circuit Steward, told me, last
evening, that he never attended such a Quarterly
Meeting before. 'Glory and praise to Jesus give,
for His' abundant 'grace!' Our congregation in
Truro is improving, and the Lord is working on
many minds. Several called on me yesterday morning for spiritual advice, and one who had long
carried her burden was enabled, while we were
conversing, to venture on Christ for salvation. I can
now walk, blessed be the Lord, with the aid of one
stick only; and have, for a considerable time, regularly rode to my places. My soul is happy in the
Lord's work, and I am asking and believing for
greater things."

Similar records of spiritual success follow, two of
which may be properly introduced.

"February 23rd, 1836—Lately many have called
for spiritual advice, some wishing to join the people,
others burdened with guilt, and some desiring instruction for obtaining all the mind of Christ. In visiting,
also, I have reason to be encouraged that the Lord
blesses me, and prospers my endeavours. This day
I have lived thirty-nine years. Glory, glory, glory,
to the Triune God, who is *my* God, for His innu-

merable benefits to the unworthiest of all His crea-
tures. O for grace to live more abundantly to His
honour and praise! Amen, Amen."

"April 2nd, 1836—The Lord has shown me abundant mercy since my last entry. I have had sharp
conflicts, but He has delivered me. He has deigned to
bless me in my labour, and to convert souls under the
word delivered by His unworthy servant. I have
begun another class-meeting at seven o'clock on
Sunday morning, and the Master has deigned to smile
on it. The work of the Lord is greatly reviving
in the Circuit, and our finances are improving. Last
quarter, after making up all deficiencies, we had an
increase of 113 members, and a good number on
trial. Glory, glory to the Lord; for to HIM alone all
praise is due. I have lately been much indisposed,
the result, perhaps, in part, of over-exertion: but
I have not intermitted my labour, and, through Divine
mercy, I am now feeling much better. May my
health and my all be unreservedly the Lord's!"

It is not to be wondered at that Mr. Wood should
speak of indisposition occasioned by over-exertion,
when the extent of his labours is considered. The
record of one Lord's day spent in Truro itself shows,
not only that he never spared himself when work was
to be done for Christ, but that he went, at times,
beyond the bounds which a *godly* prudence would
have marked out, and risked the premature decay of
his strength. After a week of great toil, having
preached in the evening of every day, including
Saturday, in some country place, and having on one
of these evenings held a love-feast afterwards, he
retired to rest on the Saturday night about half-past

11 o'clock. "About half-past 3 o'clock," he writes, "I was called up to a sick person near death. While wrestling with God, He set her soul at liberty. I met my class at seven, after about two hours of sweet secret prayer to my God and Saviour. I preached at 11, and met the Prayer-Leaders after. At half-past 2 I met a class; at half-past 3 saw some who desired spiritual advice; at 4 met the public bands; at 6¼ I preached, and afterwards held a meeting for exhortation and prayer. On coming out of the chapel, the father of the dying person I had seen in the morning was waiting, to request me to come again, at her desire, as she was near passing. I found her within a few steps of her journey's end, and retaining her confidence obtained in the morning. I prayed with her, commending her soul to God; and now, through Divine mercy, I can rejoice in my Saviour who has strengthened me for His work."

It must not be supposed that, amidst these varied labours, Mr. Wood was indifferent to the culture of his own mind, or neglected those sacred studies in which every Minister should more or less engage. There were some periods, indeed, in which he was so fully occupied that he could read little besides his Bible, *which he always carefully studied*, and attend to his immediate preparations for the pulpit. But an entry in his Diary, of the date of October 17th, 1836, shows that he assiduously improved the intervals of public service and pastoral toil. "When I first bought 'the Christian Library,'" he writes, "and for a long time after, I never intended to read it through, but to consult it as a work of reference. However I, at length, began to read it, and, finding much important matter therein, I made notes first on loose pieces of

paper. This I regret, as the papers alluded to cannot
be conveniently referred to. As I proceeded, I
extracted more largely, and entered the matter so
extracted on sheets, for the purpose of sewing them
together; that, without reading the whole of any
part of the work, I might be able, in a short space,
to see all that appeared to me of much importance.
This work I have this day completed, truly thankful
that I have been enabled, in some degree, to study
through 'the Christian Library,' and to transcribe or
abridge those parts for future use that seemed
particularly valuable." The remaining portion of
this entry relates to his personal experience, and the
prosperity of the work of God around him. "I have
lately had to struggle with long-continued, harassing
wanderings of thought and imagination. I find it
necessary to deal with this species of evil as with all
others, viz., to bring it to Christ, and cry mightily for
deliverance through faith in the atonement. The
Lord I find quickening me in His work, and He gives
us encouragement. At our last Quarterly Meeting
we had to report a net increase, on the quarter, of
146 members. Glory to God alone!"

In the month of December, 1836, Mr. Wood experienced a signal domestic mercy in having a
daughter born to him. The delicate state of Mrs.
Wood's health had awakened his apprehensions for
her safety; and his heart overflowed with gratitude
when, through the gracious interposition of God, not
only was her life preserved, but the dear child was
born alive. "This child," he writes, "has been
dedicated to God months since. O may the Lord
accept her to be His handmaid for ever, for
Christ's sake! Amen." That prayer was heard and

answered. For four years and nine months the sweet child gladdened the hearts of her parents; and then He who so graciously said, "Suffer the little children to come unto Me, and forbid them not; for of such is the kingdom of God," called her to His own presence, to enjoy His love for ever.

It was about this time that Mr. Wood was called to resign his dear mother whom he greatly loved and honoured. Calmly and peacefully she passed away, sustained by the grace of that Saviour whom for so many years she had loved and served. After recording the circumstances connected with this event, he adds, "Next to her devoted piety, and her calm and happy departure, my mind is cheered by remembering her tender affection for me, and the kind manner in which she expressed herself, particularly when I last saw her. I have nothing of which to boast, but I have the satisfaction of knowing that I endeavoured to make her latter years happy, and that, with all her affection for all her children, she appeared to regard me as her earthly stay and support in advancing life and declining age, and that, in leaving the family, she could consider me as sustaining a father's duty towards them. O may I be counted faithful, and meet her, after a short space of time, in a brighter region!"

In the early part of the year 1837 Mr. Wood had to pass through severe domestic affliction. His beloved wife, after recovering from her confinement, was seized with dangerous illness, and at one time her life was despaired of. His son was ill at the same time; a sister of Mrs. Wood, and another friend who was visiting them, were also laid aside; and, to add to their trouble, their servant was compelled to leave through sickness. But God interposed, in various ways, to succour, and at length to restore, the afflicted family. The kindness of Mr. Wood's colleague, the Rev. Samuel Timms, and that of his excellent wife, in this season of trouble, was beyond all praise. They sought especially to relieve Mr. Wood's solicitude respecting the infant so recently given to him. While Mrs. Wood lay, as it was thought, at the point of death, Mrs. Timms took the entire charge of the child, nursing her together with her own infant, and watching over her with ceaseless assiduity. During the continuance of the trial Mr. Wood's mind was graciously sustained; and although, for about a month, he had not, as he states, "a whole night's rest," yet he was enabled to continue his public labours, as well as to minister continually to his sick family. Bowing with lowly resignation to the hand of his Heavenly Father, he could say,—

> " Thankful I take the cup from Thee,
>   Prepared and mingled by Thy skill,
> Though bitter to the taste it be,
>   Powerful the wounded soul to heal."

When this period of affliction was over, other trials came upon him, which caused him the most painful exercises of spirit. But, in the midst of all, his religious consolations abounded. "While passing through these trying circumstances," he writes, "the Lord was particularly gracious unto my soul. The general character of my experience is that of steady trust in God, leading me to endeavour, at all times, to do His pleasure, but without any overwhelming sensations of joy. But during my severest exercises my joy greatly increased. When appealing to God in prayer for present manifestations of His Spirit, in

answer to the prayers of those who love Him on my
behalf, and through the prevailing intercession of
Christ Jesus, my soul has been greatly refreshed, yea,
overwhelmed. I have felt—

> ' The speechless awe that dares not move,
> And all the silent heaven of love,'

together with a breathing of 'unutterable praise.' I
have been able only to breathe 'Glory, glory, glory.'
But these words and all human language have
appeared unutterably poor, and I have longed in
some new manner to give expression to the feelings of
my soul. O were these feelings more constant! I
thought I could be well content always to carry the
cross, if I might not otherwise enjoy these condescending displays of the power of God."

Mr. Wood attended the Leeds Conference of 1837,
having taken his family to the neighbourhood of
Banwell. At that Conference he was reappointed to
the Truro Circuit, and, soon after it closed, he returned
with Mrs. Wood and his children in improved health
to the scene of his hallowed toil. At the Christmas
Quarterly Meeting he had to report a small decrease
of members, the number of persons brought into
Church-fellowship during the quarter not having been
sufficient to make up for the losses sustained through
the death and the removal of others. "This," he
remarks, "is unspeakably trying. O that the Lord
would again more mightily appear, to save immortal
souls!"

Ere long that prayer was answered. A gracious
revival of religion broke out at Perranwell, an important country place about five miles from Truro,
since transferred to the Gwennap Circuit; and whenever Mr. Wood had an evening at liberty he went

thither to assist in the religious services. "On Sunday, February 11th, 1838," he writes, "the Lord spoke in His word at Perranwell, and some were cut to the heart. Two cases were remarkable. They were two pensioners; and both served many years in the same regiment. One was discharged before the termination of the war, through a failure in his sight. He returned and was converted, but afterwards went back into the world about six years since. The other served to the end of the war. He was in all the terrible actions in the Peninsula, fought in upwards of twenty engagements, and was in the battle of Waterloo. They sat near each other on Sunday morning in the chapel, and were both deeply affected. I went up to them after preaching, and spoke to them a little. We then prayed, and the backslider soon found mercy, and was filled with joy in believing. His companion I left with our friends crying for mercy." He adds, "After preaching at Truro in the evening, we held a second, third, and fourth meeting, and some were in distress of soul. On Monday evening, at Hugus, we had a good time; and some were distressed in mind. On Tuesday we held a special prayer-meeting in the vestry at Truro, and one found peace with God. Glory to His Name!" On the recurrence of his birthday, February 23rd, 1838, he writes, "This day I have lived to see forty-one years,—years of continued and astonishing mercy from God, years of amazing neglect and unprofitableness, notwithstanding all these favours. Still God is good, unspeakably good, to me. I am happy in His service. He has taken possession of my soul. I this day renew all my former engagements to be His, wholly His, for ever. I feel that this world has less influence on my mind, and that eternity is regarded more constantly and more delightfully. I hasten through time, having one Master to serve, one business to engage my attention. My aim is to do all unto the Lord.

> ' Happy while on earth I live,
>   Mightier joys ordained to know,
> Trampling down sin, hell, and death,
>   To the third heaven I go.'

I have recently had some severe exercises, but the Lord gives me power to rise above them more easily than I could. He has also given me seasons of power, and blessed me with that which is my chief joy, even to see sinners turning to Him, and believers going on to perfection. May I henceforward only think, and desire, and act, under the powerful influence of the indwelling Spirit! Wandering thoughts in duty have greatly harassed me. Deliver me, O my God, from these foxes that hurt the vine! O let every thought be brought into captivity by Divine love, for the Redeemer's sake, Amen." This day was one of peculiar blessing. He preached in the evening at Summercourt, an agricultural village nine miles north of Truro; and on the following morning he thus gratefully records the goodness of God. "Being my birthday, I felt particularly desirous of receiving a token for good; and I praise the Lord that He granted my request. After preaching I held a second meeting, to which nearly the whole congregation stayed. On closing this, I proceeded towards the door; but one and another in deep penitence of spirit seemed anxious to remain longer. I then desired as many as were penitent to come forward to a form. Quickly six or seven came; and I seldom, if ever, felt such power in pleading with God as then. Others began to weep, and I believe full ten were in a state of true penitence, when, on account of having far to go home and the state of my voice, I was obliged to leave. Ever blessed be the Lord's most holy Name!"

The revival of religion thus graciously vouchsafed was not limited to the places named. It spread through nearly all the Circuit; and so numerous were the cases of conversion, that at the March Quarterly Meeting Mr. Wood had to report a net increase of 49 members, and 300 adults on trial, besides a considerable number of children.

While thus engaged in the spiritual labours of the ministry, Mr. Wood was not indifferent to the general intellectual culture of his people. He formed a plan for establishing a permanent library in connection with the Truro Chapel, to be open to all subscribers of respectable character; designing more particularly, to promote, by this means, the mental improvement of the young people of the congregation. After holding several preparatory meetings, he had at length the pleasure of announcing to the friends whom he called together to decide upon the rules, that he had collected about £30 towards the object, besides obtaining donations of books. On June 8th, 1838, he records, "I opened the library, consisting of upwards of two hundred volumes, being a selection from the various departments of theology, science, and literature; many of them being the choicest works on the subjects on which they treat, and others being more introductory in their character for the purpose of alluring the young to reading and study. I delivered a scientific lecture on the occasion, which was well received."

The last Quarterly Meeting which Mr. Wood attended in the Truro Circuit was one of great peace

and love; and with a glad and grateful heart he
places on record the affection shown to him, and the
improvement in the state of the Circuit which he had
been privileged to witness. "At the first Quarterly
Meeting I attended here," he says, " we were about
£100 in debt, with two preachers only. We now had
money in hand with three preachers. We then had
1,342 members of Society: at this quarter 1,932,
besides 69 under sixteen years of age, and 112 on
trial. The Lord alone hath wrought the work, and
to Him alone be all the praise! "

The Conference of that year was held in Bristol.
Mr. Wood attended it, and availed himself of opportunities of visiting his friends in the neighbourhood of
Banwell,—of preaching repeatedly to his people at
Kingswood,—and of spending one Lord's day in
Newport, Monmouthshire, where he preached the
Anniversary Sermons of the Chapel. He was
appointed to Exeter, to which Circuit he had been
affectionately invited. For some time, indeed, his
name stood for the Bristol North Circuit; but ultimately the arrangement which he had provisionally
made with the authorities of the Exeter Circuit was
carried out, and events showed that that arrangement
was indeed of God.

CHAPTER IX.

---∘∘⦂◉⦂∘∘---

PERHAPS there is no place in which Mr. Wood ever laboured where his ministry produced more blessed effects, or left a more permanent impression, than it did in the city of Exeter. To this day many love to talk of him, of his untiring diligence and exhausting toil, his readiness for every service, his holy earnestness in seeking the salvation of men, his fidelity in dealing with the cases of individuals, and the energetic manner in which he sought to keep all the instrumentalities of the Church in efficient opera- tion. The very opening of his ministry in this city— for in Exeter I now write—was marked by tokens of the Divine approval. In the early part of December, 1838, he writes, "Under the first sermon which I preached in Exeter the Lord converted two souls; and the work of conviction and conversion has been proceeding ever since. My Divine Master never before gave me such an entrance among a people. Several every week have been brought to God. The work has been extending to different parts of the Circuit, and many old members are stirred up; some of them pressing into gospel-liberty to which they had been strangers, and others seeking for and obtaining a clean heart. My own soul has been greatly quickened, and my delight is great in the Lord and in His work."

In the city of Exeter there were two chapels,—the Mint, then considerably smaller than it now is, and the St. Sidwell's Chapel, which has now, for a few years, been superseded by the larger and more beautiful chapel in Southernhay. The Circuit comprehended the towns of Crediton, Topsham, Exmouth, Budleigh-Salterton, and Sidmouth, besides several other places; but the labours of the two Ministers on the Lord's day were chiefly devoted to the city congregations. At the close of Mr. Wood's first year, however, a third Minister was appointed to the Circuit, so that greater attention could be bestowed on the important places which have been named. Mr. Wood was the Superintendent, and the late Rev. Jarvis Cheesman was his colleague during the whole period of his pastorate. The young Minister first appointed was the Rev. Thomas Vasey, who commenced his ministry in this city, but whose delicate state of health restricted his term of service here to one year.

The entries in Mr. Wood's Diary, during his first year in Exeter, record the continuance of that blessed visitation of Divine influence which marked his entrance upon this sphere of holy toil, and show that he himself enjoyed great spiritual prosperity. We may select the following :—

"January 31st, 1839.—The Lord has been pleased to pour out richly of His Holy Spirit, and many souls have been added to His Church. Few weeks have passed without fresh manifestations of our Redeemer's presence and power in awakening, converting, and sanctifying immortal spirits. To Him *alone* be all the glory for ever and ever."

"February 17th, 1839.—I preached at St. Sidwell's and the Mint, and gave tickets in the afternoon. One who never was in a Methodist chapel before last Sunday evening, at St. Sidwell's, and was convinced of sin, now found peace in the class-meeting. Several found peace in the evening at the Mint. Glory to God for ever!"

"February 23rd.—My birth-day. I believe I never spent a birthday with more sweet delight of spirit; never, when I felt more resolved to consecrate my all to God; never, when I could survey God's dealings with more gratitude, or look into the future with so lively a hope of everlasting blessedness. Last evening, while preaching, a brother of Mr. H., who had come from Ilfracombe to Exeter for his health, was enabled to believe unto the saving of his soul. O how amazing is the condescension of God, in thus employing of all His servants the most unworthy! Glory and praise to His excellent Name for ever and ever! Amen."

"Sunday, April 14th, was a very good day. The love-feast in the afternoon was a very gracious season. The body of the Mint Chapel could not accommodate all who attended, and some went into the gallery. Several were converted in the evening."

"May 8th.—I preached at Woodbury Salterton without door in the evening. I afterwards went into a house in which a Meeting has for some time been held, and formed a class of seven members."

"Thursday, May 16th.—On this day our District Meeting concluded at Tiverton. I preached there in the evening, and we held a prayer-meeting afterwards. The cause there had been for a long time in a very discouraging state; but the Lord was pleased to appear on that occasion, and to commence a blessed revival of His work. Several were converted, most of whom had previously met in class; and others went away distressed in soul. Glory to God."

"Monday, May 20th.—A special prayer-meeting for the conversion of the children of our people. It was a gracious season, and some souls were given in answer to prayer."

"Tuesday, May 21st.—I preached at Ottery St. Mary, for their chapel, in the afternoon and evening. They have long laboured under a degree of discouragement; but the Lord was pleased to appear in the evening, and several were converted to God. Glory to His blessed Name for ever! The work, I hear, still goes on."

Not long after his arrival in Exeter, Mr. Wood commenced a Bible-class on Saturday afternoon, and in the evening of that day he read and expounded a Psalm at the prayer-meeting at St. Sidwell's. This last service became very attractive to those who wished for spiritual nourishment, and was often very profitable. His habit of pastoral visitation was kept up; and the same blessed effects followed his efforts in this department which God had permitted him to witness in his former spheres of labour. Nor did he relax his pulpit-efforts. It was his delight publicly to announce the message of salvation to the unconverted, and to lead onward believers to higher spiritual attainments. When the season of the year permitted, he preached, again and again, in the open air, especially in a low part of the city of Exeter usually designated "the West Quarter." He did this very frequently on the Lord's-day, just before the evening service at the Mint Chapel, and then walked at the head of many of the poorest of the people to that sanctuary, again to preach to them and to the general congregation the word of life. He sought also to open new places for preaching, or for public prayer-meetings, around Exeter, cheerfully devoting any spare evening in the summer to preaching in the open air in some village or hamlet in which no Methodist service had been established. These labours were abundantly owned of God.

Mr. Wood was now in the fulness of his manly strength, and he rejoiced to devote that strength to the service of his blessed Master. He undertook, indeed, extra labours on the Lord's day, which would have unfitted most men for the proper discharge of their regular duties. It was no uncommon thing for him, after preaching in the city on the forenoon of the Sabbath, to ride seven or even ten miles into the country, and preach in the open air, and then return to preach to a crowded congregation in one of the city chapels in the evening, and hold a prayer-meeting afterwards. To him this toil was sweet and delightful; and the manifest tokens of the Divine blessing, which were vouchsafed on every hand, filled him with gratitude and joy. So rich, indeed, was the blessing of Christ upon the labours of His servants, that at the June Quarterly Meeting, 1839, it was reported that the number of members had increased from 633 to 872, besides many under sixteen years of age, and a large number on trial.

In some of his efforts to awaken the interest of careless and ungodly men by preaching without doors, Mr. Wood was called to encounter opposition. About a mile and a quarter from Exeter, on the Plymouth road, is the pretty village of Alphington, where Mr. Wood often took his stand, as an ambassador of Christ, to proclaim His message to the people. One scene that occurred there shall be narrated in his own words, omitting the names of the parties concerned :—

"Wednesday, July 10th, 1839.—This evening I had proposed preaching at Alphington under the churchyard-wall, on the spot where boys have their games, and where show-men take their stand. The Rev. ——, the Rector, sent a message on Tuesday, requesting that I would keep to our chapel, as he thought I might be interrupted by the boys playing there, which, he stated, he should not be able to prevent. He also wished to know the reason of my intending to preach on that spot. To this message, which was sent by one of our members, I wrote the following reply :—

'J. Wood begs his best respects to Rev. ——, and to say, in reply to the message just received, that his object in preaching in the open air is simply to seek those who do not attend the public worship of God ; and he feels encouraged to pursue this plan from having found that some, who probably attended at first through curiosity, have afterwards become regular attendants on the ordinances of religion, and have given proof of having become converted characters. The Rev. —— will readily believe that there is nothing inviting in a course which is often attended with scorn and opposition. Still, however, if he can be but instrumental in conveying spiritual good to the humblest individual, J. Wood is quite prepared to encounter any difficulties, and to bear any odium, which the discharge of these duties may occasion.'

'Verney Place, Exeter, July 9th, 1839.'

"The Rector had previously applied to a magistrate, and had been informed that a constable might disperse the congregation; and a little before preaching-time the same messenger was sent to inform me, that a Parish Vestry had been held, and that the Rector and Churchwardens had resolved to employ the constables to disperse the congregation which might assemble, warning me not to attempt to preach without door. My only reply was, that I hoped soon to be there. On reaching Alphington, I found there was great excitement in the village, occasioned by the Rector's avowed determination to oppose. I quickly began the service, by giving out the first hymn, on the spot I had intended. Several came round and joined in the singing. But we had sung only a few verses when two constables made their appearance, and one of them, standing before me, held his staff in my face and ordered me to desist. I, however, went on giving out the hymn and singing, until his frequent interruption led me to ask them their names and office. On telling me, I desired them, in the Queen's name, to keep the peace, and, stepping on a chair, I began to pray. One of them appears to have gone for fresh orders, and they soon began to talk very loudly while I continued praying. Then they laid hold on my arms, and, after pulling me for some time, they at length dragged me down while I was repeating the Lord's prayer. I then asked them, by what authority they acted. They said, by

the orders of Mr. —— and the Churchwardens. As
they were holding me, I asked them if I was their
prisoner. They said I was. I then requested them to
take me wherever they wished, and told them I
should readily go without any resistance. They
accordingly took me, first, to Mr. L.'s,—a magistrate
residing in the village. But, on coming to his house,
the servant stated that her master was not at home.
This appears to have been quite correct. After some
consultation, it was next determined to take me to the
Rector's, who, although not a magistrate, had, they
said, ordered them to act as they did, and they
thought he ought himself to talk to me. Before we
came to his gate, there came one to meet us, saying,
'Master is not at home.' However, as the people
urged the constables, and all appeared to wish to see
me and the Rector together, they pressed on and
entered the lawn to his door. Here the servants
were ranged, saying, 'Master is not at home, and
may be absent half an hour or an hour.' The constables would have taken me into the house, to await
his return; but the servants fastened the door and
said they could admit no one. After some consideration, and much urging to do something with me, they
first proposed to take me to a magistrate residing
about a mile distant; but it was said that he also was
from home. Then they proposed to take me to the
inn, and keep me until the Rector should return;
but, at length, after bringing me to the spot where
they had first taken me, they discharged me. I then
immediately began again, and, after singing and
prayer, preached from Luke xiv. 23. Just after I
began the second time, the ringers, who had been
collected for the purpose, began to ring, and, as I was

standing under the churchyard wall, the sound was very interrupting. On this case I would observe, first, I had no desire to place myself in opposition to the Rector and Churchwardens, nay, I should have been truly glad to have obliged them. But when the choice lay between pleasing men and, as I believed, serving God, I could not a moment hesitate as to the course I should pursue. Secondly, the spot on which we assembled was that on which sports, etc., are held without interruption. We obstructed no passing, as neither horse nor cart came by while we were there, and if they had, there was abundance of room. Thirdly, there was no disturbance but what the constables created, all, at the time they arrested me, being perfectly orderly and quiet. Fourthly, the men themselves said they could not help doing what they did, having been ordered to do so; not that they wished to interfere in any way. Fifthly, I was perfectly calm when pulled down and led about by the constables. My only fear was, lest any of our people should commit themselves by any expression or act, during the excitement of the time, which might have given occasion to the opposers to censure. I, therefore, had repeatedly to beg them to say nothing, but to leave the whole with me; and the Lord mercifully kept them from anything rash or improper. I now thought it would not be well to give up, and therefore published for preaching again the following evening. Accordingly, after preaching without door at Kenford, I returned to Alphington, where the proceedings of the former evening had brought a large number together from Exeter and the neighbourhood. The opposers had probably been informed of the illegality of yesterday's proceedings, so that the constables,

though there, were not commissioned to interrupt.
But, as soon as I had finished praying the first time,
the bells were set a ringing, so that I had to use
great exertion to make the congregation hear. I
concluded by exhorting to kindness and forbearance
towards those who opposed us, who, I stated, were
probably acting under some mistaken apprehensions.
Praise God for His abundant mercy! Good will surely
come of this, and all is well if God be glorified."

While Mr. Wood was thus engaged in evangelistic and pastoral efforts in his own Circuit, he was
not indifferent to the great movements that were taking
place in the Connexion. This was the Centenary year
of Methodism; and he not only exerted himself in
reference to the meeting held in Exeter, but took an
active part in similar meetings in various parts of the
District. His warm and generous heart was ever loyal
to the system of Methodism; and everything that affected its prosperity called forth his deepest interest.

As the Conference approached, he arranged to
pay a visit to his relatives in Somersetshire, for the
settlement of some family affairs, and to visit the
Kingswood Circuit, on his way to Liverpool. He
preached at Hanham three times, on Sunday, July
28th, on behalf of the Sunday-School; and he
writes, "The Lord gave us seasons of much power,
and several were in distress in the evening, whom I
left with our friends praying with them. Glory be to
the Lord! He is ever the same. The sight of many
old faces, their continued remembrance and warm
attachment, and, above all, a visit of the Holy Ghost
so much like former seasons in that chapel, I felt to
be exceedingly heart-cheering." In the proceedings

of this Conference over which the Rev. Theophilus Lessey presided, and to which the Rev. Thomas Jackson preached the memorable Centenary sermon, Mr. Wood felt deep interest. "Never did I witness," he writes, "the manifestation of so deep a feeling among the Ministers generally, to labour for souls, to live in the full enjoyment of the power of godliness, and to spend and be spent for God. Glory to our God for this spirit! O may our Centenary year be one of unexampled power and blessing throughout our Connexion!" After again visiting Langford and Banwell, and finally arranging the important business which required his presence, he returned to Exeter on August 17th, rejoicing in the goodness of God which had brought him in health and peace to his family and people. His own soul was filled with love to God. Towards the close of August he writes, "I have experienced some seasons of great refreshing during the last two months, particularly on one occasion while riding on the box of the coach over the road a little on this side Taunton. I felt I surrendered all to God, time, talents, wife, children, life, *all*, *all ;* and I had such a visit of the power of the Holy One that the earthly house was filled with the Divine Visitor. I felt as if I had as much as I could then well sustain ; and I was led to 'breathe unutterable praise.' But I have also had to encounter some furious onsets from the adversary, endeavouring to stir up unhallowed feelings in my heart. Glory to my great Redeemer, He sustains me by His Almighty right arm. But for this I should become a prey, and despair, and be damned. Never did I more sensibly feel my powerlessness for all good, separate from Him ; and never more my obligations to the atoning blood, and prevailing intercession, and present and powerful Spirit, of my God and Saviour."

In October of this year Mr. Wood was gladdened by the birth of another son, and the gradual convalescence of Mrs. Wood. But, after a fortnight, his spirit was chastened by the sorrows of bereavement. "The dear babe," he writes, "was a fine child, and thrived much. I thought, and so did his mother, that we were never so rich before, having three children living. I was also auguring good from a well-formed head and intelligent face, hoping that Divine grace might make him a useful man. But thrush appeared. He ailed about a day. On Thursday morning early, I was informed that he was ill. I nursed him for several hours, and soon after twelve o'clock he quietly breathed his last in my arms. I envy not the feelings of those who regard the death of their infant children rather as a relief than as a loss. To be 'without natural affection,' is no part of my religion. I felt the stroke keenly, as did my dear Mary Ann : but we had both given him to the Lord, and we dared not deny Him His own. Yea, we could heartily say, 'The will of the Lord be done!' "

His labours during his second year in Exeter resembled those which we have already described, and were crowned with a similar blessing. It is needless to recount them in detail ; but the record of the hallowed toil of three Sabbaths may be given, as illustrating his untiring energy, and his readiness to be spent in his Master's service.

"Sunday, September 29th, 1839.—I preached at the Mint at 10½ o'clock. Went to Thorverton, where I heard there was an opening for preaching, and preached without door in the centre of the town. Therefrom I went into a private house, and as many as the room would contain followed me, to whom I again addressed some exhortations, and explained our system and our views in coming there. Four gave their names to commence a class should we be able to establish regular preaching there. I then returned to Three Horse Shoes on the way back to Exeter, and preached, and gave tickets to the few who meet there. I then returned home, and preached at St. Sidwell's at $6\frac{1}{2}$ o'clock, and held a second and a third meeting after, the Lord being gracious unto me and strengthening me."

"Sunday, April 5th, 1840.—I preached at St. Sidwell's in the morning, and administered the Lord's Supper afterwards to an unusually large number of communicants. I then went to Cheriton-Bishop, ten miles out of Exeter on the Okehampton road, where I found a large congregation expecting me. I stood in the road near the churchyard, and felt much liberty in speaking in the name of the Lord, and the word appeared to be in power. I proposed speaking with any who might desire to serve the Lord, after concluding the out-door service, in a house adjoining. The room was large, but it was immediately filled. After explaining our object and system, I prayed and dismissed them. I then rode back to Exeter, and preached in the evening at the Mint. In commencing the service, I felt a degree of apprehension lest my voice should fail in addressing a large and crowded congregation, after the previous exertion of the day. But I lifted my heart to God, and He mercifully strengthened me, and blessed us with a time of much power. Glory to His holy Name!"

"Sunday, May 31st, 1840.—I was appointed at Topsham, where the work has long been in a most discouraging state. Although well aware that my efforts are nothing but as God may be pleased to use them, I resolved to do all I could, and to expect the promise of the Father. I therefore preached without door on the quay, at 9½ o'clock, from 'Come, for all things are now ready.' I then went to the chapel, and preached at 10½ from Ps. v. 3. Visited a sick man, and preached again in the chapel at 2½ from Rev. ii. 4, 5, and baptized a child. At 4 o'clock I preached in the street in the centre of the town from the latter part of the Apostles' creed, 'I believe in the Holy Ghost,' etc. At 5½ I preached on board a vessel to a great number who stood on the deck and on the quay from Luke v. 3. I then gave out a hymn, and sang through the streets to the chapel, where I again preached at 6½ from Prov. xxiii. 26. After this I held a prayer-meeting and exhorted; and as one soul, who was convinced at the out-door service in the morning, was in distress, we stayed and again lifted up our hearts, and the Lord spoke her sins forgiven. Glory for ever to His holy Name! When I went into the pulpit the last time, I felt in my head as if I should scarcely be able to stand: but the Lord again strengthened me, and we had a gracious season."

While thus putting forth unremitting personal efforts to lead men to Christ, Mr. Wood endeavoured to keep the members of the Church actively at work. He regularly met the prayer-leaders, and sought to extend the range of their labours, in villages and hamlets, as well as in private houses in the city. He bestowed great attention on the Tract Society, and encouraged the visitors, who soon rose to the number of 160, to prosecute their work with diligence and **earnestness.** He stood at the head of his people, to lead them onward to every good **work; and he was** the means of **quickening** the zeal, **and sustaining the** perseverance, **of many.**

Nor did he cease to take an interest in science, as far as it could be made to illustrate the Divine perfections and the Divine agency. We find him, in February, 1840, delivering some lectures bearing on natural philosophy; but he exercised a sacred jealousy over himself, lest such engagements should at all interfere with his pastoral duties, and the consecration of himself to his great work of saving souls. "I have lately," he writes, "delivered some lectures on subjects connected with natural philosophy, endeavouring to illustrate the wisdom, and power, and goodness of God. They were commenced in consequence of some inquiries made at the Bible-Class recently established. I am not quite satisfied with lecturing, as it is not preaching the gospel. To take up the time of preaching, or other spiritual meetings, by lecturing, I should deem highly reprehensible. My lecturing is extra service. Still, however, I do not intend to continue it beyond four or five lectures, lest it should assume an undue importance. I long for larger measures of the Spirit, that every thing may be savoury, and that I may bear all my Divine Master's image."

Occasionally he extended his labours to other Circuits, preaching on behalf of chapel-trusts, and other important interests; and such visits were often made a blessing to many. He sought to diffuse the spirit of a genuine revivalism wherever he went; and he greatly rejoiced when, in connection with these occasional services, sinners were brought to God. But these visits to other Circuits were always kept within such limits as not to interfere with what he felt to be his paramount duty,—the efficient care of the flock specially committed to his own charge.

Thus the year passed away in cheerful efforts to do the work of Christ, and in the enjoyment of intimate intercourse with the Triune God. In the month of July, having first taken Mrs. Wood and his little daughter to Churchill, near Bristol, he proceeded to Newcastle-upon-Tyne, where the Conference of 1840 was held; and, having spent a Sunday, on his return, among his friends in the Banwell Circuit, he reached Exeter with his family on August 21st, determined more than ever to live to God.

Among the earliest engagements of his third year in this city, was the opening of premises which had been recently taken for a Sunday-School, in one of the more destitute neighbourhoods. " When I got there," he says, "I found the congregation chiefly composed of our own people. I therefore took two or three with me to 'the Quarter,' and, after singing a few verses, when many had gathered around, I published that I was about to preach in Preston Street, and invited them to follow me; and then, singing towards the place, a crowd came after me, and we had a large company of the rough and ragged, of women without bonnets, etc. To them I preached with liberty, and the power of the Lord was in a degree displayed. I did the like the week following, and many felt it good to be there." It is beautiful to observe this manifestation of the true Home-Missionary spirit,—the spirit which leads men to seek the most degraded, and to go forth to save the lost. The

premises in question were occupied for many years
for a Sunday-School, in which great good was
accomplished; but in the year 1861, principally
through the efforts and liberality of the late William
Brock, Esq., they were superseded by the spacious
and commodious School-room in King Street. With
the same untiring energy which had marked his
former ministrations in the Circuit, Mr. Wood gave
himself up to the work of the Lord, and was encouraged by witnessing continuous prosperity. His
own soul, too, enjoyed great peace and joy in God.
Towards the close of October, 1840, he writes,
"Latterly, views of eternity have been unusually
animating to my mind. I think I feel more fully that
I am a man of another world, living below for a
time to glorify God, and to turn immortal souls to
an atoning Saviour. The Lord make me more
abundantly useful!"

In the beginning of November, 1840, he visited
Truro, to preach at the opening of a chapel at Short
Lane End, about two miles distant from the town.
He remained there three or four days, preaching
every evening in some part of the Circuit, and during
the day renewing his pastoral intercourse with the
members of the town-society. He records, with
gratitude to God, the success which attended the
Tuesday evening service at Probus. "The Lord
acknowledged His word, and good was done. I left
them at Probus late in the evening: but many were
then in distress of soul." "This visit," he adds, "has
been exceedingly animating. I took a meal at one
house, and another meal at another, and so it went
on during my stay; the intervening time being spent
in visiting from family to family, endeavouring to

render them some spiritual profit. The friends came from other parts of the Circuit, and the affection shown to me was almost overwhelming. O how good is the Lord to His servant!"

In his own Circuit he was encouraged by the continuance of spiritual success. Not only in the city, but in almost every part of the Circuit, men were subdued by the Spirit of Christ accompanying the word preached, and then found peace in believing. At Budleigh-Salterton, in particular, there was a very gracious work of God; and some who belonged to other religious communions were brought under its influence. One case of this kind may be given in Mr. Wood's own words:—"February 8th, 1841. I went to Salterton to attend a Tea-meeting. Mr. Vasey was also there. After the tea, we had some spiritual conversation and prayer. The power of the Lord was then revealed amongst us in a glorious manner. Many were cut to the heart, and several entered into the clear enjoyment of pardon. Mr. P., a gentleman who has long been connected with the Dissenters, but some of whose children have lately been converted, and who considered himself, as most others considered him, a converted character, was brought to implore mercy, finding that others were possessed of something in religion which he had not. We prayed for him, as for another penitent; and before the meeting closed, he rose from his knees, and, with delight beaming in his countenance, exclaimed, 'I never knew what religion was before. I now feel that God has pardoned all my sins.'"

It is to me a source of great satisfaction to be able to introduce here the testimony of the esteemed Minister to whom allusion is made in the last quotation,—the Rev. Thomas Vasey,—to the character of Mr. Wood's ministry in Exeter, and the success with which it was crowned :—

"I shall always account it a special privilege to have spent the first year of my ministerial life under the superintendency of the late Rev. Joseph Wood. His spirit and example, both in public and private life, were well calculated to give a young man the most exalted ideas of the work of a true Methodist preacher. He was, indeed, a man of one business. Wherever you met him, he was intent on saving souls. Whether he attended meetings on financial matters,—Tea-meetings, —Missionary meetings,—or Sunday-School meetings, —he sought to turn them to account in the way of leading men to Christ. He rarely missed an opportunity of talking to people about their salvation. In visiting at the houses of respectable people, he would manage to get a word about religion with the servant-maid who opened the door, and with the young people whenever he had an opportunity of private conversation with them. Those who did not relish this kind of talk had nothing for it but to keep out of his way. He was a true evangelist. Not content with preaching to the people who came to chapel, he would go on a week-night, before the service began, into some benighted neighbourhood,— address the people,—invite them to the chapel,—sing up the street,—and take them in with him. Sometimes, on such occasions, his congregations presented a motley appearance ; women without shawls or bonnets, and men in paper caps, with a due admixture of ragged children, all flocking in and listening attentively to the word. He did not much trouble himself with

Committees, but got tracts and engaged distributors, and found the money, and kept up the spirit of the work by frequently meeting the agents himself. He had peculiar views of Methodist preaching, as distinguished from the prevailing style of other Christian denominations, and thought it should be largely hortatory, with urgent and pointed appeals to the heart and conscience, and a larger margin left in pulpit-preparation for enlargement suggested by the influence of the Spirit and the circumstances of the congregation. His own preaching was an exact embodiment of these views. He was a very able expositor, and held a Saturday evening meeting for a series of Scriptural expositions which were very valuable and edifying. He was also a fair scholar, and well conversant with the Hebrew and Greek Scriptures, which he read and studied critically and systematically. But he showed no trace of these acquisitions in the pulpit. His style, while it was purely English and in good taste, was plain and unadorned, tending more to the colloquial than to the oratorical. His habits of private devotion were regular and were carefully maintained; and between these and pastoral duties his time was divided. I believe he never went into the pulpit without a firm faith that souls would be saved, and he was rarely disappointed. As might be expected, his visits to the afflicted and the dying were greatly prized; for he had a warm and sympathetic nature, and his prayers seemed to bring with them blessed 'airs from heaven' into the chamber of sickness. In short, I do not know any man whom I should be more disposed to point out as a model Methodist Preacher; and, at any rate, if we had many such, Methodism would occupy a much higher position than it does. The writing of this brief sketch has been most refreshing to me, by reviving the recollection of one to whom I am so much indebted for good advice and a good example."

The close of Mr. Wood's ministry in this city was marked by one of the severest trials of his life: but under it his trust in God and submission to His will were graciously sustained. The dear little girl who was born to him in Truro was naturally the object of his fond attachment. So frequently had he been called to mourn over the death of his infant children, that he looked upon her preservation as a special mercy from God; and as her mind expanded, and her affectionate disposition, sanctified even in childhood by the grace of Christ, evinced itself in the endearing scenes of domestic life, his heart naturally clung to her. On July 23rd, 1841, Mrs. Wood and his little daughter accompanied him to Bristol, on his way to the Manchester Conference. Thence they proceeded to Breach Hill, the residence of Mr. and Mrs. Capel, the latter of whom was Mrs. Wood's sister. On his return from the Conference, Mr. Wood went to Breach Hill, and had the happiness of finding his dear wife and daughter well. On Tuesday, August 17th, he preached at Chew-Stoke, in the immediate neighbourhood, and on the following day returned to Exeter, leaving Mrs. Wood and the dear child at Breach Hill, which was, indeed, included in the Bristol South Circuit to which he was now appointed. He preached at Budleigh-Salterton on Sunday the 22nd; and on Friday, the 27th, he received a letter from Mrs. Wood, informing him that their little daughter was taken seriously ill on Wednesday morning, and that the medical attendant considered her case dangerous. On the following morning a second letter informed him of her departure. But his own words form the most fitting record of this painful dispensation, and of the manner in which the grace of God sustained him under it, enabling him, though his heart was bleeding, to deliver Christ's message on the last Sabbath of his pastorate among a people that loved him, and many of whom were his own spiritual children.—"August 28th, 1841. A letter informed me of my dear child's death. O, what a stroke! I had never felt the like. When I last saw her, as if conscious it would be the last time, she could not cease from embracing me, and that with so much ardour that I feared she would injure her chest by the vehemence with which she pressed my neck in her arms, accompanied with the most endearing expressions. I had indulged the hope of her being a comfort in years to come, should the Lord prolong this commission of life. Her mind exhibited much precocity. She had a ready and clear perception, great facility and propriety in expression, much energy and ardour, and withal a most interesting appearance. But she is snatched from my grasp. The cup is unspeakably bitter. But shall I complain? Nay, I will not. I told the Lord before the second letter came, that, if He thought fit to remove her, I would still love and bless Him, kissing the rod: and by Divine grace I did so. As soon as I read the letter, I withdrew, and, bowing before God, I praised His holy and glorious Name. O, I deserved the stroke! She had been dedicated to the Lord, and was not ours. But my dear wife! She was her mother's companion, and I felt for her more than for myself; and my dear boy was dotingly fond of his sister. But God is good; and He is almighty, and will sustain. Truly 'my soul is like a weaned child.' —Sunday, August 29th. I preached at St. Sidwell's and the Mint. I feared to offend the Lord by standing back from His work; and, although my feelings were like to have gained the mastery a few times, yet He wonderfully sustained me. Glory to God for ever! —30th. Went to Breach Hill. My dear wife is wonderfully upheld.—Wednesday, September 1st. I committed the remains of my dear child to the grave in Chew-Stoke chapel burying-ground. O, what a day! Little did I think this would occur when, on Tuesday, August 17th, I preached in that chapel from Ps. cvii. 7, and the dear child was present. But 'the will of the Lord be done.' If it may but be sanctified to rendering me more devoted to God, and more useful in His vineyard, I am content. O let not the Lord withhold this desire of my heart, that I may enjoy more of His favour, and bring more glory to His name! Give, O give, me *this*, whatever Thou takest away, O my God! Amen. Amen."

* A short Memoir of this interesting child was written by her Father, and published as a Reward-Book for Sunday-Schools, at the Wesleyan Conference Office. It is entitled, "Mary Ann. By her Father, the Rev. Joseph Wood."

CHAPTER X.

THE BRISTOL SOUTH CIRCUIT.

1841—1844.

WITH a chastened and sorrowful spirit, but resolved more than ever to devote himself to God, Mr. Wood entered upon the sphere of labour assigned to him by the Conference of 1841. His bright home had been overshadowed by bereavement; but he sought solace and joy in the work of Christ, and cherished the hope that, "through the gospel," he might yet become the "father" of multitudes of spiritual children.

The city of Bristol, to which he now removed, was very familiar to him; and his Circuit extended, on one side, to the border of the Banwell Circuit, which had been the scene of his zealous efforts as a Local Preacher. The ancient channel of the river Avon formed the line of division between the two Bristol Circuits, so that a comparatively small portion of the city was comprehended in the South Circuit. The Langton-Street chapel was the principal one; and next to that in importance was the chapel in the populous suburb of Bedminster. The chief country places were Keynsham, Pensford, Chew-Stoke, Chew-Magna, and Nailsea, which last, a few years previously, had been transferred to this Circuit from the

Banwell Circuit: but there were several other smaller places.

During the last seven years, Mr. Wood had held the office of Superintendent Minister; but he now cheerfully resumed the position of second Minister,— the late Rev. Frederick Calder being the Superintendent of the Bristol South Circuit during his first year, and the late Rev. Jacob Stanley, a man of great wisdom and deep piety, combined with a most genial spirit, during the second and third.

Mr. Wood's first sermon in the Circuit was preached at Chew-Stoke on Friday, September 3rd, where, two days before, he had committed the mortal remains of his beloved daughter to their last resting-place. His text on that occasion showed how he turned to Christ for consolation and strength, and how he resolved to give himself up afresh to the work of his blessed Master :—"And He said unto me, My grace is sufficient for thee : for My strength is made perfect in weakness. Most gladly therefore will I rather glory in my infirmities, that the power of Christ may rest upon me." On the following day he came with Mrs. Wood to his house in Bristol, and on the Sabbath preached at Keynsham and Langton Street. "The Lord," he says, "gave me enlargement and power, and I believe some will have to praise God for this day for ever. Glory to His Name, that He does not forsake me, unworthy as I am."

It is scarcely necessary to say, that Mr. Wood adopted in Bristol the same methods of usefulness on which God had so graciously smiled in other places. He preached frequently in the open air; he was assiduous in the general pastoral visitation of his people ; and he was particularly attentive to those

L

who were afflicted.   In almost every part of the
Circuit he was encouraged by witnessing genuine
conversions.   A few extracts from his Diary will
illustrate this:—

"Sunday, October 3rd, 1841.—I preached at Langton Street in the morning, at Pile Hill without door in
the afternoon, and at Bedminster in the evening.
Some conversions.   Praise the Lord!   Also, after
preaching at Wesley chapel the following evening,
the Lord spoke peace to some souls."

"Sunday, October 31st.—A good day at Keynsham.   Several awakened in the evening.   Glory to
God!   This place has long remained in about the same
condition, but I trust that the Lord is at length about to
visit in power.   I went there again on the following
Thursday, and also on Friday, when I met and conversed with several promising characters who are
inquiring the way of salvation, some of whom, on
Friday evening, found peace with God."

"Sunday, December 5th.—Some professed to obtain forgiveness at Bedminster, and one purity of
heart.   Also on the 25th some found the Lord in the
same chapel; and on the 26th, at and after preaching
from 2 Cor. v. 17, 18, more than ten professed to
obtain peace to their souls.   This was a season of
extraordinary power.   One man of hard countenance,
about fifty-five years of age, for whom his wife said
she had prayed a thousand times, was brought in,
and they now rejoiced together.   One man and his
wife came forward together, and together rejoiced in
a sin-pardoning God."

"Sunday, January 30th, 1842.—A good day.   Some
felt the power of the word in the morning at Bed-

minster, and others in the evening at Langton Street. Visited sixteen families in the afternoon."

So rich a blessing accompanied the word in the Bedminster chapel, that many were attracted to it, and it became necessary to provide additional accommodation. Mr. Wood actively promoted the erection of a gallery on three sides of the chapel; and in September, 1842, he had the satisfaction of seeing that object accomplished, and of preaching one of the sermons on the occasion of the re-opening of the chapel.

During his first year in Bristol, he revisited several of the scenes of his former labours, besides rendering important services to neighbouring Circuits by preaching at the opening of chapels, or on similar occasions. He visited Exeter in January, 1842, to preach the Anniversary Sermons of the St. Sidwell's Sunday-School; and in April he went to Truro and Tuckingmill, to preach on behalf of the Foreign Missions, and connected with that visit renewed intercourse with his friends at Camborne. The Kingswood and Newport Circuits, also, which were now so accessible, were favoured with his occasional ministrations; and these ministrations were graciously owned of God. His intercourse with those over whom he had formerly watched, with pastoral tenderness and fidelity, was often very refreshing to his own spirit; and the proofs of love which met him everywhere awakened his gratitude to God.

His own religious experience, while marked, at times, by severe and protracted conflicts, was marked, also, by increased strength of holy purpose, and by richer satisfaction in the entire dedication of himself to God. On the 23rd of February, 1842, when he

completed his forty-fifth year, he writes, "'I see my
natal day return, and bless the day that I was born.'
I would on this day consecrate myself, body and soul,
anew to God, to be wholly His, and His for ever.
'Weaker than a bruised reed, help I every moment
need.' O may that help be imparted, moment by
moment, to the end of my earthly career. Amen, my
Lord, Amen!" Under the date of August 22nd,
1842, he says, "My soul has, at different times lately,
been sorely assailed by the great adversary. In-
jections of evil thoughts, and imaginations forcibly
presented to the mind, from which I had been free
for a long period, harassed me day after day. My
abhorring them in my heart, and crying to God for
deliverance, did not prevent the tempter from continuing his suggestions under various forms, so as to
engage the attention and obtain a hearing. But the
allowing the mind to muse thereon I found to be very
injurious; and, although I felt I would rather die
than do anything to grieve my God, yet I felt that
'the permitted thought of iniquity is sin.' I have been
taught, over and over again, that I have no might
but as God upholds me; and my comfort and victory
appeared to come more fully while considering these
words, 'Not by might, nor by power, but by My
Spirit, saith the Lord.' O the mercy of being delivered! It is only when He who bruises the serpent's
head arises to rebuke him, that the adversary retires."
The entry on the closing day of the year 1842 is
well worthy of being preserved:—"December 31st.
Held a watch-night at Bedminster. The Lord mercifully acknowledges the labour of a worm in some
degree. But few Sabbaths pass without some evidence
of conviction or conversion; sometimes more than

one or two. Still, however, 'what are these among so many?' Multitudes slumbering on, while death is rapidly approaching, and one after another is falling around. O for more of the power of the Spirit! We want a mighty awakening. And where is the hinderance? O that we might see the lighting down of God's mighty arm! My soul has been more free from severe conflict for some time past. I go on smoothly, having but occasional trials and exercises, which we all must expect. I want more panting ardours after God,—more intimate converse with Him,—more power and prevalence in prayer,—more spirituality in all I think, and speak, and do. I have been encouraged by some evidences of good in pastoral visitation, and in attending the beds of sickness. But I want to be among the people as fire among dry stubble. O for a richer anointing of the Spirit! I feel my will to be swallowed up in the will of my Heavenly Father; but I have not that distinct perception, at all times, of what that will is, in circumstances of occasional occurrence; and I long for that Spirit of wisdom which shall be my momentary guide in every affair of life, and which 'shall abide with me for ever.'"—On the next recurrence of his birthday, February 23rd, 1843, he writes, "Through God's abundant mercy I this day see the completion of my forty-sixth year; and I never delighted more in my Master's work, nor looked forward with more pleasing anticipations to eternal life. Death-bed scenes continually admonish me. My labour in sick-visiting is not a little. I have upwards of thirty names now on my sick-list,—a greater number than usual,—and several of them will die. And more than this,—some of them had left the work unper-

formed, and on visiting them I found all to do. But
this day the Lord relieved one burdened mind, while
I was endeavouring to plead the atonement on her
behalf, and the fear of death gave place to humble
confidence. Glory to my Master! He is unspeakably
condescending in that He deigns to employ a worm.
O for a heart more ardently loving, and more
zealously doing, all His will! My one object is to
please God. This, however, I can only do by His
upholding power; for never was there a weaker
worm of earth, if left by Him. I stand; for he holds
me up. I urge on my way; for He leads me forward.
Never will a soul in heaven have to ascribe more to
the riches of sovereign grace. Hallelujah! Praise
the Lord!"

Mr. Wood's pastoral labours occasionally brought
him into contact with cases that were deeply affecting,
and that filled his heart with unspeakable sorrow.
The very next entry in his Journal, which he has
preserved, illustrates this; and the circumstance is
here recorded, in the hope that it may prove a
warning to some who are in danger of being
"hardened through the deceitfulness of sin."—"On
March 8th, 1843, I visited a backslider. He told me
that he knew the way well,—that he once enjoyed the
power of godliness,—that he had mixed with worldly
men and drunk into their spirit,—and that now, in
bodily weakness, he saw his danger, but could not
feel. 'And, Sir,' said he, 'I would not convey any
wrong impression to your mind respecting my state.
My heart is as hard as *steel.*' I urged the necessity
of his immediately crying to God for the gift of His
Spirit, adding that, although then sitting at the fire-side,
he might be called into eternity before the morning, and

prayed with him. The next morning I found that he was no more. Soon after I left him the previous evening he went to bed. His pious wife perceived that he was growing weaker, and begged him to pray. He was inclined to be drowsy. Before morning rose, his spirit fled. The last words he uttered, a little before his departure, were, 'What is a man profited, if he gain the whole world, and lose his own soul? or what shall a man give in exchange for his soul?' O let me work while it is day! The night is falling on many, and I can render them service no longer."

The course of Mr. Wood's ministry in the Bristol South Circuit was not distinguished by any extraordinary incidents requiring special mention. It was a course of uniform and sustained labour for Christ, in the several departments of service which the ministerial office includes; and it was a course of continuous blessing, for "the hand of the Lord" was with His servant, and many, through his instrumentality, were saved. He moved among his own people as an ambassador of the Lord Jesus, and a faithful and affectionate pastor; and he went, as opportunity served, to neighbouring places, to promote the work of God. The following extract from his Diary will show his readiness to undertake occasional services, as far as was consistent with his duties to his own Circuit; and it records also his merciful preservation in a time of danger —"Sunday, April 16th, 1843. Preached at Cam their chapel Anniversary Sermons. Good day.—Monday, 17th. Preached afternoon and evening at Downend for their chapel, and attended a tea-meeting between the services.—Tuesday, 18th. Preached twice and attended a tea-meeting for their chapel at Lydford, in the Glastonbury Circuit. A gracious influence was vouchsafed in the services of this week. Glory to our God!—On Saturday, May 20th, as I was returning from assisting at the Missionary Meeting at Tintern, after crossing the Passage, on getting upon the mail coach behind, the coachman drove off without giving notice. I was thrown from the place where I stood near the guard, and fell upon my back upon the ground. My hat was thrown from my head by the fall, so that no protection was afforded by it. I was greatly shaken, and felt the effects in a degree for some time: but, through God's kind providence, I was preserved from serious injury. O may the rest of my days be more fully than ever His! I went on the same evening, through heavy rain, to Timsbury, in the Midsomer-Norton Circuit, where I preached for their Sunday-School the following day."

In this Circuit, also, as in former ones, Mr. Wood sought to promote the general intellectual improvement of his people. We find him delivering some lectures on different branches of Natural Philosophy, in connection with the Langton Street chapel, though, as we have already seen, he was very jealous over himself, lest any engagement of this kind should lessen his attention to his proper work as a Minister of Christ. "On January 3rd, 1843," he writes, "I gave a lecture at Langton Street on Caloric and Hydrostatics, and another on the 26th on Pneumatics and Optics. I begin and close with singing and prayer, and found my remarks on a text, conforming my address as nearly as I can to our regular public services, although avowedly of a different character, with a view of leading our hearers to cultivate their minds.

This is done in evenings that are unemployed in the regular work, as I could not supersede a service professedly religious by anything of this sort."

Mr. Wood took a lively interest in the Educational movement in our Connexion in the year 1844, and attended several meetings to promote it; and he exerted himself to establish a Wesleyan Day-School at Bedminster. Indeed, all the agencies and interests of Methodism were regarded by him with thoughtful sympathy. And that sympathy extended to the whole Church of Christ. He cheerfully took part in meetings intended to cement the union of believers of different denominations, and to manifest their oneness to the world. He rejoiced, also, to be present at each of the Conferences held during his three years in the Bristol South Circuit. Nor was his attendance on the annual assembly of his brethren casual and irregular. He took an interest in every part of the business, and made notes of the proceedings for his own private use. At the Conference of 1844 he was appointed to the Birmingham West Circuit, to which he had been previously engaged; and at the close of August he left Bristol to enter upon that important sphere of sacred service.

CHAPTER XI.

THE Circuit to which Mr. Wood's labours were devoted for the next three years differed, in one respect, from those which he had previously occupied. It embraced *several* large town Chapels, while the country places were comparatively few; so that his ordinary ministrations were, for the most part, given to Birmingham itself. In his first year, the Rev. Edward Walker was the Superintendent of the Circuit, his other colleagues being the Rev. John Burton and the Rev. James Laycock: in his second and third years, the chief pastoral oversight of the Circuit was entrusted to the Rev. George Turner, and the place of Mr. Laycock was filled by the Rev. William Hurt.

The spiritual state of the Societies, at the commencement of his ministry, was low and discouraging; and at the first two Quarterly Meetings a decrease in the number of members was reported. But in connection with the latter of these Mr. Wood writes, "Things are assuming a more healthy state. We had a love-feast yesterday, which the friends say was the best for some years. The Lord is with us, and I think we have seen our lowest ebb. O for a mighty spring tide of mercy!" To secure such a visitation

of grace, the Ministers and people adopted the
right course. The last day of the year 1844 was
observed as a day of fasting and humiliation before
God ; and the opening day of the new year as one of
special prayer for the outpouring of the Holy Spirit.
These occasions were marked by blessed tokens of the
presence of the Lord, and the Ministers and office-
bearers were greatly cheered. Arrangements were
made for a series of special services in the Cherry
Street chapel ; and in these many were brought into
the liberty of the children of God. Mr. Wood says,
" God graciously owned the effort. We had, on some
occasions, the communion-rail filled from end to end
with penitents."

While thus earnestly engaging in revival-services,
Mr. Wood did not diminish his attention to his regular
pastoral work, nor did he overlook the advantage to
be derived from the systematic instruction of the
young in the Holy Scriptures. He adopted a plan of
co-operation with the Teachers of the Cherry Street
Sunday-School, which was calculated not only to
encourage them, but greatly to add to their efficiency.
Under the date of February 28th, 1845, he writes, " I
commenced meeting the Teachers of the Sabbath-
School, Cherry Street, to go over their Bible-lessons,
with a view of preparing them to give more efficient
instruction to the children on the following Sundays.
This is a matter of much importance ; but it involves
a considerable increase of labour to myself, if it be
properly attended to." It is much to be regretted
that such an arrangement cannot be generally adopted
throughout our Connexion. In many Circuits, indeed,
the engagements of the Ministers are so numerous,
and distributed over so wide an area, as to render it

impossible; but wherever it is practicable, it is likely,
under the Divine blessing, to produce the happiest
results.

About this time we find an entry in Mr. Wood's
Diary which indicates the beginning of the decline of
his strength.   He had, indeed, scarcely passed the
prime of life, having just completed his forty-eighth
year : but he had so severely taxed his energies in
the work of his beloved Master that it is not surprising
that symptoms of weakness now appeared.   " For a
considerable time," he writes, " my health has suffered.
I have felt an oppression in my breathing, and an
inability arising therefrom to walk fast.   My labours
have been performed with difficulty.   My mind, however, has been led to a deeper consideration of eternal
realities, and I feel more than ever loosened from
earth.   What it can give, and what it can inflict, sink
greatly in my estimation.   O for an entire swallowing
up in God!"

In connection with the painful consciousness of
diminished strength, Mr. Wood was just now called
to endure domestic affliction, and to experience the
anxiety which only a father's heart, that has been
repeatedly smitten with bereavement, can properly
estimate.   His wife had only recently recovered from
a serious illness, through the blessing of God on his
assiduous attention to her, night and day, when they
received tidings that their only son, whom they had
left in Bristol preparing for the duties of professional
life, was laid aside by dangerous sickness.   They
hastened to Bristol to see him; and Mrs. Wood
remained to nurse him and promote his convalescence.
There is a beautiful combination of genuine natural
feeling with high religious principle, in the record

which Mr. Wood has made of this circumstance. "He is our only child left to us. No heart but a parent's can estimate a parent's feeling under the circumstances. But I have often offered him to God, and I dare not recall my dedication even if I could. I have hope of his being spared to us, if it be the will of my Heavenly Father. But I have no will apart from His, so far as I know my heart. And doth this abate natural affection? Nay, but it controls and purifies it. I have left my dearest with our dear son, and I return somewhat solitary and not yet well, to endeavour to do a little in my Master's service." Very mercifully this affliction was removed. In about six weeks Mr. Wood had the happiness of receiving his dear wife and son in Birmingham; and though his joy was chastened by a renewed attack of illness in the case of the latter, yet this, too, passed away, and on May 18th, 1845, he gratefully records that "Joseph and his mother were able, for the first time since his affliction, to attend public service."

In July of this year he undertook a journey to the south-west of England, visiting several of the scenes of his former labours. On the 2nd, he opened a chapel at Downside, a hamlet in the Bristol South Circuit, into which he had been the instrument of introducing Methodist preaching about twenty years before, when he was a Local Preacher.[*] On the following day he preached at Kingswood, and thence went forward to Camborne. There he preached, "with comfort and the power of the Spirit," on the Lord's day, and at Kingswood again on his return, in the course of the following week. Such visits were always a source of sacred pleasure to himself, and

* See Chapter IV. pp. 54, 55.

were often owned of God in the conversion of the
ungodly, as well as in the establishment of believers.

Mr. Wood attended the Conference of 1845, which
was held in Leeds, but returned before the close of
its proceedings, to allow one of his colleagues to be
present during part of the time. He speaks of the
session as "one of great cordiality," and of many
of the public services as "attended with much
power." With unabated diligence, though with
less of physical strength, he resumed his labours in
Birmingham, and occasionally visited other Circuits,
where he not only preached, but held prayer-meetings
o secure the fruit of the gracious impressions received under the word. His own soul was ripening in
holy affections. Towards the close of December he
writes, "This morning, before day, when lying
awake, these words were powerfully applied to my
mind,—indeed, I awoke with them,—'filled with all
the fulness of God.' I had thought on these words
and preached from them, but never before that hour
felt that, by simply claiming the blessing, I so fully
realised their meaning. O may I never cease to exert
the same faith, and ever receive the same power in its
plenitude of blessing!"

In the valuable record which forms the chief
source of this narrative, there is, unhappily, no
account given of Mr. Wood's labours during the year
1846. Writing towards the beginning of the following year, he says that, on looking over his daily
notices, he had not courage, under the heavy pressure of varied engagements, to transcribe the whole.
"I must, therefore," he adds, "pass over the past,
hoping to be more attentive in future, if spared,

to mark such evidences of the goodness of God as appear especially fitted to be set up as 'pillars of witness' to the power of Divine truth and the riches of Divine mercy." But there is one fact, which transpired in the month of January, 1846, which is supplied by the Rev. George Curnock, in his interesting and valuable tract entitled "The Railway Navigator, or Recollections of Robert Blake." In a visit which Mr. Wood paid to the neighbourhood of Exeter, in that month, he was the means of leading to Christ a young man, who afterwards, during his brief career, was made eminently useful. "My earliest recollections of Robert Blake," Mr. Curnock writes, "recall a young man of about twenty-three years of age, standing nearly six feet high, with a fine, open countenance, beaming with interest and kindness; a clean white slop covered his ordinary working dress as he sat and listened with deep attention to a sermon preached in the Wesleyan Chapel, Crediton, by the Rev. Joseph Wood, of Birmingham. The text chosen was 'The precious blood of Christ.' That theme which has softened the hearts of millions, produced its proper effect upon the heart of Robert. There he thought upon his ways; the past, with all its guilt and consequences, crowded upon his mind; he trembled before God, while tears of penitence gave evidence of deep inward sorrow for sin. During a prayer-meeting after the sermon, the Minister spoke to him, and urged him to come and kneel at the communion-rail. For some time he remained earnestly pleading with God, while the Minister and the writer endeavoured to encourage him to 'behold the Lamb of God,' and exercise that full reliance upon 'the precious blood' which brings peace and joy. He did believe. To use his own language,

'My chains fell off, my heart was free.'

He rose from his knees a new man in Christ Jesus, and began to praise God in the presence of a large congregation."

It was on February 23rd, 1847, when he completed his fiftieth year, that Mr. Wood resumed the record in which he designed to preserve those incidents of his life, and those exercises of his mind, which he thought deserving of remembrance. "What has led me to open this book to-day," he says, "is a desire to bear testimony, on the day on which I am permitted to see my fiftieth year completed, that God is faithful, a God keeping covenant, who has dealt with me now, for half a century, in great forbearance, in stupendous grace. I have no resource but His unlimited, everlasting, ever-abounding mercy in and by my only Lord and Redeemer, whose infinite merits have availed and do now avail for me, and whose Spirit lays hold upon a worm, and blesses me, even me, washing my poor soul by an application of Christ's precious blood in its merit and virtue, so that I still dare to draw nigh; and, covered with that all-availing merit, and upheld by that free, almighty Spirit, I stand amidst the bright splendours of Jehovah's infinite purity and power, and cry, 'Abba, Father! my Lord and my God.' Hallelujah to God and the Lamb, by the Spirit of holiness! To my Triune Jehovah, Father, Son, and Holy Ghost, I ascribe, and will ascribe, glory, praise, and blessing. And by His own power, without which I can only wander and sin, I now renew my dedication; crying for wisdom, that in all things I might know, and for grace, that in all things I might both do and suffer all His will, through life, in death, and to all eternity. Amen, my God, Amen! And do Thou say so too. Then I am happy. I have my heart's desire. I ask nothing higher. I would have nothing besides. God's will only; God's will always; God's will for evermore. Confirm it, O my Father, through Christ Jesus, by the sealing power of the Holy Ghost, even this day, and the glory shall be Thine throughout eternal ages! Amen! Hallelujah!"

In the early part of the year 1847, the failure of the potato-crop in Ireland, combined with other causes, was producing severe distress in that country, and involving it in the miseries of famine. By the appointment of the Government, Wednesday, the 24th of March, was observed as a day of national fasting and humiliation, and collections were made for the alleviation of the sufferings of the Irish poor. Mr. Wood entered into these services and efforts with deep feeling; and he writes, "I have never known a day of the kind so generally observed. The places of worship were crowded. A gracious feeling was vouchsafed; and I trust that the prayers of the people of God will be answered, averting His descending wrath by which multitudes in Ireland and Scotland are perishing by famine, and scarcity begins to be seriously felt in this favoured land."

Soon after this he visited Exeter and its neighbourhood, to preach on two or three occasions of considerable local interest; and this visit, like others, was attended with spiritual success. The entries in his Diary are as follows:—"March 30th, 1847. Went to Silverton, Devon, and preached for their chapel.—31st. Opened the new chapel at Cheriton-

M

Bishop. Seven years since I was enabled, through Divine mercy, to preach without door in that place, and my heart rejoiced in being permitted to open a small chapel, well adapted for the neighbourhood. Glory to God alone! When first visited, in April 1840, they were exceedingly dark, having for a long period had no evangelical Minister in the church, indeed, *never* that any one could recollect, and no other religious denomination being in the neighbourhood.—April 1st. Preached in Exeter for a Sunday-School, although very hoarse from a cold. 2nd. Re-opened the Exmouth Chapel, after the erection of a gallery. In the evening, after preaching, while I was urging the importance of instant decision, and observing that many were 'cheated' by Satan, by allowing him to keep them in their seats with their penitential sorrows, instead of coming forward to obtain the aid of instruction and special prayer, one stout rough-looking man exclaimed, 'He shall not cheat *me*,' and bustling out of the pew, and pressing through the people as for life, he fell on his knees at the communion-rail, and quickly entered into Gospel liberty. Several followed, among whom was one who had, for some years, been an avowed infidel."

Similar instances of success occurred, again and again, in connection with Mr. Wood's ministry in his own Circuit. The records which follow those just cited illustrate this.—"Saturday, April 3rd. Returned to Birmingham.—Monday, April 5th. At the Sunday-School Tea-meeting at Harborne the Lord was with us. Some were in distress of soul. Among others, a young female, an acquaintance of a young man who was accustomed to attend the Socinian chapel. He endeavoured to comfort her by repeating, again and again, the words, 'Let not your heart be troubled.' The young person was not to be so consoled; and, after a while, the would-be comforter got into trouble himself, and upon his knees sought redemption in that precious blood which he had lightly esteemed.—Sunday, April 11th. Several persons professed to find peace with God after preaching in the evening."

An interesting notice is found, in his Diary, about this time, of the only work, of any considerable size, that he ever published. He mentions that, on April 17th, 1847, he corrected the last sheet of his "Help to Extempore Prayer," and adds, "May my gracious Master bless this humble attempt to add a mite to the treasury of devotion! A new edition having been called for, Mr. Mason applied to me to know if I wished to make any alterations. It was originally written when I was a youth; and, on examination, I found it impossible to do less than recompose nearly the whole, excepting the Scripture quotations."

In the month of June, 1847, Mr. Wood's health so far failed, that his medical advisers insisted upon his taking rest. On the 9th of that month he was seized with inflammation of the liver, which, in the opinion of his medical friends, had long been coming on, as the result of excessive exertion, continued with scarcely any intermission. For a few days he abstained from his regular work. His entry respecting Sunday June 13th, is, "I was a prisoner, but happy in God." But on the following Lord's day he resumed—though, as the result proved, prematurely—his beloved work.—"Sunday, June 20th. Unwell still, and in pain: but we had a blessed season at Cherry Street in the evening, when many professed to find peace with God. This exertion threw me down again, and we were obliged to return to former remedies. I am told that there *must* be rest, partial or final; and I have resolved to yield to the urgent advice of doctors and friends, and go, for a time, into the country. My Birmingham friends have shown the utmost kindness. May the Lord abundantly bless them!" In accordance with this resolution, formed evidently with great reluctance, Mr. Wood went, in the course of the week, to Bristol, and afterwards to Nempnett and Banwell, where he remained until July 9th. During this season of rest his health greatly improved, though he did not fully regain his former strength. His people in Birmingham, with affectionate solicitude for his comfort, wished him to remain away longer: but he was anxious again to minister to their spiritual welfare, and again to lead souls to Christ. "I preached," he says, "on Sunday July 11th, twice, and was graciously supported; as also on the 18th, when the Lord acknowledged His word by saving some."

There were many occasions in Mr. Wood's history on which his catholic spirit was manifested; and he was ever ready to respond to efforts made by evangelical Ministers of other Communions to bring about spiritual fellowship among all who truly love the Lord Jesus. A pleasing instance of this occurred at this time. In reference to July 20th, he writes, "I spent the afternoon with some other Ministers at the Rev. J. C. Miller's, Rector of St. Martin's, Birmingham," (now Dr. Miller, of Greenwich,) "an amiable, liberal, and truly evangelical Minister of Christ."

But the close of his ministry in Birmingham was now rapidly approaching. His friends, anxious for the establishment of his health, arranged to make excursions to some beautiful spots in the neighbourhood, and prevailed on him to accompany them. "On July 23rd," he writes, "I went with some friends to the Clent Hills, and spent an agreeable day. On August 6th, a few went to Sutton Park. I spent a part of the afternoon in visiting in Sutton, where, I hope, some seed then sown may be found after many days. On the 10th we went to Warwick, but the day was not propitious. On the 20th a pleasant day was spent at Chillington Hall. I have entertained an antipathy against these little parties, and consented to accompany our friends chiefly because I would not appear insensible to the kindness which led them to form these arrangements, in great part, to give me and those of my fellow-Ministers who went a pleasant 'out,' and relaxation for our benefit. But they have passed off so well, having in each case been connected with worship, and bringing parties into more friendly intercourse, that my prejudices are in a great measure removed. Still, however, they need to be carefully guarded; otherwise levity and general spiritual deterioration will be the inevitable result." Two days afterwards, on Sunday, August 22nd, he preached in the Islington Chapel, Birmingham, and says of the services, "A blessed day. Many resolved for the kingdom of heaven." On the 28th he removed to his new sphere of labour, cherishing the most affectionate regard for the people whom he was leaving. "I praise my God," he writes, "that I was ever appointed to the Birmingham West Circuit. For many friends there I have a very strong attachment, which I believe will never decline. I have enjoyed many great blessings, and I trust I have been rendered, in the

hands of my Master, instrumental of permanent good.
All glory be to the Father, to the Son, and to the Holy
Ghost, for ever and ever! Amen. O God, for Christ's
sake, pardon all my sins and negligences, and bless
Thy people in Birmingham!"

CHAPTER XII.

1847—1853.

AT the Conference of 1847 Mr. Wood was appointed to the Bristol North Circuit, for which his services had been earnestly solicited. It was most agreeable to him to return to the city of his early associations, in one part of which he had already laboured as a Minister for three years, and in which his only son was now resident, and was likely to become settled in his profession. Every thing seemed calculated to promote his comfort, while there was before him the prospect of extensive usefulness.

At the very commencement of his labours, God gave him a token for good. At the Grenville Place chapel, near the Hotwells, where he preached on Sunday, September 5th, 1847, "several," he says, "professed to feel the power of the word, and some testified to having found peace with God. This was the beginning of a gracious revival."

But here, alas! the interesting record that has furnished us with an insight into the inner life of Mr. Wood, while it has brought before us so many facts of deep interest connected with his public and pastoral labours, is interrupted. An interval of four years occurs in which no entry is made in the book before me, in which my honoured friend was accustomed to insert what he deemed it right to preserve of his daily memoranda, together with general statements, and reflections on his experience and the events of his course. The next entry bears the date of November 17th, 1851, more than twelve months after his ministry in Bristol had closed, and contains only a very brief review of the leading facts of that ministry. With a sorrowful and bleeding heart the affectionate Pastor relates how the abundant spiritual prosperity with which God crowned his labours and those of his esteemed colleagues, of whom most affectionate notices occur, during the first two years of his residence in the Bristol North Circuit, was followed by a season of discord and desolation. The storm of agitation which succeeded the Conference of 1849 burst upon the city of Bristol with peculiar severity. I know that, in refraining from giving permanent publicity to the few details which Mr. Wood specifies, I am only acting in accordance with what would be his own wish were he still among us. To my mind there is something very touching in the remarks with which his statement is introduced :—" I have so long delayed to make any entry in this book, that it has become a task to resume it. I am particularly reluctant to attempt any thing like a detailed account of what has taken place since my last entry, as it includes two years of dire agitation in the Church, over which my soul mourns with deep sorrow, and the very remembrance is sickening and humiliating beyond expression." He then goes on to mention that, during his first year in the Bristol North Circuit, when he was under the superintendence of the Rev. Thomas Martin, having as his other colleagues the Rev.

Willson Brailsford and the Rev. John M'Lean, the number of members in Society greatly increased. It rose from 1,916 in September, 1847, to 2,236 in the following March, and, notwithstanding some adverse circumstances, "the work," he says, "continued to advance, and souls were every week, if not daily, added unto the Lord." At the Conference of 1848, Mr. Wood was appointed the Superintendent of the Circuit, his colleagues being the Revs. John M'Lean, William Hurt, and Thomas S. Monkhouse, together with the Rev. Anthony Ward, who was sent to assist Mr. M'Lean whose health had seriously failed. During this year, also, the members continued to increase; and the abundant blessing of the Lord Jesus rested upon the Circuit. It had been arranged for Mr. Wood to attend the Conference of 1849, which was held in Manchester; but, while he always loved to be present at the Annual Assembly of his brethren, and while it seemed important that he should be there, as the Superintendent of the most influential Circuit in the Bristol District, his sense of duty to his own people, and his zeal for the conversion of dying men, led him to forego that privilege. The summer of 1849 was marked by a fearful visitation of cholera, in many parts of our country; and in the city of Bristol it raged with destructive violence. "While numbers were sickening and dying around," Mr. Wood says, "I felt it to be my duty to remain at my post. Having made arrangement on 'the Plan' for the supply of my places, with the view of attending the Conference, I had my time more at my disposal, and considerably extended my without-door preaching, especially in the most neglected spots, and where the plague was the most prevalent. The people, partly influenced by novelty, and partly 'moved with fear,' came in great numbers to hear the word of life, and the power of the Lord was often present both to wound and to heal. Many on their knees in the streets cried for mercy, and some there found salvation. After preaching, I often gave out a hymn, and our friends assisted in singing to the nearest chapel, where we continued the meeting in exhortation and prayer. Many were thereby led to the house of God who had previously been strangers to the sanctuary."

At this Conference Mr. Wood was re-appointed to the superintendency of the Circuit, retaining as his colleagues the Revs. William Hurt and Thomas S. Monkhouse, and receiving the late Rev. Dr. Etheridge in the place of Mr. M'Lean. It is a pleasure to insert here his brief notice of his association with the profound scholar, the eloquent preacher, and the generous friend, who a few years since passed away, but of whose Christian excellencies and services to the Church no fitting record has yet appeared. "I had known Dr. Etheridge," he says, "many years before, when I was stationed at Exeter, and he resided, for a time, in a part of that Circuit. I always admired his choice spirit, but never had the opportunity of appreciating his excellencies as now that we were united as fellow-labourers, and had to struggle with difficulties as well as to labour for God." The year opened with bright promise; the number of members in Society having continued to increase, there being also an extensive religious awakening in the city, and a plan having been formed, and generously supported, for liquidating all the chapel-debts in the Circuit. But "the dire hurricane of agitation," as Mr. Wood designates it, "broke upon the Circuit,

withering and scattering on all hands." It was to
him a year of unspeakable anxiety and distress ; and
after he had left the Circuit, the unholy strife issued
in a secession which reduced the Society to less than
1,000 members.

Mr. Wood removed, at the Conference of 1850, to
the Sheffield West Circuit, again taking the position of
second Minister under the late Rev. William Allen, who
was his senior in the ministry, and who had already
superintended that Circuit one year. Here also he
remained three years; and in the last of them, Mr.
Allen having removed to another sphere, he again
undertook the laborious and responsible duties of
chief pastor.

Of the first sixteen months of his ministry in
Sheffield no record has been preserved by his own
hand. The volume which contained a brief notice of
every day's engagements during the time which he
spent in the Bristol North Circuit, and the earlier part
of his residence in Sheffield, appears to have been
destroyed; and the brief record dated November
17th, 1851, from which extracts have just been given,
forms the only statement founded on these memoranda
which he deemed it right to preserve. It is on
January 1st, 1852, during his second year in Sheffield,
that his Diary is resumed, furnishing me with the
incidents of his daily life, and occasionally indicating
the progress of the work of God in his own soul.
But it gives me pleasure to be able to introduce a
brief statement of the Rev. Dr. Waddy respecting
this period of his ministry, and, indeed, respecting
the whole of his ministry in Sheffield. "Mr. Wood
was so constantly and diligently engaged in his
pastoral work, that he seemed to have no time for

anything else. In this he was very eminent, and
exemplary, and useful. The virulence of the agitation
was somewhat abating when he came to Sheffield.
He was ever true to his principles and to his brethren ;
but he mourned over the losses of our scattered flocks,
and laboured very diligently to restore the fallen and
to bring back the wanderers. His ministry in
Sheffield was richly evangelical and spiritual, and
many will be his ‘crown of rejoicing’ in ‘that day.’”

The notices of Mr. Wood’s labours in Sheffield
during the latter portion of his time there, which are
now before me, abundantly confirm the statement of
Dr. Waddy. It is evident that he applied himself
diligently to every department of pastoral work, and
that he sought assiduously to win back to cordial
co-operation with the Ministers some whose attachment to our system had grown cold, and who, amidst
the controversies of that period, had adopted views
which tended permanently to alienate them from our
Communion. He took a lively interest, also, in every
agency which was calculated to diffuse knowledge and
piety. He sought to uphold the Day-School connected
with the Bridgehouses chapel, attending all the meetings
of the Committee, and doing everything in his power
to encourage and sustain the master. He took
charge of a Theological Class, and endeavoured to
promote the intellectual improvement of the young
men who belonged to it, availing himself occasionally
of the help of his colleagues in delivering lectures to
them. And he valued the relation into which, as a
Sheffield Minister, he was brought to the highly
influential College established in that town, then
under the governorship of the Rev. Dr. Waddy. He
attended the meetings of the Directors, and gave his

best attention to everything that bore on the efficiency of that valuable Institution; and he availed himself of opportunities of direct personal appeal to many of the students on the subject of religion. Frequently he was gladdened with tokens of spiritual success; but the agitated state of the Connexion greatly interfered with the progress of the work of God, and the number of members in the Circuit was greatly reduced by a large secession.

In the month of January, 1852, he visited some of the scenes of his former labours. Two or three days were spent in Bristol in pastoral visits to several members of his old flock, and even to some who had been led away from the Society. "Finding," he says, "considerable discouragement · among our friends, I endeavoured to cheer them by assurances that, if we are faithful to God, He will assuredly appear for us, and send a blessed time of heart-reviving grace. On Thursday evening, the 22nd, I preached in the Ebenezer chapel from Zech. xiii. 1, and held a prayer-meeting, when some came forward penitently seeking salvation, and a few professed to find peace with God." From Bristol he proceeded to Exeter, having been earnestly solicited to preach on the occasion of the jubilee of the Strangers' Friend Society, with the assurance that his expenses should be paid without touching the collections. The Exeter Circuit had suffered, in common with the Connexion generally, from the fearful agitation of the two preceding years; but a better feeling had begun to prevail, and it was hoped that a visit from one whom God had made so useful in former years might prove of great advantage. Some notices of this visit will be read with interest by many.—"Sunday, January

25th. I preached in the Mint Lane Chapel, in the forenoon from 1 Cor. xiii. 8, and in the evening from Psalm cvii. 30. In the afternoon I held a love-feast. My heart was cheered and well-nigh overwhelmed by the testimonies of some to whom the Lord had condescended to employ me as an instrument of good in years gone by, and during former visits. What am I, a worm, that the Lord should show me so much mercy as to use me for His praise! Blessed be my God and Saviour for ever and ever! In the evening many professed to obtain salvation through faith in Christ Jesus. Hallelujah!"—Mr. Wood attended a Tea-meeting on the Monday afternoon, and afterwards a public meeting in the Mint chapel; preached at the St. Sidwell's chapel on Tuesday; and again at the Mint on Wednesday and Thursday evenings. On each of these occasions some obtained the assurance of forgiveness, while others continued in penitential distress. Reviewing this visit, he says, "I praise my good Lord for this visit. I have been greatly refreshed myself, and filled with grateful joy in beholding a repetition of former displays of grace. I called on about seventy different families, paying them, in most cases, but a very short pastoral visit. I regretted that a few were passed over; but my conscience bore me witness that I had gone to the limit of my time and strength. In some cases I was much cheered, especially at Mr. N.'s. who invited his workmen from the shop to come in when we had prayer. Only two, however, came. The others said that Mr. Wood might come to them, not expecting that I should, and our friends were apprehensive lest I might encounter insult if I went. This, however, gave me no concern. I stepped away to the shop, spoke to them, and prayed with them. On leaving, I shook each of them by the hand, and spoke to each. They received what I said with seriousness, and treated me with respect. May the good Lord bless the seed sown! Going over part of the premises, Mr. N. led me into a smaller room, where a man was working alone. I spoke to him. He burst into tears, and I found that he had been in distress since last Sunday evening. I prayed with him, and the Lord spoke in mercy to his soul. Blessed be the Name of the Lord for ever and ever! Amen."

Some entries in his Diary, during his residence in Sheffield, show that he kept up his acquaintance with the original language of the New Testament, and that he valued those clearer views of Divine truth which the careful study of the very words of inspiration often suggests. On February 14th, 1852, he writes, "Finished reading through my Greek Testament for the twenty-second time. This time I have read it through on my knees, and have found some light shed on my mind on some portions of the Sacred Records hitherto unperceived." And on June 25th, in the following year, he says, "I finished philological notes calculated to assist in reading the Greek Testament. I regret that when I began this exercise, more than thirty years since, I did not adopt the plan with which I concluded it, after more than twenty-seven years' intermission. I may yet, perhaps, if spared, go over a portion of the former part of the work again. It has obviously no merit beyond evincing a degree of application and perseverance. The exercise has been attended with pleasure, because it is the word of God."

The Conference of 1852 was held in Sheffield, and

Mr. Wood took his full share of labour in making preparation for it, and regarded its proceedings with great interest. At this Conference, as we have already intimated, he undertook the chief pastoral oversight of the Circuit, having as his colleagues the Revs. William Jackson and John Clulow, who now entered upon their second year in Sheffield, and the Rev. George Mather, who was just appointed to the Circuit. It was impossible for him to feel a deeper interest than he had done in the spiritual welfare of the Societies; but in his altered position he had an increased burden of care, more especially as unusual difficulties then attended the working of the Methodist economy. But God sustained him, and gave him to see some fruit of his labours.

One very beautiful development of his character, as combining thoughtfulness and sympathy with the energy and zeal which were its prominent features, has been mentioned to me by the Rev. William Jackson, who was his colleague, during two years, in this Circuit. But I refrain from entering upon this subject here. The circumstances alluded to shall be stated in Mr. Jackson's own words, in a paper with which he has kindly furnished me, and with which this chapter closes.

In the course of this year Mr. Wood originated a scheme for the reduction of the debts on the Ebenezer and Bridgehouses Chapels, and had the happiness of seeing it brought into active operation. That scheme, indeed, was crowned with complete success. Just before he left the Circuit, a Tea-meeting was held to receive the report of the Fund provided and of its application. "We started," Mr. Wood says, "to raise £1,500. We have raised about £1,590 net, besides paying £62 to the Missions, as the ladies could not hold their usual bazaar for the Missionary work, and only about £37 remains unpaid." But this local effort did not prevent Mr. Wood and his colleagues, and the noble friends in Sheffield who sustained them, from entering heartily into the Connexional movement which was then made, to relieve the Funds of the Connexion from embarassment, and to extend the evangelistic action of Methodism. "The Relief and Extension Fund," which was inaugurated that year, under the second presidency of the late Rev. John Scott, was well supported in Sheffield, and in its success Mr. Wood greatly rejoiced.

His own soul continued to prosper. On the day on which he completed his fifty-sixth year, February 23rd, 1853, he thus reviewed his career, and acknowledged the abounding goodness of God:—"What mercies have attended me! What unutterable forbearance has been exercised by a God of infinite compassion! Still He blesses me. He will be gracious because He will be gracious. He seems to have set His heart on showing favour to me, a worm. My soul pants after Him with strong desire for more intimate communion. O for the fulness of the Spirit! that God, in condescending grace, would deign to order and control every thought of my heart, all the imaginations of my soul, all the tempers of my mind, and my whole life, that so I might enjoy the liberty, the happiness, the honour, of doing only, doing always, and doing with all my might, all the good pleasure of the Triune Jehovah, who is my covenant-Friend. Glory be to God the Father, God the Son, and God the Holy Ghost, and may the whole earth be filled with His glory! Amen and Amen."

Just after this, he experienced a merciful preservation in the midst of imminent danger. Having engaged to preach to his old friends at Camborne, he went on Friday, February 25th, to Bristol, and proceeded at once to the steam-ship "Cornwall," which was to sail that evening for Hayle. "It promised," he says, "to be a fine night and a good passage. I conversed with the Captain, after prayer in the evening, and found that he was seeking salvation. About eleven o'clock I retired to rest. Soon after the wind blew a gale from the north-west, which continued with great violence through the following day. Our Captain got under the shelter of Lundy Island, and intended to cast anchor there until the storm should abate. But, before this was done, the wind, during a squall, 'chopped round' more to the north, when Lundy can afford no protection, and we were compelled to face the winds and waves. By the change, however, the wind became more in our favour; and, after long buffeting with the waves, we got to the place of our destination just in time to pass over 'the bar' at Hayle between six and seven o'clock in the evening, contrary to the expectation of the officers on board. This storm visited, according to the newspaper accounts, a large portion of the coast; and on Saturday there were many wrecks. It is said to have been especially violent on the coast of Devon and Cornwall. Of course we were in the whole of it; but we were mercifully preserved by the good providence of our God. On getting to Hayle, I found that a friend had been waiting for me with his gig from ten o'clock in the morning until four in the afternoon, when, the steamer not being in sight, they told him we could not get into the harbour that night, and he returned.

I hired a conveyance, and went on to Camborne, where I had my home at Mr. Smith's,"—afterwards Dr. Smith,—"thankful for my preservation." The public services at Camborne, both on the Lord's day, and on the following Monday and Tuesday evenings, were marked by manifestations of the Divine presence. On Wednesday Mr. Wood preached at Truro; and "some," he gratefully records, "found peace in the prayer-meeting." He stayed that night at the house of a lady who kept a boarding school for girls; and, as usual, he sought to lead these young people to the Saviour, and with very blessed results. On the day on which he returned to Sheffield, he received a letter from this lady, informing him that several of her pupils had found peace with God.

At the March Quarterly Meeting, 1853, he was gratified to report a small increase in the number of members in the Society. It was the turn of the tide after a lengthened period of depression and loss. "We had a good Quarterly Meeting," he writes. "The Circuit had been going down in numbers every quarter since Midsummer, 1849, until this quarter. Our increase is now 16, with 42 on trial. 'Praise God from whom all blessings flow.'"

From that time until the assembling of the Conference, he continued to labour with his usual assiduity, and to watch over all the interests committed to his charge. The Conference met this year at Bradford, Yorkshire, for the first time; and Mr. Wood was hospitably entertained in the town of Halifax. Under the able presidency of the Rev. John Lomas, the important business which came before it was transacted with great harmony. Mr. Wood speaks of it as "a happy, united, blessed Conference." He conducted a love-feast, on a Sunday afternoon, in the Eastbrook Chapel, the Rev. Thomas Collins, one of the Ministers of the Circuit, being also present; and he says, "The chapel was crowded; and such bursts of warm-hearted, sound, Methodist feeling I have not witnessed for a long period. My own soul was refreshed, and I thanked God and took courage."—Many tokens of affection were offered to him, as he closed his arduous labours in Sheffield; and, after a brief visit to Banwell, and taking part in the anniversary services of the St. Philip's chapel, Bristol, in which God again graciously owned his efforts, he removed to Peckham in the Southwark Circuit, to which he had been affectionately invited, and to which the Conference had appointed him.

I am happy to be able to close this chapter with a beautiful delineation of Mr. Wood's ministerial character, as it was developed in Sheffield, from the pen of the Rev. William Jackson, now the Governor of the Didsbury branch of the Theological Institution:—

"My personal acquaintance with the late Rev. Joseph Wood began after the Conference of 1851, when I was appointed to the Sheffield West Circuit, in which Mr. Wood had spent one year. I had heard much of the saintliness of his character, his never-wearying activity, and his generous bearing towards his colleagues; and I soon found that there was no exaggeration in anything that I had heard. The Circuit had just before been rent by agitation; and, though the storm had in a great measure subsided, there were occasional mutterings, proving that the angry elements were not perfectly at rest. Added to this, there was the depressing influence of

thinned congregations and Societies; and, though
many valued friends in that town and neighbourhood
rallied round their Ministers, upholding their hands
by earnest prayer and self-sacrificing contributions,
it was a time of undoubted trial and discouragement.
At this period Mr. Wood proved himself a true
shepherd of the sheep. He was indefatigable in his
efforts to keep them from wandering out of the way,
or stumbling in it. While his faithfulness to what
he believed to be the truth both in doctrine and
discipline was never relaxed, he manifested the
utmost forbearance towards the erring, seeking to
win them back to the fold. In this he often succeeded; and, though the sad effects of agitation were
long felt in Sheffield, I am persuaded they would
have been much more serious if it had not been for
the tender, loving, yet discriminating, forbearance of
Joseph Wood.

"A few months after my entrance on the Circuit,
I was laid aside for some weeks by severe illness. It
was then I proved the brotherly sympathy of my
excellent colleague. Scarcely a day passed without
his visiting me, not to talk on Circuit-matters, for
from these he considerately abstained, but to speak
of the love of God in Christ, to bring to mind some
precious promise, and then to close by such a prayer
as only a soul conscious of Divinely-imparted strength
and of its own utter weakness could have poured
forth. I was very much impressed, during these
visits, by Mr. Wood's power to adapt himself to the
requirements of a sick room, and of a nervous invalid.
In public I always thought his tones a little harsh;
but in visiting the sick,—and I have heard this
remarked by others as well as myself,—his voice

was modulated to the gentlest accents, his footfall
was scarcely heard, and his whole bearing had a
soothing and tranquilising influence on the sufferer.

"Never shall I forget his anxiety that I should
not resume work too soon, or the difficulty that I had
in persuading him, the first time after my affliction
that I started with him into the country, that I was
strong enough to bear the ride. He almost insisted
on my stopping at home; and, though never willing
in the least degree to spare himself, he was full of
fear lest the burden might prove too heavy for a
weak brother. There was something very remarkable in his consideration for his colleagues at all
times. Wonderfully active as he was himself, and
unremitting in the work of pastoral visitation, he
never made his own power the standard for others,
never exacted so much and such kind of work
from his junior colleagues, but allowed every one
of them to maintain his own individuality in his
mode of work, satisfied that this was best for 'the
edifying of the body of Christ.'

"On the removal of the late Rev. William Allen
in 1852, Mr. Wood became the Superintendent of
the Circuit, when he devised and successfully carried
out a plan for the relief of some of the heavily-bur-
dened chapel-trusts. In the management of its
various details he combined great tact with courtesy,
offending no one by neglect on the one hand, or
undue pressure on the other, and, as nearly as possible, interesting every one in the promotion of his
object. The directly spiritual part of his work,
however, was at all times his great delight: for this
he laboured night and day. When reviving influences
came down on the congregations, and sinners

anxiously inquired 'What must I do to be saved?'
or believers were seeking after a fuller consecration
to the Lord and His service, then the heart of this
faithful Minister of Christ glowed with love unutterable towards his Divine Master, and expanded in
sympathy towards every seeking soul, and his very
countenance seemed to catch a ray of the Divine
glory.

"I feel it to be one of the great privileges and
responsibilities of my life, to have been associated
with so holy a man,—a man from whose lips I never
heard a word that might not have been uttered before
the assembled universe, who was, I believe, incapable
of a mean or selfish action, and whose whole life was
an embodiment of all that is true, and lovely, and
honourable, and of good report. May the Lord, the
sovereign Distributor of blessings to His Church,
bestow upon it many such pastors and teachers as
our revered friend Joseph Wood!"

CHAPTER XIII.

WHEN Mr. Wood came to London, after the Conference of 1853, the storm of agitation that had swept over the Connexion had passed; but its withering effects remained. The Southwark Circuit had suffered severely; but it was gradually reviving through the blessing of God on the judicious management and the faithful labours of the Ministers appointed to it. No arrangement, probably, could have been better than that which made Mr. Wood the colleague of the Rev. Henry H. Chettle, who had already superintended the Circuit for two years. Though his physical vigour was abated, Mr. Wood was yet strong to labour for Christ, and he retained his quenchless love to the souls of men. His piety was mellowed; and his eminently devout and benevolent spirit enabled him to exert an influence for good, both in the official meetings of the Circuit, and in the homes of his people.

At the very commencement of his labours, he was favoured with some encouraging tokens of the presence and power of the Spirit of God. His first Sunday evening was spent at Peckham; and the prayer-meeting which followed the public preaching of the word was marked by a spirit of holy desire and expectation. A fortnight afterwards he preached in the Southwark chapel, on behalf of the Sunday-School. There was a large congregation; and he gratefully records, "It was a time of power. Several came forward as penitents, and some professed to find salvation. Glory to God and the Lamb! At the close a young person wished to see me, and, on coming into the vestry, told me that, six years ago, I had detained her in a meeting in Bristol, to pray with and for her, that she at that time obtained pardon, and that she still enjoys the favour of God."

The incident just related was only one among many in which Mr. Wood found in London the fruit of his former toils. Several came to him after his public services to relate how, in Bristol, or Kingswood, or some other place, he had urged upon them to become decided for God, and gratefully to acknowledge the grace which had kept them in the narrow path. And some to whom he had been made useful in former days, but who had fallen away, were recovered through the blessing of God on his faithful and affectionate ministry. He mentions one who was brought in at Bitton, in the Kingswood Circuit, when he was stationed there, and who for twenty years ran well. This person, having left the neighbourhood for a while, found, on his return, that the Society was rent by the fearful agitation that troubled the Connexion, and, his own mind becoming unsettled, he did not re-unite himself to the Church. He lost his religion, and became, as he stated, "unutterably wretched." But seeing an announcement that Mr. Wood was to preach at the Grove Chapel, in the Southwark Circuit, he came to the service, and "the first words which he heard on entering the place,"

Mr. Wood remarks, "were blessed of God to inspire some hope. He obtained restoration; and since then his wife and some of his family have been brought to God."

In the Diary before me, Mr. Wood has mentioned the topics of an address which he delivered at a special Society-meeting in the Southwark chapel, about a month after his arrival; and I gladly record them, as showing the pointed character and the practical wisdom of his pastoral counsels. "I spoke," he says, "of the visitation of absentee members by other members of each class,—of not resting while any member of the class remained without a clear sense of pardon and purity,—of family worship,—of the duties of mothers, especially that they should take their young children once a day alone with them, and pray for each of them aloud, as they knelt around,—of avoiding to speak of the faults, real or supposed, of religious people before their children,—and of a holy life before them. Also of endeavouring each one to gather souls from the world into the Church by kind invitation and much prayer." At this meeting the pastoral address of the Conference was read by the Superintendent; and Mr. Wood's exhortation was followed by several prayers. Such meetings of the Society have often been found to be occasions of more than ordinary spiritual profit.

Mr. Wood applied himself in this Circuit, as in others, to pastoral visitation; but he remarks, in two or three places, that he experienced much difficulty in finding the members, "through incorrect or insufficient information, and the defective state of names and numbers in the streets." This, however, did not cause him to desist. While he regretted the loss of time which was thus occasioned, he continued his efforts, and was rewarded with the esteem and gratitude of his flock.

His own spiritual life was graciously sustained by the Spirit of Christ; and there were some seasons of peculiar enjoyment in communion with God. On Saturday, November 5th, 1853, he writes, "A favoured time in prayer in the course of the afternoon in my study. The Lord gave me a power and going forth of heart, and a wrestling of soul for a deeper impression of the Spirit's seal. I felt as if I could have gone on for a very long time in this exercise, and wished for a solitude in which I might have given vent without restraint to the aspirations, and longings, and adoration, of my spirit. O how condescending is the Lord!" Thus endeavouring to live in fellowship with the Triune Jehovah, he maintained great tenderness of conscience; and if, at any time, he was betrayed into a hasty expression, he deeply lamented it. I find, about a month after the date of the above extract, the following entry :—"I spoke sharply to a workman who, I thought, meant to insult me by affirming what I thought wrong; but I suffered afterwards greatly in my mind on account of it. My ardent, precipitate spirit requires to be continually guarded, or I say more than I intend."

In some of the occasional services which Mr. Wood undertook in other Circuits, he was favoured with great encouragement and success. He preached at Poplar, on Monday, January 16th, 1854, from Acts xvi. 30, 31, and this service was greatly owned of God. "Many," he says, "came forward as penitent seekers of salvation, and some professed to obtain a clear sense of pardon. One of them, a young married

man, went afterwards to show me the way to the
Railway Station, and spoke to the following effect,
and, as nearly as I recollect, in these words :—'I once
knew the Lord, but I yielded to the influence of evil
companions and left the good way. I have long been
very unhappy; but in all I have felt that the Methodist
chapel was my home, and I never left that, but
attended on Sundays. Lately my misery has increased; and I felt so under the preaching this
evening that, if you had not come and spoken to me,
I could not have gone forward to the communion-
rail, for I felt that if I had attempted it I should have
sunk down on the floor. I have parents who are
good people. My father has been a member, I
believe, forty-five years. I had a letter from him last
week, in which he told me that he and my mother are
so distressed about those of their family who are
unconverted, that they lie awake at night, weeping
together respecting us. I answered my father's letter
to-day, and I had not heart to refer to that part of it;
for as I could not say what would make them happy,
I said nothing. But to-morrow I will write again,
and tell them what God has done for my soul. Now
I want my wife to be converted too.' He also told
me that they had one child, and promised to go home
and at once begin family-prayer. May the Lord
preserve him, and grant that he and all the others
who were this evening led to obey the Divine call,
may be found approved in the day of the Lord Jesus!
Amen."

On the 24th of the same month he preached at
Woolwich from Matthew ix. 29. "The Lord favoured
me," he writes, "with liberty, and gave power with
His word. Several came forward, amongst whom

was a very interesting young soldier, a non-commissioned officer, who professed to find comfort, and another soldier who was wounded deeply, and who also professed to find deliverance. His countenance, beaming with serenity and peace, indicated the inward change. His wife, who is a member, sat by him, the subject of deep feeling when I invited him to come forward. Afterwards, in the vestry, while he sat with others, and gave his name to become a member, she again sat by him, her infant in her arms, but was weeping for joy. I returned home after the service, praising God for the work of His grace."

The labours of the Lord's day following, January 29th, 1854, spent at Deptford, were similarly blessed. "I preached," Mr. Wood says, "on behalf of the Strangers' Friend Society, morning and evening, addressed the Sunday-School in the afternoon, and held a prayer-meeting half an hour before the evening preaching. The Lord was pleased to clothe the old truth with power. In the evening, after the sermon, several professed to find salvation. One pious father found among those who obtained mercy a daughter, the child of many prayers. When about to give glory to God for some who could rejoice in His pardoning mercy, a man whom I had not invited forward, not having got to that part of the chapel, stood up at the back of the pews, and with a loud voice praised God that He had healed all his backslidings, and had filled his soul with peace and joy. Blessed be the Lord God of Israel for ever and ever, and let the whole earth be filled with His glory! Amen and Amen."

On some occasions, throughout his ministry, Mr. Wood preached on portions of Holy Scripture which forcibly struck his mind, with very little previous preparation; but he has placed on record his deliberate conviction that, unless under very extraordinary circumstances, such a procedure is not wise. He mentions, about this time, preaching on a week-evening, in one of the smaller chapels of his Circuit, from Rev. iii. 11, and adds, "There did not appear to be much influence. The preparation by previous thought was very little. The passage had struck my mind, and I spoke from it with a degree of liberty; but it did not appear to me to *tell*. I am persuaded that, whenever there is opportunity, careful attention, close application of thought, and earnest prayer, must precede our speaking in the name of the Lord, if we would look with confidence for success." Another extract, bearing on the choice of subjects for the pulpit, may be added. Most Ministers have occasionally felt a difficulty in deciding on what portion of Divine truth they should address their people; and on such occasions earnest prayer to God is the fitting resource. Mr. Wood writes, "Thursday, February 9th, 1854. Being at a loss as to a subject, I cried earnestly to the Lord, and He opened my mind to the words, 'Having therefore obtained help of God, I continue unto this day,' and He opened my mouth in speaking from them. I propose, by Divine aid, to seek from my God more earnestly my message to the people. May He deign to order and command me!"

On the recurrence of his birthday, February 23rd, 1854, he thus reviews his career, and dwells on his prospects of the future: "A child of numberless mercies, preserved during fifty-seven years of unworthiness, imperfection, and sin. How wonderful are the

condescension and forbearance of God to me, a poor
worm of earth. Yet He blesses me,—forgives me,—
saves me,—makes me happy,—deigns to employ me,—
gives me a degree of success in labouring for Him,—
and opens before me a hope in heaven. I am not
weary of life. I gladly live on, to do my Master's
will, and, if He sees good, to suffer also. But my
country is above. I hasten to do my work, for the
evening is at hand. I, however, anticipate no night,
but the rising of an unclouded day of eternal purity
and peace. I yield my soul anew to Him who is
my God, my All. O may He more deeply stamp
the seal of conscious approval, impressing the full
image of Christ!"

In April of this year, Mr. Wood took a leading
part in a series of special services held at the Union
Street chapel, near the Blackfriars Road, with a
view to induce the attendance of many who habitually
neglected Divine worship. His narrative of this
Home-Missionary effort will be read with interest.—
"Monday, April 3rd. I took a list of our special
services to a great number of houses, not omitting
one, and kindly invited the people to attend. Not
more than three or four refused to receive the papers,
and *they* were not offensive in their refusal. One, on
taking the paper, said, 'I wish you would bring some
money.' Another, who kept a respectable shop in
Blackfriars' Road, on my asking if he would allow
me to leave a list of our religious services, said, 'O,
yes; you may leave anything you like, so that there
is nothing to pay.' Many of the houses are kept by
prostitutes, and no man should enter them alone. I
adopted the precaution not to pass over the threshold,
and not to stay longer than to give a brief invitation.

My soul was grieved at the deep degradation and wide-spread ruin; but I felt that nothing but kindness and compassion was suitable in addressing them. By a kind and respectful manner I found that very rough-looking men appeared to be subdued. Before commencing the service in the chapel, I obtained the assistance of a few friends to sing through the streets, thinking thereby to remind them of the service and of the bills I had delivered. Many collected, and I believe some were thereby led to come in. While singing down the street, a young female came out to me, as I was walking at the head of the little party, and offered me a penny. This was, of course, intended as a jest, as much as to say, 'We will give the poor street-singer a penny.' I declined taking it by a respectful bow and waving of my hand. The Great Master, however, recompensed me for any little annoyance not worth naming, by giving me much power in speaking His truth. Some of the senior children of the Sunday-School came forward, and with weeping sought the Saviour's mercy; and the people of the Lord were richly visited by the influence of the Eternal Spirit. Glory to my God for ever!"—"Wednesday, 5th. Visited many more houses with a list of services and an invitation. in the neighbourhood of Union Street."—"Thursday, 6th. Sang again through the street, adding this evening another street near. Just as I began to preach, I observed Mr. C. take his hat and leave the chapel. I feared that he was taken ill. He, however, soon returned, and soon afterwards a hale man, perhaps a little above thirty years of age, with an intelligent countenance, came in. He heard with fixed attention; and as he stayed to the prayer-meeting, I spoke to him. He told me that, during the sermon, he had obtained what he had not felt for nine years, and that he had peace with God through our Lord Jesus Christ. On leaving the chapel, Mr. C. told me that he had visited this man in the afternoon, but not seeing him in the chapel he went out for him, when the man told him he would be quickly there. He came and found the Lord. What might not be accomplished if God's people would follow sinners, and give them no rest until they yield to the call of mercy? A very poor woman, far advanced in life, and apparently almost despairing, came in because of the singing in the street, and seeing the same Minister whom she had seen so engaged several months since. She said that her heart was dead, still repeating, 'Ever since I bore my last child, my heart has been dead, I cannot pray. I have no feeling.' I induced her to come forward. She, at first, objected that she was so filthy. True she was. But she had a soul. She came and knelt down, and we prayed for her; and although she did not find pardon, her countenance brightened with hope, and she felt that her heart was not dead. Some children came weeping and telling me that they wanted to find the Saviour."

While thus actively engaged in evangelistic efforts in his own Circuit, and ever ready to promote such efforts in the Circuits around him, Mr. Wood felt a lively interest in all the affairs of the Connexion, as well as in every movement affecting the Church of God at large. He attended regularly the meetings of all the Committees of which he was a member; and he availed himself of his residence in London, to be present at the Anniversary Services of many of the religious and benevolent Societies which adorn our land. Occasionally, too, though very rarely, he took a day, or a few hours, for relaxation and viewing the beauties of nature.

An incident which came to his knowledge in the month of June, 1854, shows how a few words uttered for God may, after the lapse of years, be the means of awakening individuals from a state of sinful indifference. After preaching at the Albion Street chapel on the evening of one Lord's day, a member of the Society walked with him to the Old Kent Road, and narrated the circumstances under which he was brought to God. "When you travelled," he said, "in the Kingswood Circuit, you called at my father's house at Hanham. My mother was a member ; and, when you left, you put your hand upon my head, and said, 'God bless thee, my child, and make thee as Samuel of old.' I was then very young. I grew up in sin, and became very profligate. I imbibed infidelity, and was a professed Socialist. I attended no place of worship, but ridiculed religion. When about nineteen years of age, I went with one or two other young men, in the employ of a master-painter in Bristol, to paint a house in Banwell. While there, I was one evening in the shop of Mr. Wilcox, a stonecutter, a Methodist, and seeing some females going by, dressed as Methodists, I inquired who they were. Mr. Wilcox told me they were the family of the Woods. I asked him if they were related to Mr. Wood, the Minister. He said that they were of the same family. Immediately the words you uttered in prayer for me when I was a very little boy came to my recollection in a way I never felt before. I left the shop, and went with one of my comrades for a walk on the Bristol road. The sun was going down in the west behind us, and Banwell wood was before us, which I thought appeared full of solemn gloom, as if indicating my doom. My companion had been singing a song, and I had been dancing as I went on by him, trying to drive away the serious impressions which I had just felt in the shop. But my feelings were too mighty. My companion inquired, 'What is the matter? You look as if frightened.' I replied that I knew what was the matter, and would go no further. I returned back, but could find no rest. I returned to Bristol and Kingswood soon after, and continued seeking the Lord in deep distress of soul for ten months, until on a Monday morning, after being encouraged by some experiences which I heard in a love-feast on the Sunday, while I was praying at my bed-side, the Lord broke in upon my spirit, and filled me with His pardoning love." After mentioning the circumstances under which this man came to London, where he was now comfortably providing for his family, Mr. Wood adds, "Who would have thought that the little seed cast into the heart of a little child, after being buried under many years of resolute iniquity, would nevertheless be the chosen seed of the Spirit for life eternal? And who would have expected that means so simple, in the stone-cutter's shop, would be employed by the Holy One to communicate to that seed its vegetative power. Truly 'the wind bloweth where it listeth.' O may I be found more diligent in sowing, and with increasing confidence look to God the Holy Ghost for success, although it may be after many days!"

We have seen that the robust health which Mr. Wood usually enjoyed, in the earlier part of his career, had now begun to give way. During his residence at Peckham, attacks of illness occasionally interrupted his labours. On one Lord's day, when he was unable to preach, he writes, "I awoke early, and should have rejoiced, had it so pleased my great Master, to have risen for a day of labour in a vineyard where there is much to be done. But He knows best what to do with His servants. I might have done no good, but some mischief or other. I had some meditations of a cheering kind, and while all but myself this morning were at the chapel, I found it good to pray for God's people and ministers who are engaged in public worship, and to meditate on the holiness which should be connected with the house and service of our King."

At the Conference of 1854, Mr. Wood was appointed the Superintendent of the Southwark Circuit, with the Rev. Charles Prest as his colleague. The intimate knowledge of all the interests of that Circuit, which he had acquired during his first year's labours, qualified him for the special duties which now devolved upon him; while his zeal for the salvation of souls was unabated.

In the early part of October he paid a visit to his friends in Camborne, and was abundant in his labours on the Sabbath and the two following days. It was both to them and to himself an occasion of spiritual blessing. "The services," he gratefully remarks, "have, in general, been crowded. On Sunday evening, especially, the presence of the great Master was felt. I have much enjoyed this visit. My home was at the house of my dear old friend, Mr. George Smith, who, with his beloved wife and affectionate family, did everything to make me comfortable. The intervals of public duty were chiefly occupied in visiting old friends; but the time was insufficient for seeing many whom I wished to call upon."

Among cases of special interest which occurred in the course of his regular ministry, we may select the following:—

"Sunday, November 5th, 1854.—Union Street; evening. After preaching I administered the sacrament of the Lord's Supper. I permitted any who were determined for God to remain, although they might not come to the Table. Some promising young persons, who were Teachers in the Sunday-School, stayed, and, while closing the service, one young man was so deeply affected that he could not conceal his feelings. Others followed. The first was clearly made happy in God, and some others professed to find consolation. I then proposed that they should receive the sacrament, to which they readily assented; and, returning to the communion-place, I administered to them the tokens of the Redeemer's love. It was a touching and powerful occasion. Praise to my great King!"

"Sunday, November 19th.—Silver Street Chapel Anniversary. I preached short in the morning, and publicly examined the children of the Sabbath-School in the former part of the history of Elijah. After the evening service we held a prayer-meeting, when several came forward as penitents, and some professed to find salvation. One found pardon before the prayer-meeting commenced; and some who did not come forward appeared to be decided to serve God. Glory to the blessed Name of my Lord and Master for ever!"

"Sunday, February 25th, 1855.—Southwark. I

felt very stupid until the evening service, when the Lord graciously revived both body and mind. There was a largely attended prayer-meeting afterwards, when a few appeared to obtain peace. The case of one fine young man was very marked and decided. He struggled mightily in prayer, and was gloriously delivered. 'Glory to God in the highest!' I was encouraged to find that one of the family whom I visited last Sunday afternoon was led, after I left the house, to get to God in earnest prayer, and again found 'the joy of His salvation,' and testified in her class-meeting to this grace of God."

"Monday, April 16th, 1855.—Visited several. After leaving a poor backslider in Baalzephon Street, I came out at the end of Kent Road, just as the Emperor and Empress of the French passed, who had come up by way of the Bricklayers' Arms Station. I should have liked well enough to have seen them, but enjoyed much more the sight of a weeping backslider with whom I had been praying."

"Thursday, July 10th.—A gentleman met me to-day in the High Street, and, grasping my hand warmly, said, 'I was to-day suddenly seized in such a way that I did not know but my end might be near. I reverted to your discourse on last Sunday morning, and felt comfort and confidence. I was prejudiced against your preaching before then. I had never heard you; and I was, therefore, prejudiced in ignorance. But since last Sabbath I have felt differently from what I ever did before; and if I do not come to see you it will be from inability, for I shall come whenever I have the opportunity.' I had met him in an office before, and his wife is connected with us; but I believe he is an Independent. On

Sundây morning I felt less liberty than I sometimes do, and feared that the sermon was not likely to be productive of much good. The Lord, however, gave me to feel that, if HE was glorified, I was content to be abased, for 'of Him, and through Him, and to Him are all things, to whom be glory for ever and ever. Amen.'"

In connection with a visit to Bristol, to preach occasional sermons at Bedminster, and subsequently to Banwell, in August of this year, Mr. Wood mentions some cases in which he endeavoured to speak to his fellow-travellers about their salvation. Under the date of Saturday, August 18th, he writes, "In travelling I always watch for an opportunity to speak some word for my Master, but often find it difficult to do so with success, and to know when to speak and when to be silent. But this week I have had some encouraging cases. On Tuesday, coming from Banwell to Bristol, I spoke to a young man who is employed on the line, and found by his answer that he had heard of Divine things before. I suspected that he had been a scholar in a Sabbath-School, and asked him if it was not so, when he acknowledged that it was, and that he had a mother who used sometimes to talk to him; but he said that it was many years since any one had spoken to him about his soul. He appeared glad to be advised for his spiritual good, and I hope that the seed sown when he was a lad will bring forth fruit to life everlasting. In the afternoon of the same day, I went from Bristol to Swindon, and fell in with a young man who had recently left college in the United States, and was on his way, with another young man, to the Paris Exhibition. He said that his health was not very good, and that, in the spring of life and of the year, he had resolved to make a tour. I expressed my earnest wish that he might obtain much advantage, and realise much enjoyment, in the prosecution of his plan. But I reminded him that, as this was the spring-time of life, it was of much importance what kind of seed we sowed, and that according to this seed would be that harvest for eternity which assuredly awaited us. He received it very kindly. I had to get out at Swindon, having to preach there. He expressed his regret at parting with me, and our conversation appeared to be mutually agreeable.—The next morning I went on from Swindon to London, and was joined by a party going to Brighton for a summer-visit. We had to wait some time at Didcot, and I remarked to them, that our passage through life was by express train, and that we never should get a stoppage until we ran into the terminus at death; and that, as we could only obtain a preparation on the passage, it behoved us to make the most of our moments. They silently assented, but with looks of wonder from the juniors at this sort of talk in a railway-carriage. They soon fell to a manifestation of agricultural hilarity, which, not being censurable, I did not frown upon, lest it should lead them to suppose that religion would prevent innocent cheerfulness. On getting to the terminus, I was glad to be able to render them some service, in seeing them in a right omnibus. They evidently had begun to regard me with a degree of interest and deference. May our good Lord cause the seed to grow!"

One method which he occasionally adopted of

conveying religious truth to the minds of persons who
neglected public worship, was the giving **away** of
religious tracts, as he went **to** his appointments **on the**
Lord's day. He says, in reference **to Sunday, August**
19th, 1855, "In my way to **Silver Street this morning,**
I distributed upwards **of ninety hand-bill tracts,**
speaking some word kindly **to all who received them,**
not in the way **of conversation, for I had not time for**
this. They **were received kindly by all : but there**
was one man standing **with others, who** appeared **to**
be an arch, **shrewd fellow, who said, on my asking**
him if he **would take a tract, 'O yes, I will take one.**
I am going **for a** Missionary, **Governor.'** I replied,
'**You** and I are going into **another world ; but** I
cannot say which **of us** will **get there first.'** At this
he appeared to be taken aback, **and had no** ready
answer; **and, although he wished to have said some-**
thing **more, I had no time to wait while he sought a**
rejoinder. I felt much satisfaction **in this work, and**
pray that **some of the seed, at least, may appear, if**
it be **not until after many days." A few months**
afterwards, **he mentions a similar effort on the Lord's**
day :—"I distributed **a number of hand-bill tracts in**
my progress from place **to place. I feared that the**
few last would **be lost, as several** rough **boys who**
were playing noisily in **the** street, on seeing me **give**
one, came to be supplied, and pressed around me so
eagerly that I gave them the **few** I had left. Instantly
they ceased **from play ; and, the tracts** being chiefly
hymns, they began in their **way** singing **them and**
then reading aloud, and, **as** they walked **on orderly**
at some **distance** behind me through part of **two**
streets, **I waited** before I entered **the chapel and**
spoke to them, when they all heard with signs of

interested attention. Shall not some of the seed spring up to the glory of the Lord of the vineyard?"

In the autumn of the year 1855 Mr. Wood's health was frequently affected, but he continued his arduous labours, encouraged, again and again, by decided cases of conversion. The affectionate invitations which he gave to seekers of salvation to come forward and avow their decision for Christ, in the prayer-meetings that followed the Sunday evening preaching, were generally responded to; and many who thus penitently sought the Lord were blessed with "joy and peace in believing."

In the month of November he went on a Missionary deputation to the Bedford and Northampton District; and at Dunstable he met with an incident which deeply affected him. He had preached there on the Lord's day; and several professed to receive the assurance of forgiveness. On the following morning, as he was walking towards the chapel, an aged woman abruptly stopped him. "She was rather tall," he says, "and erect, with an intelligent countenance, careworn and furrowed by age. Her gait was trembling from feebleness, and she carried in one hand a small white basin containing apparently leavings from some kitchen. She said, 'I *must* stop you. The Lord bless you; and blessed be God who sent you here yesterday;' with many similar expressions. On looking in her face, I found she was one whom I had seen in the prayer-meeting last evening seeking salvation. She told me that she now felt happy in God, and she still loaded me with blessings. How sweet is religion to a poor forlorn soul, tottering into eternity!"

During his third year at Southwark, Mr. Wood

and his colleague were cheered by a small increase of members, after a lengthened period of depression. At the Christmas Quarterly Meeting, 1855, he was able to report a net increase of twenty-two; and in June, 1856, just before leaving the Circuit, he mentions that, at the Quarterly Meeting, he had to announce "a small addition," and that the meeting was marked by "a very cordial feeling."

He continued to labour, amidst scenes such as we have described, happy in God himself, and made the instrument of blessing to many. In his occasional visits to other Circuits, and especially to the scenes of his former ministerial toil, he was gladdened by meeting with persons who came forward to welcome him, and to tell him that, in former years, he had been the means of leading them to Christ. His ministry in Southwark closed at the Conference of 1856; but its blessed effects still remain. The general features of that ministry, and the honour put upon it by God, are well described by his colleagues in that Circuit, each of whom has favoured me with a brief communication on the subject. The Rev. Henry H. Chettle says, "It was my privilege to be associated with the Rev. Joseph Wood for one year in the Southwark Circuit. He very soon impressed me with the simplicity and sanctity, the zeal and energy, of his character; simplicity, without weakness,—sanctity, without sanctimoniousness,—zeal, without presumption,—and energy, without coarseness. He had a clear perception of his object; and to accomplish it, was direct in his aim, and unwearied in his efforts. Devoted to Christ, ready *always* for every good work, he laboured and prayed, on all occasions, to win souls: and he succeeded, for God was with him." The Rev. Charles

Prest remarks, "I had the happiness of being associated with the Rev. Joseph Wood for two years, labouring in a densely-peopled part of the metropolis, where his ministry was intelligent, powerful, and converting. His pastoral care, though largely called upon, was never lacking, but was abundantly manifested to the lasting profit of many souls. 'Instant in season, out of season,' he embraced every opportunity of doing the work of a Home Missionary, and this with great success. So diligent a visitor I have never known, and his tender fidelity to the sick and the sorrowful has been rarely equalled. Somewhat rustic in his address and manner, he was, however, a thorough man, and an unsophisticated Christian gentleman. He was 'the soul of honour,' and nothing little, mean, or sinuous, ever obscured his frank, generous, and transparent conduct. He commanded my respect, and secured my affection. I mourn the loss of such a friend, but rejoice in the assurance that, whilst he possesses the blessedness of 'the dead who die in the Lord,' his 'works do follow him.'"

CHAPTER XIV.

―∞⋄∞⋄∞―

ON leaving Southwark in August 1856, Mr. Wood became the Superintendent Minister of the Chelsea Circuit, to which he had been affectionately invited. Like the other metropolitan Circuits, this presented a large and most important sphere of labour; while the fact, that the Westminster Training College was included in it, invested it with a peculiar interest. The spirit and teaching of the Ministers stationed in that Circuit, from time to time, contribute to form the character of many who, as Day-School Teachers, will exert an important influence on the minds of the young in many parts of our country, and even in distant lands.

In entering upon the Circuit, Mr. Wood felt very grateful to God for permitting him, notwithstanding the decline of his physical strength, of which he was conscious, still to undertake the full duties of the Christian pastorate. On the Saturday before he commenced his public labours, he writes, " For some time I felt so much over-wrought, and such a diminution of vigour, that I did not know but my Master might be about to lay me aside. If He had, I could not have complained, but felt I could adore and praise Him. But He has given me another part of His vineyard to labour in, and I trust in Him for bodily, mental, and spiritual strength for the work assigned to me. May He bless me, and take all the glory!"

His first Sabbath was spent at Westminster, where he preached twice and administered the sacrament of the Lord's Supper, being assisted in the latter engagement by the late Rev. John Scott, the beloved and honoured Principal of the Normal Training Institution. It was not long before his labours, both at Westminster and at Chelsea, were crowned with visible success. At the prayer-meetings with which the public services of the Lord's day were generally closed, it was no uncommon thing for persons to come forward as penitent seekers of salvation. At Westminster, in particular, he was made very useful. On the second Sunday which he spent there, he preached in the afternoon in the open air; and he continued this practice, whenever opportunity was afforded, and his own strength permitted him to do so. Some of his notices of these services, and of the prayer-meetings that followed his evening ministrations, are well worthy of being preserved.

"Sunday, September 21st, 1856.—Westminster. I addressed the Sunday-School briefly in the afternoon, after which I went to the Broadway, and, standing by the pump, conducted a religious service in the usual form, only that I did not take a text. The congregation was very attentive, and I hope that some good may result by the blessing of God. After the evening service, we held a prayer-meeting in the body of the chapel. Many remained. The power of the Lord was present, and several testified clearly of His saving mercy. Amongst others was a mother, who once knew the Lord, and who gave her infant into charge of another woman, while she came forward seeking mercy. Also a man and his wife, who promised that evening to set up family prayer; and a young woman who had long been seeking God, and who, on finding mercy, exclaimed, 'How was it I did not believe before? Why, all the world might come and find mercy!'"

"Sunday, October 19th, 1856.—Westminster. A powerful season in the prayer-meeting. Several professed to find the salvation of God, and some departed in great distress of soul. I felt some misgiving on going to preach without door in the afternoon. lest it should prove too much for my voice, having the evening service before me. But the Lord greatly assisted me. The attendance was large, and amongst them some very rough-looking persons of both sexes; but they behaved with exemplary attention, and I was greatly pleased to see some of these hard-faced men endeavouring to join in the singing after my address."

"Sunday, November 30th, 1856.—Westminster. I felt much liberty to day. In the evening some appeared to decide for God. I spoke to two rough men on the gallery stairs who were looking on. One came forward with his white flannel jacket, but said he did not know how to pray. I prayed as a penitent seeking salvation, and he repeated after me. The other said that he had a pious father and mother who, with the other members of the family, were Methodists and respectable people, but that he had gone astray, and by his own wickedness had got into disgrace and misery,—that he had not been in a place of worship for twenty years before then,—and that he had not then come into the chapel with any good intention. While he was telling me this, and more of the same kind, the tears stole down his face, and I constrained him to come forward and kneel down. O that mercy may reclaim this prodigal!"

While Mr. Wood was thus intent on doing everything which he himself could do to bring men to God, he was anxious to enlist the hearty co-operation of all the office-bearers in the Circuit, and the members of the Society generally. He made arrangements to hold a tea-meeting of the Leaders and Stewards, both at Chelsea and at Westminster, to promote mutual love and united efforts in the work of Christ; and these opportunities were occasions of great spiritual profit.

In some cases, when he had felt discouraged at not witnessing the spiritual success for which he had hoped, he was afterwards cheered by learning that the Spirit of God had been silently moving on the hearts of some, and that they had attained to peace through believing. His record of the services of Sunday, October 26th, 1856, and the following day, is, in this point of view, very instructive. On the former of these days he preached the Sunday-School sermons at Chelsea; and he writes, "Rather straightened in the morning; at least, I had not that ease and enlargement which I have sometimes experienced. Much liberty in the evening; but, although a few came forward in the prayer-meeting, no one professed to find salvation. I feel humbled at what appears to be the day's result, for which I had entertained more hope. May the Lord forgive me all my own want of spirituality and power, and bestow

a mightier baptism of the Holy Ghost. Visited a
few in the afternoon." On Monday, the 27th, he
says, "As I was going to the chapel for the noon
prayer-meeting to day, a man accosted me, wishing
to communicate to me the information that, last
evening, while I was speaking to the penitents who
were at the rail, he again apprehended the salvation
of God. Many years ago he enjoyed religion; but
he entered the army, had been abroad, returned, and
is now one of the guard belonging to the Queen's
household. In the prayer-meeting he, with great
propriety of language and deep feeling, prayed and
praised God for the work wrought. After the feeling
noticed above, I feel the more thankful at the condescension of my blessed Lord and Master in owning
His servant."

His method of dealing with individual cases often
evinced great spiritual discernment; and his faithful
warnings, as well as his affectionate encouragements,
were frequently blessed by God. He mentions, on
one occasion, that, after preaching, an elderly woman,
who had been a member, and seeking salvation for
fourteen years, entered into the enjoyment of peace
with God. "Our friends," he adds, "had been nursing and encouraging her; but it appeared to me that
they were nursing her unbelief, by pitying her as if it
had been a lame hand which she could not help. I
administered the strong medicine of the gospel, by
showing her that she was dishonouring Christ, and
pleasing the devil, who was holding her soul by her
doubts, as a wicked boy the poor cockchaffer by his
thread, and that her doubts formed her sin, which she
could never take to heaven; and the Lord mercifully
blessed the word."

P

On the 23rd of February, 1857, Mr. Wood completed his sixtieth year.   No thoughtful man can come
to such a period of life without a solemn review of
the past, and an equally solemn reference to the
future.   On that day we find the following entry in
his Diary:—"This day I see the completion of my
sixtieth year.   I wonder, while I write it, that I have
been so long in the world, for the period that has
elapsed since I was a young man, entering upon the
activities and responsibilities of life, seems as nothing.
I also wonder at the infinite kindness and forbearance
of God towards me.   I cannot but be aware that the
Lord, in stupendous grace, has condescended to use
me as an instrument for good in conveying comfort
and assistance to many, and in leading some to Christ
and salvation, which I adoringly acknowledge, and
for which I praise His holy Name.   I also feel under
infinite obligations that He has enabled me to labour
with some diligence to do His will, and that I have
not fainted.   But I am unspeakably humbled that I
have known so little of the power of saving grace,
and have done so little for the honour of God and the
good of mankind.   Still I rejoice in having attained
the age of sixty.   I feel as if I had attained some
vantage-ground, and that the prospect before me is
more animating.   I bound away as from a new start-
ing-point, and long to do with greater spirituality and
power all the will of God.   The Lord have mercy
upon me, and apply the atoning blood with far greater
power by the Eternal Spirit, moment by moment!
Amen."

It is almost needless to say, that Mr. Wood
adopted in the Chelsea Circuit, as he had done in
others, a plan of systematic pastoral visitation.

Though his declining strength prevented him from accomplishing as much in this department as in former years, yet his visits were numerous, and were often connected with a special blessing. Under the date of Monday, March 30th, 1857, we find the entry, " I visited in the morning and afternoon, although weary from yesterday's labour. But some whom I have seen could ill spare a pastoral call, as they are in trouble and affliction. What a hidden life of sorrow and privation is spent by some among us, whose trials are unsuspected by those about them, and not always known to the members of their own families, but are communicated to a sympathising pastor, to whom they can open all their griefs!" On the following day he writes, "Visited a good deal to-day, and am thankful for strength and for a disposition to do it, and for the kindness and affection with which I am received." Sometimes, in the course of pastoral visitation, he met with cases of special interest which he has placed on record. He mentions that one day he visited in three of the wards of the Brompton Hospital for consumption, and adds, "One interesting young person, who wished to see me, spoke to this effect, and nearly in these words, 'I was, several years ago, very happy in the enjoyment of God; but an acquaintance was formed with one who was worldly. I felt it was not right, and my mind became beclouded and unhappy. I wished to get free, but was held fast, and did not know how to break the acquaintance off. At length this was done, and I felt relieved, and obtained a return of peace. Still I was without that full enjoyment of God which I had before felt. A small memorial remained in my possession, and it was a hinderance to me. The acquaintance having·been broken off, and he married to another, I felt that I had no right to retain it, and I threw that last memorial into the fire. Immediately my soul was fully freed, and I can praise God for the deliverance, and I know that all is well for time and for eternity.' How often has some 'little memorial' wrought distance from God!" About a month after this, that young woman died rejoicing in her Saviour. In one of his pastoral visits he was brought into contact with a man who avowed infidel sentiments. "I visited several," he writes. "One man, who enjoyed religion when a young man, twenty years ago, has since drunk into infidelity, and questions whether all he ever felt was not mere excitement, as idolaters are highly excited in their rites, so as to endure tortures, and submit to death voluntarily. I, of course, showed that they were acted upon by perfectly opposite influences ;—that the believer, in proportion to the subjection of his mind to the power of truth, was led to the more earnest pursuit of purity, and to more zealous efforts to promote the glory of God and the welfare of mankind; whereas in proportion as the idolater was excited by his rites, he became the more intensely selfish and impure, and that the circumstances connected therewith were of the most polluting character. I left him, after praying with him and his wife and children, not without hope. O that Divine mercy may yet visit that soul!"

Again and again he was encouraged by instances of powerful awakening under his ministry. He mentions that, when meeting the leaders at Westminster on a Wednesday evening after preaching, a young person came to the vestry door, requesting him to come to her father's house. "I soon went," he adds, "and found a sister of that friend in great distress of soul. They told me that, a month before, she had heard me at Westminster, and had been ever since labouring under a heavy burden; that she had come from Blackheath, where she resides and to which she was to return this evening, wishing again to hear the same Minister; and now her sorrow became overwhelming. I talked to her and prayed. While we were on our knees her soul was set fully free by the power of the Holy Ghost. Glory to the Triune God for ever! and may she praise God to all eternity!" On one Sunday in May, 1857, he preached at Battersea in the forenoon, in the open air at the bottom of Sloane Street in the afternoon, and in the Sloane Terrace chapel in the evening. "There was a gracious feeling," he says, "at the evening service, and in the prayer-meeting that followed. I trust that some will have to praise God for this in the day of eternity. I was much exercised myself before the service, as I have often been, especially lately, when the Lord has favoured me and His people with a time of power afterwards. It has seemed to me that I have nothing but weakness, and unworthiness, and unfaithfulness; and then the Lord has deigned to reveal 'the excellency of the power' which is with Himself alone. 'Even so, Father, for so it seemeth good in Thy sight,' in dealing with a worm from whom Thou condescendest to hide pride."

Mr. Wood's conviction of the value of out-door preaching, as conveying Divine truth to the minds of some who cannot be induced to come to the house of God, was so strong, that he often engaged in such efforts in connection with his visits to other Circuits. Two or three instances may be given in his own words.

"Richmond, July 12th, 1857.—I was not quite well; but, the day being fine, I could not well keep within, and was thankful to be able to proclaim salvation in the Park to some who probably seldom hear the truth. I stood at the hither end of Lord John Russell's premises, where many collect on the Lord's day. Immediately after preaching, a young man came up to me, wishing to speak with me. He told me that when he was a lad, at the time I was in the Birmingham West Circuit, I sometimes called at their house and talked with him, but that he used to get away when I was coming. He added, that for some time past he had been thinking more seriously about his soul's salvation, and had wished to speak to some one; that he had recently come to Richmond as a shopman, and that, seeing me in the Park, he gladly embraced the opportunity of speaking to me. Some appeared decided in the evening."

"Brentford, July 26th, 1857.—I preached without door in the afternoon at New Brentford, over the Canal Bridge, by the side of the high road, under the shade of some trees. Several heard with attention; some of whom evidently worshipped nowhere, as they were in their working dress, only perhaps rather neater than on other days, and had the appearance of being 'navvies.' After the evening preaching there was a good prayer-meeting, and I trust that some were decided to serve the Lord."

In connection with his attendance on the Liverpool Conference of 1857, he gave one Sunday to Wigan, preaching for the chapel morning and evening, and in the afternoon in the open air. "A good time," he writes, "in the morning. I offered to speak without door in the afternoon, and our friends advised my going to *Scholes*, a part of the town occupied mainly by Roman Catholics. The rain came down so heavily, that I questioned the propriety of remaining ; but I thought that I ought not to leave while any were disposed to stay. A considerable number remained, who evidently would otherwise not have heard the word anywhere ; and I never before saw such a number of young persons, from twelve to sixteen years of age, that stood packed together, and with attentive gaze heard the word. Some older persons of sullen mien became softened into attention, and I hope some seed was sown that will spring up to life everlasting. In the evening I had not much enlargement ; but there was a power in the word, and in the meeting following the communion-rail was filled with seeking penitents, and several professed to find salvation. Blessed be the Lord !"

It is interesting to note some of the texts which Mr. Wood chose for his open-air addresses. Passages like Luke xiv. 23 naturally suggested themselves :—"And the lord said unto the servant, Go out into the highways and hedges, and compel them to come in, that my house may be filled." But his favourite text for such services appears to have been Rom. iii. 22, which sets forth, in a clear and impressive manner, the evangelical method of justification, and offers "righteousness" to all, without exception, who, in the renunciation of sin and of self-dependence, fly to the Lord Jesus Christ.

During his first year at Chelsea, he paid a visit to his old friends at Exeter, to preach on behalf of the St. Sidwell's Chapel. Here again God graciously owned his labours, both in the public services and in social and pastoral intercourse. During the two week-days which he spent in this city, he visited more than forty families, besides attending a public meeting on the Monday evening, and preaching on Tuesday: but these exertions, he adds, were "beyond his strength."

Similar visits were paid in the autumn of 1857 to two other Circuits in which he had laboured,—Kingswood and Bristol North. In the latter case he preached the anniversary sermons of the Ebenezer chapel, and was greatly comforted and encouraged. "There was a good attendance," he writes, "in the morning; and in the evening the chapel was crowded. At the prayer-meeting some came forward seeking salvation, and I hope a few were blessed. One young man, the first who came forward, told me that he was convinced of sin when I preached in Bristol last, but had not found salvation. This evening he was delivered from his burden. O that the Lord may make him a valiant soldier of Christ!"

Towards the close of the year, Mr. Wood went to the neighbourhood of Banwell, to settle some business arising out of the trusts which he held for the benefit of various members of his family. As a cousin was driving him in a gig to Nempnett, the horse suddenly fell, and Mr. Wood was thrown out with violence, and his head and neck were severely bruised. The horse rose and moved forward; and one wheel of the gig passed over his legs, injuring more especially the left leg, which, many years before, when he was in the Camborne Circuit, had been crushed by the fall of a horse. He was so disfigured by this accident, and his whole system was so shaken, that he was necessarily laid aside from his work for several weeks. After resting for a few days among his relatives in Somersetshire, he made an effort to return to his home, which he reached on the evening of Saturday, December 19th, 1857. The passive graces of the Christian character were now called into exercise. Mr. Wood's greatest trial was to be laid aside from his beloved work of preaching, and from pastoral intercourse with his flock, when he felt that the Circuit needed all his efforts. But he was enabled to bow in meek submission to the Divine will. Occasionally, indeed, he feared that he had gone out of his providential path, in visiting Somersetshire at that time : but he strove to cast all his care upon God, and to derive spiritual benefit from the dispensation. The record of his feelings on two of the Sabbaths which he spent in the retirement of his own house, will be read with interest:—

"December 20th, 1857.—My place has been at home. Through infinite grace I willingly and thankfully bow to my Master's order, crying to Him that the visitation may be greatly sanctified. The first two days after the accident, I had but little going out of heart. I was quiet before the Lord, and wondered that my soul was not more taken up with love, and prayer, and praise. Perhaps the general shock of the system had something to do with this. On Friday I began to have more feeling in duty ; but my mind was awfully assailed by all kinds of wandering thoughts and vain imaginations. But here I am, at the feet of my Lord, imploring a deeper stamp of the Spirit's seal. O for a fulness ! O for the mightiest power of sanctifying grace, even *now*, O my God, yea, even *now*, in honour of the covenant of grace, and truth, and love, in Christ Jesus, by the power of the Holy Ghost! Amen."

"January 3rd, 1858.—Still a prisoner, but happily proving that the Lord is not confined. This afternoon, while our servant was at the covenant-service, my dear wife and I held the service by ourselves in my study, closing it by partaking of the Lord's Supper. We both felt the presence of our Master, and were enabled to rejoice in His salvation. In the evening, I read a part of the evening service with her, and we then had our social prayer. This has been a good day, and I am enabled to submit beneath the mighty hand of God, adoring Him for every exercise. I have thought on the words of the Psalmist, 'I will sing of mercy and of judgment.' But in my case it is 'mercy' all. I have not to 'sing of judgment,' in this sense of the word, except of 'judgment' deserved, but never inflicted."

On the Friday of this week, Mr. Wood went out for the first time since his return from Somersetshire, and presided at the Quarterly Meeting of the Circuit. At this meeting the Circuit-debt was paid off, and he greatly rejoiced in this result of many earnest efforts and liberal contributions on the part of the friends of Methodism around him. He speaks of the meeting as "a very united and gracious season;" and his spirit was evidently refreshed by mingling with the leading office-bearers of the Circuit. On the following Lord's-day, January 10th, he was enabled to conduct the forenoon service in the Sloane Terrace chapel. "I had to be taken to the chapel," he writes, "in a wheel-chair, and to get a contrivance for supporting my injured leg by kneeling. Reading the prayers I found quite enough to manage, and my leg was uneasy: but in preaching very little of this remained. The Lord opened my mouth, and bestowed an unction with the word. I returned home nothing the worse for the effort, praising the God of all grace for His abounding mercy on this behalf." A fortnight afterwards he ventured to preach twice, and on the following day resumed his pastoral work by visiting a few sick persons. From this time, although walking was often difficult and painful, he continued to attend to all his work, devoting himself assiduously to the varied interests of his Circuit, attending the several Connexional Committees of which he was a member, and occasionally undertaking services in other Circuits.

In the labours of the months that intervened between this time and the Conference, he was again and again cheered by cases of conversion, and by the manifest blessing of God both on his public ministrations and his pastoral counsels. The Conference of 1858 was held in Hull; and Mr. Wood attended its sittings, and took a lively interest in its proceedings, and in many of the public religious services. He speaks, in particular, of the gracious unction which attended the delivery of the Ex-President's official sermon; and it is pleasing to recall that memorable season, inasmuch as the honoured Minister whom God so richly anointed for that service has passed away. Under the date of Monday, August 2nd, Mr. Wood writes, "I heard the Rev. F. A. West, the Ex-President, this morning from 'Be filled with the Spirit.' He preached under a mighty influence. It was an extraordinary season. I do not remember to

have been present on such an occasion for years.
On the announcement of the text,—one on which I
had myself endeavoured to preach,—I thought, 'I
trust I shall obtain some richer baptism of the Holy
Ghost in the course of the sermon.' But again it was
suggested to me, 'Why not *now*, at the beginning,
and not wait for the sermon?' I thought I knew that
this was from the Holy One, and then and there I
made anew a full surrender, and my soul was filled
with the Spirit. I then enjoyed the sermon exceedingly, and was greatly edified. Glory to God, the
Father, the Son, and the Holy Ghost!"—One Lord's
day during the Conference was spent by Mr. Wood
at Ruddington, in the Nottingham South Circuit,
where he preached the anniversary sermons for the
chapel. At the close of the Conference he went to
Gloucester, where he had engaged to preach on the
Lord's day; and thence he proceeded to the neighbourhood of Banwell, to arrange some matters of
business, and to preach again among the people to
whom his earliest ministrations had been addressed.

Soon after his return to Chelsea, he was seized with
violent pain, and the disease proved to be an obstinate
obstruction of the bowels, that no remedies, for a
time, could reach, and that brought him very low.
Six Sabbaths passed away before he was able
again to attempt to " preach the unsearchable riches
of Christ." On one of these silent Sabbaths,—September 12th, 1858,—he writes, "My weakness is
great; and I did not rise until between 11 and 12
o'clock. I have derived comfort from hearing my
dear wife read from this month's *Magazine* as well
as from the everlasting word of God; but I have felt
scarcely adequate to any effort. I can only be quiet,

and wait, and trust, resting my poor unworthy self, my all, on God's free mercy in Christ Jesus for present and everlasting life. I am cheered and thankful to hear good tidings from the sanctuary. O that the Lord may be with His people this evening in great power!" When he was sufficiently restored to be able to leave home, he went, with Mrs. Wood, to Deal, for change of air, and afterwards accepted the invitation of Mrs. Budgett, of Kingswood, to spend a little time at her house. He found the journey fatiguing; and on the first Lord's day after his arrival, he says, "I much wished to go to the means, but could not, and was glad to lie down instead." On the following day he has this entry in his diary :—" Felt refreshed this morning, and walked round the gardens. My friends here are, as always, very kind. But I miss my late friend, Mr. Samuel Budgett. All seems as fresh to me as if he had recently passed away. His manner, his kindness, our last walk together round these gardens, our last conversations, recur vividly to my mind: and I am admonished that I also have symptoms of decreasing strength, such as he exhibited some time before he passed away."

On Saturday, October 16th, 1858, Mr. Wood returned to London; and on the following day he once more preached in Sloane Terrace chapel. "I had proposed," he writes, "to make a first attempt to preach, since my illness, in the evening. But I felt that, humanly speaking, there was a risk; as I am by no means well and strong. But the people of the Lord prayed much for me, and I also felt that I could rely on the Lord for special help. And He did graciously assist me while I spoke from Isaiah xxviii.

16. Bless the Lord, O my soul, for this His great mercy!" In the course of that week he took two other preaching-appointments, and applied himself to various matters of business connected with the management of the Circuit. From this time he resumed his regular work, and persevered in it, although often the subject of much weakness and exhaustion. Nor was he left without decided encouragement. Under the date of December 26th, he mentions that in the prayer-meeting that followed the public ministry of the word in the evening, in the Sloane Terrace chapel, "a backslider found his forfeited peace, and was enabled again to rejoice greatly in the God of his salvation." "Another young man," he adds, "under deep feelings of amazement and distress, also came forward. On the first being filled with the joy of forgiving mercy, I told him to speak to the second who was still in anguish of soul. After some time the second young man found salvation, and stated that he was a son of pious parents, that his mother had been for fifty years a member of the Methodist Society, and that he had a brother a Local Preacher; but that he had himself been an avowed infidel, and had read the Scriptures only to cavil and oppose, but that he then proved the truth which he had before denied. May the Lord keep them, and add hundreds more!" Three weeks later he writes of a Sunday evening service at Westminster, "I had not much enlargement, but the Lord gave power with the truth, and some came forward seeking salvation. Among these were a man and his wife, probably about fifty years of age. The wife was in great distress, and the man told me that he had been the subject of deep conviction, that he had for years

attended the chapel, and often felt deeply, but that
this evening was the first time he had stayed at a
prayer-meeting. May the Lord make them both
steadfast in His service! One was a woman about the
same age, who received consolation. She said that
she had been seeking the Lord, but that this was the
first time she had come into our chapel, though she
had a child who came to the Sabbath-School. In
addressing the School in the afternoon, I sent a message by the children to their parents, to invite them
to the chapel this evening, and to tell them that the
Minister intended to speak of a Physician who heals
gratis. It was probably this which brought her in
the way of being healed." In the month of February
1859, he conducted a special service at Dalston in
the Islington Circuit; and he says of it, "Four of the
family with whom I took tea were at the communion-
rail after preaching. Some promising young men
came forward also, with some females of respectable
appearance. One youth, the son of a pious mother
and grandmother still living, who have long prayed
for him, but with little apparent success, as he has
been a most intractable and ungovernable youth, was
the first to come forward and found salvation. On
speaking to a respectable young married man, who
with his wife was in their pew, he dropped his face
on my neck, and with sobs of joyous emotion informed
me that he had that evening, during the service,
found the salvation of his soul. Praise the Lord for
ever!"

About this time, also, Mr. Wood records the satisfaction which the healthy religious state of some of
the classes in his Circuit, which he met for the renewal
of tickets, afforded him, and the gratitude to God

which was thus called forth. His own soul, too, was kept in peace, though he was not without occasional conflicts. On February 23rd, 1859, he writes, "This day I complete my sixty-second year. It has been a happy day. My mind serene, and reposing on my covenant-God in Christ, with cheering hopes of fuller devotedness to the glory of Him whose I am, and to whom I surrender my all by His grace, for time and for ever." But the once strong man was now frequently depressed with languor. His earnest spirit prompted him to continue, as far as possible, the incessant labours of former years; but he often retired from his public engagements weary and exhausted. It is affecting to read the record of one Lord's day spent at Westminster and Justice Walk :—"June 6th, 1859. I felt weak in walking to Westminster and in returning. I rested in the afternoon, not without heart-searchings if I might not, as I have heretofore done on Sundays in the afternoon, in fine weather, preach without door. But I felt that to attempt it would be wrong; and with all my rest I had no strength to spare in the evening, small as the demand was upon me. This might perhaps have been occasioned, in part, by the oppressive state of the atmosphere; but before my affliction I did not suffer from atmospheric influences as I do now." Still, however, he went forward in his work, attending early prayer-meetings, giving himself up, as his strength permitted, to pastoral visitation, and rejoicing, after the service of the Lord's day evening, to gather around him penitent seekers of salvation. Occasionally, too, though now but very rarely, he visited other Circuits to preach occasional sermons, and endeavoured to avail himself of the opportunities afforded him of leading the members of the families entertaining him to a saving knowledge of Christ.

Thus his last year in Chelsea passed away. He attended the Conference, which was held in Manchester, under the able presidency of the Rev. Dr. Waddy, and after a brief visit to his old friends at Perranwell, in the neighbourhood of Truro, and to some other parts of Cornwall, where he renewed the associations of former years, he returned to Chelsea, to take his leave of a Circuit endeared to him both by his anxieties and efforts on its behalf, and by the success which God had vouchsafed to him. Arrangements had been made for a Tea-meeting at Westminster, to assure him of the esteem in which he was held, and to acknowledge, with gratitude to God, the blessing which had rested upon his labours. The Rev. John Scott, the Principal of the Training College, took the chair, and both he and the Rev. Michael Coulson Taylor, with many of the leading friends of the Circuit, spoke in a manner which deeply affected him. "Their observations," Mr. Wood remarks, " at once humbled me, and led me to feel grateful to the great Master, who has owned me in this place, and given me favour in the eyes of His people. Blessed be His holy and glorious Name for ever!" It is an affecting thought, that all three of these esteemed and honoured Ministers have now passed to the presence of "the Chief Shepherd," from whom their graces and their differing gifts were derived, and by whom they were upheld in their career of faithful service. On the following Sunday evening, August 28th, 1859, Mr. Wood preached at the Sloane Terrace chapel, and afterwards met the Society. "Thus," he says, "I finished my public

labours in this Circuit.   My heart is deeply impressed
with a sense of the unspeakable condescension and
mercy of God, in holding me up and enabling me to
be of some service in this place.   I am thankful that
our numbers have steadily, although slowly, advanced ;
that great and pressing financial difficulties have been
overcome ;   and   that   every   department   prospers.
How great and how good is the Lord!   'Bless the
Lord, O my soul!'   Six years have elapsed since I
came to labour in London ; and in leaving it, while
deeply conscious of innumerable infirmities, yet I
adore the abundance of that free grace which has
enabled me, in conjunction with others, to bring some
glory to God, and to promote the spiritual and
financial prosperity of His cause.   O for pardon !   O
for grace !"

CHAPTER XV.

—◦○◦◦——

AT the Conference of 1859, Mr. Wood was appointed a second time to the Bristol South
Circuit. Eighteen years before he had gone to that
Circuit, full of manly energy, though his heart was,
at the first, bowed down by the bereavement which
had wounded his tenderest sensibilities as a father.
Now his strength was declining; and, though his
zeal in his Master's cause knew no abatement, he had
often to complain of weariness and languor. Then
there was before him the prospect of lengthened and
abundant usefulness in some of the most important
Circuits of the Connexion. Now he had many pre-
monitions that his day of active service in the Church
was drawing to its close. He was in his sixty-third
year; and the incessant toils of his lengthened
ministry, and the severe attacks of illness which he
had recently experienced, had told upon his system.
He was the ripe Christian, the wise, faithufl, zealous
Pastor, and he still did the work of an Evangelist:
but he could not exert himself, to the large extent to
which he formerly did, in evangelistic effort.

The Circuit, too, had passed through a period of
severe trial, and had sustained considerable losses.
On the first Sabbath on which Mr. Wood stood in the

Langton Street pulpit, he was deeply affected by the change which that beautiful chapel presented. "The first Sunday in September, eighteen years ago," he writes, "I commenced my ministry in Bristol South, and I regarded a renewal thereof to-day with mingled feelings. Since then agitation had spread desolation over this fair field; and, although it has begun to revive, and under the superintendency of my predecessor, with the aid of the Chapel Fund, £2,000 of debt has been paid off from the Langton Street chapel, yet when I entered the pulpit in the morning, and saw how sparsely the gallery was occupied, and contrasted this with former times, my spirit sank within me. The circumstances of the riot created in this chapel also rose up before me. My mind was greatly exercised, and I felt as if I should be glad to preach anywhere but there. Still I was enabled to speak words of truth, and was a little cheered at the close. In the evening, after a great struggle, the Lord gave me some reviving, and I was enabled to speak with freedom. A good prayer-meeting followed, but no one came forward."

In the course of his first week, a Tea-meeting was held to give him a hearty welcome to the Circuit. "The occasion," he says, "was very interesting, and, I trust, edifying." Two influential members of the meeting belonged to the Society at Nailsea, which formed part of the Banwell Circuit when Mr. Wood laboured in it as a Local Preacher, but which had, for some years, been transferred to the Bristol South Circuit. They had been present, and had voted, at the meeting at which he was recommended as a candidate for the ministry; and now they came to welcome him as a venerable Pastor whom God had signally honoured. Mr. Wood, after specifying this circumstance, adds, "Several addressed the meeting in a manner very encouraging to me; but I endeavoured to show them how incapable I am of benefiting the great Master's cause unless HE deigns to use me, and that our united prayer must be for 'power from on high,' and that we must faithfully use the grace given."

The expressions of warm affection with which he was everywhere greeted called forth his gratitude to God, and cheered him in his course of holy toil. An incident which occurred on the third Sabbath which he spent in the Circuit, led him to record his feelings on the subject at some length. "After the morning service at Bedminster one good friend, after bringing her family to me, and expressing the usual congratulations with unusual feeling, on account of my being again with them as their Pastor, exclaimed, 'I hope you will never again leave us till you "clap your glad wings, and tower away."' The feeling of sincere and deep affection manifested by all has much affected me. In visiting this and other old Circuits, I have been cheered by the very kind manner in which I have been received. But I have never before accepted an invitation from a former sphere of labour, although such have been many times kindly tendered, and could not therefore know that a visit differed from an appointment, so much as I have found it to do. The first is the visit only: the second is the return home of an esteemed and beloved member of a family, after many years' residence abroad. As such a member I seem to be greeted in every household; some telling me of a sick member of the family whom I once visited, and who is now safely lodged in

'Abraham's bosom,' others calling to my recollection stirring incidents which I had forgotten, or referring to the time when they or some belonging to them were led to decision under my ministry. I am greatly humbled by this goodness of God."

The return of Mr. Wood to Bristol enabled him and Mrs. Wood to enjoy the society of their only son, who had now been married about four years, and who had settled at Redland. He was, as we have seen, a man of strong domestic affections; and it was a merciful arrangement that, as he was drawing near to the close of his active labours, he was placed where his son could often visit him, and where his heart could be gladdened by the fond affection of his little grandchildren. In Bristol, too, he was very near the scene of his earliest toils, which, indeed, he was occasionally required to visit, not only to conduct public religious services, but also to execute the trusts which had been reposed in him for the benefit of some of his relations.

It was not long before he realised direct and manifest spiritual success, both under the ministration of the truth, and in connection with his system of pastoral visitation. On Friday, September 16th, 1859, he writes, "Visited several. While praying with a lady and her servant, in the course of my pastoral visitation, the young person professed to find peace with God. Praise the Lord!" His notice of Sunday, September 25th, is, "Preached at Langton Street in the morning, and was much assisted in holding forth the truth of God. Addressed the Sunday-Schools in the afternoon, and led the Teachers' prayer-meeting. The evening service at Bedminster was, through mercy, a time of power, and some appeared to decide for God. A good prayer-meeting ensued." The following Thursday was spent in pastoral visitation at Bedminster, where, also, he preached in the evening and met the Leaders. He says, "I took dinner and tea at Mr. C.'s, Southville. Visited morning, afternoon, and evening. I believe I have not had such a day of pastoral visitation, in which I have visited and prayed with so many for years, and still had strength given to me for the public service in the evening. This has much cheered me, leading me to think that I shall yet be able to serve the Master and His Church, and not be a comparatively inefficient Minister in this Circuit. Still 'the will of the Lord be done,' whether by active performance or passive endurance."

In this Circuit, as in his other spheres of labour, Mr. Wood sought to call into activity the energies of his people. He re-organised the Tract Society, and evinced the liveliest interest in its operations. He engaged some ladies to conduct a female prayer-meeting in a low neighbourhood in the afternoon of a week-day; and among these ladies Mrs. Wood, delicate as her health was, took her place. He established, also, a public Band-meeting on Saturday evening, and a Bible-class for young men, to promote among them the consecutive study of the Holy Scriptures.

It was no uncommon thing for persons to accost their beloved Pastor, as they met him in the streets, or came to him after some religious service, to tell him of good received under his ministry in former days. Such circumstances filled him with gratitude to God, while they deepened the feeling, that he himself was nothing, and that it was in infinite con-

descension that the Holy Spirit had used him as the
instrument of conveying spiritual life to some who
were "dead in trespasses and sins." But he felt, as
it was right that he should feel, a peculiar regard for
those whom he had "begotten through the gospel;"
and the consciousness of his spiritual relation to them,
and of a holy sympathy with them resulting from the
common indwelling of the Holy Ghost, was connected
in his mind with sacred joy. On October 7th, 1859,
he writes, " Visited to-day. I met a man whom I did
not know, but who told me that he was a boy when I
went to the Kingswood Circuit, that God had used me
as the means of his conversion, and that he had ever
since held on his way. Called at Mr. E.'s office, who
reminded me that his wife was one of my spiritual
children. Before I got home, a woman met me and
stopped me, saying, that she had not seen me for
several years, but that she had to praise God that I
was the instrument of her salvation. I felt that
encouragements fell thick about me, and I praised
the Lord." Soon after this, as he was travelling to
London, to assist his friends in Chelsea to wind up a
movement for the relief of their chapels which he
had inaugurated, he met a gentleman in the train
who said to him, "You are my spiritual father. I
heard you preach a little before you went out to
travel, and I was then awakened." Mr. Wood adds,
" On inquiry he told me that it was at Allerton in the
Banwell Circuit. He also told me the text, and the
words with which I closed the sermon, and the
manner and tone of voice which the Holy One blessed
in leading him to decision for God. He is now a
wealthy farmer, and has, through all the time, retained
the love of God, and has recently been engaged in

promoting a new chapel in the place where he resides. If I mark this pillar, it is to praise the Lord."

During a considerable portion of this appointment to Bristol, he was able, in addition to his regular duties in his Circuit, to undertake some occasional services in other Circuits. We find him, shortly after his arrival, preaching in the neighbourhood of Salisbury, and afterwards at Marlborough and Chippenham. In the month of December, 1859, he spent a Sabbath at Weston-super-mare, the Minister of which place had occasionally to change with those of the Bristol South Circuit. "I was much impressed," he writes, "with a recollection of the past. In 1815 Christmas day was on Monday. On the Sunday previous and on Monday I preached at Weston for the first time of being appointed there;* and here I am, after forty-four years of labour, still upheld, while of our friends of that day I can scarcely find one. That was in the first small chapel. This was followed by a larger, of which I was one of the Trustees; and this by the present commodious and very good building. Praise the Lord!"

The holy zeal which filled Mr. Wood's heart made him look around for new openings for evangelistic effort. He engaged a large room in Avon Street in the Temple parish,—a very low and poor part of the city,—for preaching and other religious services, and he bestowed on this place special attention. He often began the service without doors, and led many to the room, who, probably, would not otherwise have been induced to come to it. Here, too, he commenced an evening school, engaging the services

---

* See Chapter iii. p. 22.

of some of his young friends as Teachers, and himself encouraging them by his presence, when his
other engagements would allow. He was greatly
cheered by a blessed revival of religion which took
place in this neighbourhood; and, when he was
detained from the earlier sittings of the Conference
of 1860 by the illness of Mrs. Wood, he devoted
the evenings which he had to spare to this sphere of
Home-Missionary effort. The work of three successive evenings is thus briefly recorded :—

"Monday, July 30th.—Avon Street. About a
quarter before eight I went to Ash Lodge, sang and
gave an invitation, and then sang on to the room.
Several were in distress, and some appeared to
obtain consolation. The room was filled."

"Tuesday, July 31st.—Avon Street.—Visited part
of the day. Sang, as usual, through some streets
before going into the room, which was filled, and
several seeking salvation: two or three also professed to find peace to their souls. We praise the
Lord, but wait for mightier visitations of the Spirit.
May the Lord gloriously appear!"

"Wednesday, August 1st.—Avon Street. I gave
a brief address. Began, as usual, without door. The
room was again filled, and some decided for life
everlasting."

Another of these evangelistic efforts may be here
mentioned, though not in the exact order of time. In
the course of his second year in the Bristol South
Circuit, Mr. Wood again introduced Methodism into
the beautiful village of Brislington, about two miles
from the city. The entries in his Diary show how he

proceeded in this attempt. "I have long wished," he writes, on Monday, April 22nd, 1861, "to preach in Brislington, and yesterday I spoke to two members of Society who reside there, and they promised to inform their neighbours. On coming, I found the people assembled. The room was greatly crowded, and I was enabled to speak the word of life to a people who appeared eagerly to listen. I promised to go there again, D.V. O for an open door and an effectual one in this village!" A week later he says, " I took tea at Mr. ——'s, and engaged him to take charge of a class in Brislington, if I should succeed in raising one. Went to Brislington, and sang, prayed, and gave an address without door. Preached within, and, after preaching, explained the nature of our church-fellowship, and invited any who desired to join to offer themselves as members. In addition to two who meet in Bristol, five gave their names. Some others appeared to linger on the question, but I did not press them. I proposed to form a Tract Society, and some offered to become Distributors. May the Lord favour this beginning, and take all the glory and praise; for to Him alone is all due!"

The extent of Mr. Wood's labours on the Lord's day, even now that his strength had begun to decline, and he often felt depressing languor, may well fill us with astonishment. It must, we think, be admitted, that he frequently went beyond the limits which Christian prudence would have marked out; and that it would have been better for him not to have crowded so many services into the day of sacred rest. But he felt that that day afforded golden opportunities for accomplishing his Master's work; and he was anxious to improve them all. He attended, whenever he was not absolutely prevented from doing so by illness, the 7 o'clock morning prayer-meeting in the vestry of the Langton Street chapel; finding, in that means of grace, refreshment to his own soul, and seeking to keep up among his people, the spirit of united devotion. In the afternoon, during the summer, he often preached in the open air; and when he did not, he usually visited the Sunday Schools. The following extract from his Journal will show how many of his Sabbaths were spent :—

"Sunday, April 8th, 1860. (Easter Sunday.)— Prayer-meeting at 7 a.m., and had some quickening, but felt more dull than usual. In the forenoon service at Langton Street, I was favoured with power, especially towards the close. Visited the Langton Street Sabbath-School in the afternoon, to endeavour to put forward the Juvenile Missionary Association; and therefrom went to Bedminster and addressed the Sunday-School, proposing to extend the Juvenile work to them. Before going from the vestry into the chapel to give the address, I was seized with giddiness so great that, if a chair had not been at hand upon which I instantly sat, I believe I must have fallen. After the address I visited Mr. M., Jun., then his father who is suffering from gout. I also visited a sick man to whom the Lord had sent a message by His unworthy servant, while preaching on the wedding-garment. I then called on a person recently come from Cornwall, who is a member, as also his wife and children. Took tea at Mr. G.'s.—Was blessed with power in preaching in the evening, and some appeared to decide for God. Weary, but grateful and happy. Praise the Lord!"—Soon after this entry, we find him expressing the conviction, that he must forego paying pastoral visits in connection with his preaching on the Lord's day. Under the date of July 22nd, 1860, he writes, "I visited before preaching and afterwards; but felt as if I must decline this work in connection with Sunday preaching, desirable as it is to continue it, and accustomed as I have been to it since the commencement of my ministry. Yet I have a feeling of exhaustion in visiting and praying with two or three sick cases in immediate connection with Sunday preaching, without resting between the services. On week-evenings I do not suffer so much from this cause, the labour in preaching being less."

But the consciousness of exhaustion after efforts that were, in former years, comparatively easy, was not the only intimation that he had that his public efforts and pastoral toils must be abridged, and that the time was drawing near when he must glorify his Saviour chiefly by the manifestation of the passive graces of the Christian character. On Sunday, October 7th, 1860, he attended the 7 o'clock prayer-meeting, and in the forenoon preached in the Langton Street chapel. "During the giving out of the second hymn," he says, "I found that I could not read the words but by closing my right eye. On opening it, I found that there was another set of letters in a different place, so that both together involved perfect confusion, and were not only unreadable but bewildering in the extreme. It seemed a little relieved when I read my text; but I felt it to be a solemn moment, and I determined to persevere, holding the pulpit with both my hands that I might not fall, and by degrees it passed away. I felt disconcerted for a time; and I praise the Lord that it did not continue, or I must have ceased." But, after this service, he administered the Lord's Supper; then, in the afternoon, visited the Langton Street Sunday-School, and thence proceeded to Bedminster, where he visited two families, and afterwards preached and again administered the Supper of the Lord. And, as if this was not enough, he visited two afflicted families on his way home. He adds that, at the close of the day, he was "very weary, but thankful."

It was always a delight to Mr. Wood, as it must be to every earnest Minister, to be assured that some were actually led to a closure with Christ under his preaching every Lord's day. So great was his solicitude for present and visible success, that he was at times in danger of being unduly discouraged when he did not witness it. Still he did not overlook the value of those gentler operations of the Spirit which lead minds of a certain order to retire from the sanctuary to pour out their penitential sorrows to God in secret, making them willing also openly to confess Christ by an avowed union with His Church. Under the date of the next Sabbath, October 14th, 1860, he says, "I was favoured in the evening, at Langton Street, with a season of much liberty and power, and the congregation heard with fixed attention. Still, however, while some were impressed, no one came forward as a penitent. It is cheering to see present effects: but I would not 'limit the Holy One of Israel.' May the Lord work as He will; only let Him work mightily to save from eternal death!"

In the course of his second year in the Bristol South Circuit, he paid a visit to his old friends in

Exeter, and preached twice on the Lord's day, and again on Monday and Tuesday evening, besides filling up the morning and afternoon of the latter days with pastoral visitation. A few months afterwards he went to Camborne, to preach on the occasion of the re-opening of the Centenary chapel. On each of these visits he was cheered by the proofs of love which met him on every hand; and in Exeter, in particular, by numerous instances of conversion in connection with his renewed labours.

Mr. Wood attended the Newcastle Conference of 1861. His home was at Sunderland; and there is reason to believe that his brief sojourn was made a blessing to the kind family that hospitably entertained him. Immediately on his return, he had so severe an attack of giddiness as to cause great alarm to his family and friends. He had gone with Mrs. Wood to Burnham, to spend two or three week-days in quiet before entering upon the active duties of his Circuit. Writing on Thursday, August 15th, 1861, he says, "After a hearty breakfast, we set out intending to take a long walk. But we had not proceeded far on the esplanade, when I felt a giddiness come on. This I have been subject to for some months; and sometimes it has been so severe that, in walking the streets of the city, I have felt that had it proceeded a little further I could not have kept my feet. But this morning it was worse. Mrs. Wood was holding on my arm, as usual, and, perceiving that I staggered, inquired if I was giddy. Just then I was near a lamp-post; and, feeling as if I should fall, I grasped it with my arm. Immediately it seemed as if the post bent to the ground, and I fell. I had consciousness, but no sight. A man was just then passing with a tilt cart. He ran, and I felt him and my wife lifting me up to the seat, which still seemed to be falling down. In a short time, however, I gradually recovered and walked home. But, my dear wife being very much alarmed, we returned to Bristol in the evening."

Notwithstanding this severe attack, we find him meeting his class and attending the public prayer-meeting on the following day, " though," he says, " I felt it to be as much as I could well bear." He preached also, on the Lord's day, at Bedminster and Langton Street, and met a class in the afternoon. But in the course of this week a very painful affection of another kind, to which he was occasionally liable, came upon him in an aggravated form, causing extreme suffering, and rapidly reducing his strength. But though this last attack confined him to his bed, during the greater part of each day, yet his heart was intent on his work as a Christian Pastor. On the day after it came on, one of his people, not being aware of his illness, called to ask him to visit his dying son who greatly desired to see him. Mr. Wood rose from his bed, at great risk, and went in a cab to see the dying youth. " I was thankful," he says, "to visit him once more. Having prayed with him, he held fast my hand, and with eyes bright with joy he looked to his mother, and exclaimed 'I am happy *now*, mother.'"

The Sabbath came round, and Mr. Wood attempted to rise and go to the morning prayer-meeting, hoping not only to attend this, but to take his appointments to preach. But the pain returned so severely as to frustrate all his hopes. His appointments were supplied; and, in his retirement at home, he wrote, "I bow, I trust, in entire submission to my Heavenly Father's gracious disposal of me, deeply conscious that I deserve no good, but richly merit His chastening rod. To be kept from labour is more trying than physical suffering. But the good Lord knows how and where to strike, and I well know that a Father's hand afflicts, as well as sustains and preserves, and that infinite wisdom, love, and mercy will attend every stroke. O for a sanctified use of all! I feel as if I had as yet done nothing in the world for the honour of God, and the good of mankind, that will bear inspection. So little done, and that little in so poor a way, so overlaid with self, and marred by innumerable imperfections, infirmities, forgetfulness, wanderings, and perversities. It is of stupendous grace that I have not been dismissed from the vineyard many, many times, for want of more full consecration to my Master's service. O may the Lord again, and more mightily, visit me, and make the remnant of my life 'a whole burnt-offering' to Him!" On the following Wednesday, he persevered in the effort to preach at Langton Street, and afterwards met the Leaders for a short time. "It was a considerable effort," he says, "to preach, and I did it with a feeble voice, but felt much of the Divine influence, and it was blessed to my own soul." At the close of the week, he went for a few days to Banwell, hoping to gather strength for his work. On the Lord's day he gladly attended Divine worship in the chapel, and heard an esteemed Local Preacher. After the evening service, he gave an address and led a prayer-meeting. "It was a gracious season," he observes, "but I appeared to feel the effect of that small exertion. I felt it profitable to wait upon the Lord,

although it was in the way of standing aside for
more favoured servants to discharge the active duties
of the day. Praise the Lord that I have any place
among those who belong to His house, although
utterly unworthy to occupy the humblest station in
His family."

On his return to Bristol, after this very brief
period of relaxation, Mr. Wood, though still in feeble
health, resumed his work ; and on six successive
Lord's days he preached twice in his own Circuit,
besides meeting classes, and took his appointments
also on the week-days. But the indications of failing
power continued. Under the date of Sunday, October
6th, 1861, he writes, " We had a good prayer-meeting
at 7 o'clock this morning. I had felt profit in meditating on the subject of this morning's discourse, and
the leading thoughts were very familiar to my mind :
but in the course of the service some considerations
that I thought might prove most edifying were taken
from me, and every effort to recall them was unavail-
ing. I continued to speak, but not to the points I had
intended ; and I felt how easy it was for the Master
not only to give me notice to leave the vineyard, but
also to incapacitate me for labour. I felt languor in
the afternoon, but was strengthened for the evening
service and blessed in it. I administered the sacrament of the Lord's Supper after the morning and
evening preaching, and visited three sick cases. I
could not venture to attempt more, and was thankful
to be permitted to do this."

Some of his friends now interposed to urge him to
take the needful rest. The Rev. John Lomas, who
was spending a little time in Bristol, kindly offered to
preach for him on one Lord's day, on the express

condition that he would rest while he did ; and, soon after this, he was induced to avail himself of the invitation of his esteemed friend, Mrs. Budgett, of Kingswood, to stay awhile at her house with Mrs. Wood. While there, the Chairman of the District, the Rev. Samuel Romilly Hall, called on him, and affectionately begged him to desist from labour, proposing to ask from the President the services of a young man as an assistant for three months. To this proposal Mr. Wood was unwilling to accede ; but he promised to abstain from public engagements for a month. One of his silent Sabbaths was spent in bed, as he was too unwell to leave it. " I did not rise to day," he writes on November 24th, 1861 ; "but I hope it has not been an unprofitable day, although on the bed of affliction. I have been cheered with the intelligence of good being done in connection with the special services held evening after evening. How strange it seems that I cannot mix with the people of the Lord in their efforts to do good. Truly my great Master is showing me, that He can do very well without me. This, of course, I have well known and often acknowledged, but perhaps never more deeply felt than now ; and I do not recollect that the feeling of this truth was ever accompanied with such an acquiescence in the Divine will." On the following Lord's day, also, he was confined to his lodgings in Banwell, Mrs. Wood remaining with him in the morning, and her sister in the evening. "We were not without gracious influences," he says. " While musing, the glow of Divine love kindled up, and it was good to speak of the lovingkindness of the Lord. Sometimes it seems as if I shall be speedily restored, and my soul longs to declare more fully, and with more spiritual power than ever, 'the gospel of the grace of God.' But, again, after a little application, I have felt as if I was a broken vessel, incapable of active service, and only fit to be set on one side, to wait the Master's disposal. Well; be it so: only let grace be imparted to do or to suffer in such wise that God's merciful designs may be accomplished, and His great Name glorified."

Again he returned to Bristol, and resumed his work; and through the great mercy of God, he was enabled to continue it until the Conference of 1862. Indeed, he was so far restored as to be able to visit Exeter in January of that year, to undertake exciting and laborious public services, and to pay pastoral visits to many who loved him, and for whose spiritual welfare he was solicitous. On a few occasions he visited some other Circuits, to preach; but he wisely restricted his engagements of this kind. From time to time the giddiness to which he was subject returned; and he felt that he had not the same control of his thoughts, nor the same readiness of utterance, which he used to have. All things seemed to intimate, that the time had come for him to retire from the more active labours of the Methodist itinerancy, and to devote himself, in a more limited and less responsible sphere, to the advancement of the work of God. He bowed meekly to the will of his adorable Master, and at the Cornwall Conference, held in the town of Camborne, in which he was so greatly beloved, and in which his ministry had been made so useful, he took his place among the honourable band of Supernumerary Ministers. His feelings, when the arrangement was actually made by the Conference, were such as only they to whom the preaching of the Lord Jesus has been the joy of life can estimate. He was present at that Conference, and he writes on Wednesday, August 4th, "I was set down as a Supernumerary for one year. Great kindness was expressed by the President, the Rev. Charles Prest, who said he had heard me preach before he was himself a Methodist, alluded to the fact of my having been his Superintendent, and expressed his obligation for my having been at that time useful to his family. Blessed be the Lord who has deigned in any way, however humble, to use a worm! I can scarcely realize the fact of being laid aside. I have felt, up to the period of my affliction, as if just in full work, with retirement, if ever, far ahead. Sitting in the Conference Chapel, I could not but contrast my present position with that when, thirty years ago, in high health and full of zeal, I entered upon my appointment in this Circuit. But 'good is the will of the Lord,' and the will of the Lord be done! Amen." He returned to Bristol, and on two successive Sabbaths preached to his people "the unsearchable riches of Christ," devoting the afternoon of his last Lord's day to visits to the Langton Street Sunday-School, and that in Avon Street, over which he had watched with a father's solicitude and love.

CHAPTER XVI.

———∞⚬∞———

WHEN Mr. Wood became a Supernumerary, he retired, in the first instance, to Banwell, the place of his birth, and the centre of his earliest labours in the cause of Christ. Many things conspired to draw him towards the home of his childhood, although there were strong inducements, on the other hand, to settle in Bristol, or one of its suburbs.

Throughout his ministry he had maintained, in a greater or less degree, his connection with Banwell; and while the chief management of the family-property there devolved on him, he had ever cared for the interests of Methodism. Recently he had exerted himself to promote the erection of a larger and more beautiful chapel in that village. That chapel was now approaching completion; and, soon after he went to reside there, he had the happiness of taking part in the services connected with its dedication to the worship of Almighty God. The late Rev. F. A. West preached in the afternoon of October 28th, 1862, from Heb. xi. 6; and in the evening of that day a Public Meeting was held, at which Mr. West, the Ministers of the Circuit, and Mr. Wood delivered addresses. On the following Lord's day, the Rev. S.

R. Hall, the Chairman of the District, preached in the morning and evening, and Mr. Wood conducted the afternoon service, designed chiefly for the young, and especially for the children of the Sunday-School. A fortnight later he preached in the new chapel on the Lord's day evening; and under this sermon a young person from the village of Henbury, near Bristol, who was present, was powerfully convinced of sin. Under the date of Monday, November 17th, Mr. Wood writes, "In the prayer-meeting Miss ——, who was awakened under the sermon last evening, came in distress of soul, seeking the Lord. We concluded the meeting, but few, if any, left; and while praying with the penitent, the light of God's countenace arose upon her soul, and she was filled with peace. I rejoiced greatly in being permitted to gather and offer this first-fruit of conversion, so far as known, in the new chapel. Bless the Lord, O my soul!"

Many of Mr. Wood's Sabbaths were now spent in listening to the Christian message as proclaimed by others. Nothing but illness kept him from the house of God. It is interesting to read the brief and striking comments which he has made on the discourses which he heard. Occasionally he himself preached: but the tendency to giddiness, from which he habitually suffered, prevented him from undertaking many services which he was requested to conduct. Still he had the heart of a pastor and an evangelist; and, when he felt able to do so, he endeavoured to find opportunities of conveying Christ's truth to those who were "ignorant and out of the way," as well as of comforting the poor and sorrowful. Under the date of Sunday, October 26th, 1862, we find the record, "More than forty years ago I remember visiting the Banwell Poor-House, to hold religious service with the inmates. This afternoon I went in quest of some one who would open a room for that purpose. An aged man and his wife gladly heard my proposal, and took me to an adjoining room, where a widow resides in whose apartment a young man occasionally comes and reads. I went at six o'clock, but would not consent for Mrs. Wood to accompany me, that no one less might be at the chapel but myself. I expounded the case of the jailer, (Acts xvi.,) and there appeared to be a gracious feeling amongst the few, chiefly aged people, who came. Feeling I can do a little, I am not satisfied to be entirely silent on the Lord's day." How beautiful it is, to see a venerable minister of Christ, who had been accustomed, for many years, to preach to large and influential congregations, gladly availing himself, in his retirement, of an opportunity of speaking of the Christian salvation to a few poor aged people, and regarding such an exercise as a privilege and a joy!

In the closing months of the year 1862, Mr. and Mrs. Wood frequently came over from Banwell to Bristol and Kingswood, to spend a few days with their son, or with those who still loved him for his past labours. On one of these occasions he heard the Rev. James Smeeth preach at Kingswood in the forenoon and evening of the Lord's day, and himself assisted in the administration of the Lord's Supper after the latter service. "Perhaps," he says, "I never more fully rendered up all in renewed covenant to God, to be entirely and eternally His, and never more clearly apprehended my entire dependence upon the Holy One both to will and also to do of His good pleasure; so that should my life be prolonged, and my strength increased, it might be entirely for the glory of God, and I only asked for this on the condition that He would deign to control me, and cause me to choose and to do all His will, and nothing but His will, for ever. This was accompanied with great refreshment of soul, and I was therein delivered from varied, continued, and violent temptations." On the last Sabbath evening of this year he preached in the Kingswood chapel. "The Lord gave me strength for the occasion," he writes, "but I had none to spare. I commenced a prayer-meeting which was replete with gracious feeling. After a few had prayed, I handed over the conduct of the meeting to Mr.——, and returned to my home at Mrs. Budgett's."

It is pleasing to be able to record an instance of that brotherly love among Christian Ministers of different communions, which ought always to prevail: for, surely, they who hold the same fundamental truths, who live under their power, and who are savingly united to Christ Himself, should ever be ready to welcome each other, and to manifest to the world their oneness in their common Lord. The Vicar of Banwell, at the time of which we are now speaking,—the Rev. Mr. Turner,—was a man of a kind and catholic spirit, and had given a subscription towards the new Methodist chapel. Soon after Mr. Wood settled in the village, a meeting was held on behalf of the Church Missionary Society, in the National School-room, which he felt it to be a pleasure to attend. "On getting to the door," he says, "the Vicar met me, and begged me to go to the platform; and, being called upon by him to speak, I could not

resist the invitation, and for the first time addressed
an assembly of Church of England Foreign Missionary
supporters."

In the early part of the year 1863, Mr. Wood
ventured to visit Exeter and Taunton, to preach
occasional sermons. In reference to the Lord's day
services in the former city, he says, " I felt it to be as
much as I could well do to keep on my feet at the
beginning of the forenoon service at St. Sidwell's ;
but when I began to preach the sensation passed
away. My Divine Master granted a special and
sensible supply of strength, both physical and spiritual,
and vouchsafed a gracious influence. Several, during
the prayer-meeting that followed the evening service
at the Mint, professed to find salvation. I returned
to my domicile, happy and thankful to the God of all
grace, who had again so graciously visited me in this
sphere of my former labours." He preached, also,
more frequently in Banwell, and some other places
in that Circuit, on the Lord's day, besides frequently
attending a Mothers' meeting, and assisting in a
Bible-class for the youths connected with the Sunday-
School. In the month of April he undertook a
journey to London, and was refreshed by intercourse
with his friends there, though he does not appear to
have conducted any public service. Soon after this
he had a very severe attack of the giddiness to which
he was now always liable, and which usually followed
any considerable exertion. He had preached twice
in Banwell on Sunday, May 10th, and had attended
the service at the parish church in the afternoon,
partly out of respect to the Vicar; and when he
rose on Monday morning, he found that he could
scarcely stand, and must indeed have fallen to the

ground had not a chair been at hand. These
painful sensations, however, passed away, so that in
the evening of that day he was able to go with Mrs.
Wood to Bristol, to attend the session of the District
Committee on the following day. He had fondly
hoped, at times, to return, at the next Conference,
to the full work of the ministry; but that hope he
was now compelled to relinquish. After the District
Meeting closed, he came to Exeter, at the urgent
request of his friends, to spend a few weeks. He
remained about a month in this city, paying many
pastoral calls, and having social intercourse with
nearly all his old friends,—intercourse which he
always sought to turn to spiritual profit. In connection with this visit, he conducted two public religious
services. His record of Sunday, May 31st, is, "I
preached in the Mint chapel, in the forenoon, from
Ps. lxxviii. 41, 'They limited the Holy One of Israel.'
I have scarcely ever felt more on taking a service.
The tremor of the over-wrought frame continued for
a considerable time; but at length I was lifted above
this also, and felt a degree of power. On breathing
my soul to God for help, when commencing the
service, He, in condescending grace and mercy, said
to me, 'I am with thee.' It seemed like an audible
voice, communicating with the word a peculiarly
reviving power, and assuring me that I should not be
forgotten. I hesitated if I should name that which
filled my soul with grateful love; but why should
I not declare, to the praise and glory of infinite
mercy, the lovingkindness of my God and Saviour?
—I much wished to go to the Mint in the evening;
but the exertion in the morning required that I should
remain quiet, and I felt it to be a duty to avoid

another large assembly to-day. But Mrs. Wood and myself had a little service, with prayer for those who were assembled in the great congregation." On the following Sunday he undertook the evening service in the large Mission-Room in King Street. "I began to sing," he says, "in my old standing-place in 'the Quarter,' now somewhat altered, and we sang away to the new chapel in King Street, where a large number had previously collected, and I preached from Rom. iii. 22, 'There is no difference.' The presence of the great Master was felt, and some came forward to get the prayers of those who were ready to aid. I remained as long as I could, and, leaving the meeting with them about 9 o'clock, I went away rejoicing."

At the close of June, 1863, and during the early part of July, Mr. Wood visited his son at Redland, and rejoiced to be present at some of the opening services of the beautiful Victoria Chapel, Clifton, of which his son was the architect. Afterwards he went to Ilfracombe for a fortnight, hoping to derive benefit from the bracing air of that romantic watering-place; and in his walks he sought to deposit the seed of Divine truth in the hearts of some who conversed with him. Returning to Bristol, he was earnestly solicited by many of his friends to come and settle among them. Several houses, which seemed to be suitable, were looked at; but difficulties presented themselves which deferred Mr. Wood's final settlement at Redland until April of the following year. Referring to the solicitude of his friends on this subject, he says, "I am ashamed that our friends should be so pressing to have us residing amongst them. It is true that, when I had full health, I was much engaged in pastoral

duties, and could go on for hours in succession, talking
and praying from family to family. But now I am
compelled to make my calls without praying, except in
cases of sickness or trouble, or unless those friends
who knew my former manner should ask for it. So I
tell them I can no longer serve them as I once did,
and that they will be disappointed after all their
efforts to have me near them."

Throughout his ministry, Mr. Wood had ever been
ready to administer spiritual advice and consolation
by letter to his friends who were involved in affliction,
or visited with bereavement. Many such letters of
his are doubtless preserved, and, were they collected,
would form an edifying volume. One specimen,
belonging to this period of his history, must here
suffice. On his return from Ilfracombe, he received
information that one of his most attached friends in
Exeter, Mr. John C. Guest, had met with a serious
accident; and he addressed him as follows :—

"3, Exeter Buildings,
Redland, Bristol,
July 23rd, 1863.

"My Dear Sir,

I returned from Ilfracombe last evening,
and learnt, by a letter from Mrs. Guest, that you
have, through a fall, got a fractured arm; but I am
thankful to find that it is doing well. How small and
unlooked for an incident may occasion the loss of
limb or life! Let us then be ever ready for any event
of Providence, and prepared to meet our God. I
want to know that you preserve an abiding manifestation of the favour of your Heavenly Father. Do
you *now* feel, 'I am my God's, and He is mine'? and

are you pressing into the fulness of the blessing of
the gospel of peace ? O let this visitation be sanctified
to your present and eternal welfare! So shall it
become the forerunner of great and permanent blessings, and not of heavier strokes.   Every afflictive
dispensation improved will become the subject of
grateful thanksgiving, but if we neglect or rebel in
insubordination, it will be steeped in the bitterness of
a curse.   Some of the old divines used to say, ' It is a
great loss to lose an affliction', *i.e.*, to lose the benefit
it was intended to convey.   I apply to myself the
lessons which I write for you.   May we both enter
into all God's design, and find the end of all our
sorrows in the joys that are at His right hand !   How
happy are those that have left us since the brief
period that has elapsed since I was last in Exeter !
How soon may we follow !

> ' Ready winged for their flight
> To the regions of light,
> Our convoy attends,
> A ministering host of invisible friends.'

O let there be no hesitation, when they appear with
their commission !

"Mrs. Wood unites with me in kind regards to
Mrs. Guest, yourself, and family, hoping soon to hear
of your full restoration.

"I am, my dear Sir,

Yours affectionately,

JOSEPH WOOD."

"Mr. GUEST."

After his return to Banwell, towards the close of
August 1863, Mr. Wood cheerfully exerted himself, as
his strength permitted, in occasional preaching, in

visiting the sick, in addressing the Sunday-School, and in tract-distribution. If, however, he ventured to preach twice on the Lord's day, he usually felt very unwell on the following day, and, on several occasions, had an attack, more or less severe, of giddiness. On October 9th he had so painful a seizure, that he could not again attempt to preach for a whole month. But, as soon as he could, he gladly resumed the work to which his life had been devoted. He preached at Axbridge on Sunday, November 15th, and was greatly cheered by the tokens of his Master's presence and blessing. "I was sent for," he says, "in the morning, by Mr. ——, and sent home in the evening. The same man who came last time drove the conveyance, and I was glad to learn that, since that time, he has set up family prayer, and is earnestly seeking the salvation of his soul. A few times in the course of the day I felt my head getting very light, with an intimation of approaching vertigo, but through the goodness of God it passed away. In the afternoon I called on two families, but feared to visit the Sunday-School, as I was conscious I had gone as far as I could without presumption. I was aided in the morning, and had a time of much power in the evening. The Lord greatly encouraged me, and some penitents came forward seeking salvation. It seemed something like old times, and my soul was greatly cheered."

It is interesting to mark how his love for the critical study of the New Testament was maintained during his retirement. He procured, at this time, a copy of the recently-discovered Codex Sinaiticus, which he studied with great care, noting the variations in it from the received text. He derived great comfort also from reading the lives of eminent Christians, and often got Mrs. Wood to read such works to him for their mutual edification. Soon, however, he found that lengthened application to reading brought on the painful affection to which he was liable, and that he was unable to fix his attention, for any considerable time, on any subject, without injury.

He entered upon the year 1864 with a consciousness of diminished strength, and was compelled by illness to spend the first Sabbath of that year in his own house, being unable to fulfil an engagement to preach at the village of Ubley, in connection with the opening of a new chapel. On the last Sunday of January, however, we find him preaching twice in the Banwell chapel, and after the evening service conducting another for the renewal of the covenant. He gratefully acknowledges the gracious help of God vouchsafed to him in the delivery of His word, and adds, "At the close of the sermon I felt as if I could scarcely go further, but my Divine Master renewed my strength for the remainder of the service. I praise the Lord for this day, and pray that covenanted grace may be imparted to keep my vows. 'I will cause you to walk in My ways, and ye shall keep My commandments and do them.' I yield all in the strength of grace, and I look to God to work within me to will and to do. Amen, my God, Amen."

On the following Sunday he preached twice at Churchill, and at Banwell again on February 7th. Then came four silent Sabbaths, on one of which he was unable even to go to the Lord's house. He writes, on that day, "Another precious Lord's day spent in the house. Last evening I was much tired, but I felt a sweetness in the night, while breathing my soul to God, and looking for present answers. There may be many reasons why mercies intended for us are for a time delayed, but having grace patiently to submit under these circumstances is the most valuable answer we could receive. I believe for every thing promised in the covenant of grace in Christ Jesus; but for blessings of Providence, not specifically expressed, I feel it a high privilege to be enabled to ask in submission to the Divine will, perfectly assured that my Heavenly Father will bestow the blessing implored, or will give some benefit that will prove a greater good. I should gladly be engaged to-day in active duty; but the Master shows me that He can carry on His work without me; and having, for many years, put the honour upon me to use me, in some humble degree, for His praise, He now bids me learn the lesson of patient submission, and stand aside and wait. With profound abasement of soul, and imploring Divine grace that the words may be indeed the language of my heart, I would say, 'Even so, Father, for so it seemeth good in Thy sight!'"

Several of the entries in his Diary, about this time, show how he delighted in communion with God, and how his soul was refreshed by meditation on His truth. On February 23rd, 1864, he says, "Being my birthday, each of my grandsons wrote me a sweet note. I this day complete my sixty-seventh year. I am amazed at myself, when considering the bottom-less mercy and long forbearance of my God and Saviour, and my littleness of love to Him and zeal for His glory and the salvation of souls. Still, through grace Divine, I hold on in the way, having

S

no will but that the will of my Heavenly Father should be done in me, by me, and upon me, both in time and in eternity. Vain thoughts would often draw away my attention from devotion and the great things of God's law; and my cry is, that every thought of my heart may be cleansed by the mighty sanctifying operations of the pure, eternal Spirit of truth and love. Amen. Amen." On March 9th, he writes, "I felt it profitable yesterday in prayer, and during waking time this morning to meditate on the words, 'No man knoweth the Son, but the Father; neither knoweth any man the Father save the Son, and he to whomsoever the Son will reveal Him.' I felt I did, at His bidding, come to Him ; that Christ did reveal Him to me; and, in the power of the Holy One, I did claim Him as my God, reconciled to me in Christ Jesus, and my soul was filled with peace and joy in believing. I clearly saw and felt that, when God calls, it is His intention that I should come,— come then,—come direct,—that on coming, Christ stands by, as it were, to introduce to the favour and blessing of the Father all who come through Him. Strengthened by the Holy Ghost, and inclined to render up all to God without reserve, I am, by His own power and grace, enabled to claim the full salvation of the gospel, to be kept by the same power and sovereign grace."

An interesting notice occurs of the labours of Sunday, March 13th, 1864. That day was spent by him at Axbridge. A gentleman resident there sent, as usual, his man-servant with a conveyance to fetch Mr. Wood, and afterwards sent him home in the evening. To this man Mr. Wood had talked about Christ and salvation; and he now gratefully records,

" The man who drove me could now tell me that he had found salvation, and his wife also, and that they have both joined the Society as members. I was heavy and tremulous in the morning, but was refreshed by keeping quiet in the afternoon, and in the evening I was favoured with a time of liberty and power, which seemed, in a degree, to recall memories of the past. But I had to leave the prayer-meeting as soon as I commenced it, feeling it enough to do to support my weight." These appear to have been the last public services which he was privileged to conduct in a Circuit in which the zealous efforts of his youth and early manhood had been put forth, and to which he ever cherished a warm attachment.

In the beginning of April, 1864, Mr. Wood removed from Banwell to Bristol, having taken a house in Woodland Terrace, Redland. At the request of the Ministers, he at once commenced leading a class in his own house, the meetings of which were usually occasions of rich spiritual blessing ; and in the early part of the following year, at the earnest solicitation of the Rev. W. M. Punshon, he began a class of young ladies at the establishment of the late Mrs. Wansbrough. Whenever it was possible for him to do so, he attended Divine worship at the Portland Street chapel, and greatly valued these opportunities of uniting with God's people in the services of the sanctuary. Occasionally, when unable to walk so far as Portland Street, and yet well enough to leave his house, he went to the little chapel on Durdham Down, now superseded by the spacious chapel at Redland. He engaged, as far as his strength permitted, in pastoral visitation, and frequently took part in prayer-meetings. Sometimes, also, he

attended the meetings of the Committee of the Bristol
Auxiliary of the British and Foreign Bible Society,—
a Society which he had always loved; and, in one or
two instances, he went over to New Kingswood
School, to attend the meetings of the local Committee
of that Institution. His strength was now easily
exhausted, and new forms of suffering came on. At
times he had a rheumatic affection in one foot, which
was exceedingly painful; and a slight attack of
paralysis caused his right hand almost constantly to
shake. The last Lord's day on which he preached
appears to have been August 21st, 1864, when he
conducted the worship of God in the forenoon at
Westbury; and it is an interesting circumstance that
his text, on that occasion, was, "The precious blood
of Christ," his sermon on which had, in former years,
been repeatedly owned of God in the awakening and
conversion of men. His account of that service will
be read with interest:—"I awoke," he says, "question-
ing if it would be right for me to attempt to preach
at Westbury this morning, and the tremor throughout
my frame would speedily have convinced me that I
could not. But, by the gracious influence of the Holy
One, I was enabled to lay the affair on my God and
Father, who knew that my motive was to glorify
Him, and that I was willing, if He saw good, to fail.
Determining to proceed with God, or to stop with
God, I next endeavoured to get the right subject. I
had felt my mind drawn to Psalm xviii. 30, 'The
word of the Lord is tried,' but with greater sweetness
and force to 1 Peter i. 19, 'The precious blood of
Christ.' It was, however, suggested, 'Perhaps this
preference arises from the latter being a favourite
subject of mine,' and, to settle the question, I put it

to this decision, viz., 'This may be the last time of my attempting to preach, my health being so uncertain, and were I sure that it would be the last time, on what subject should I preach?' The instant reply was, on '*the precious blood of Christ.*' I took it and was greatly aided. I baptized a child, and was taken back to the Down, by the man who fetched me with his trap." After this time, he went, on several occasions, to the Sunday-School at Durdham Down, to address the children, especially urging them to present decision for Christ, and exhorting them to bring neglected children to the School. He preached, also, on a week-evening, in the little chapel at the Down, to meet a case of emergency, his text being John i. 16, "And of His fulness have all we received, and grace for grace." But now his public work was done. Still he continued his pastoral visits to many whom he knew, ever breathing the spirit of devotion, and glad to be employed in any way in working for his Master.

In the month of February, 1865, he commenced the work to which reference is made in the Preface, writing down the chief incidents of his childhood and youth, and intending to preserve out of his Diary whatever he might deem worthy of being handed down to his family. These papers evince great care, and must have cost him much labour; for the tremulous movement of his right hand had become such that, towards the close, they are scarcely legible.

Thus, in meek submission to the will of God, and cherishing habitual gratitude for the mercies which had crowned a life of earnest labour for Christ, he spent the years of feebleness and languor which preceded his entrance upon his heavenly rest. His words of love and faithfulness were, even now, often blessed to those whom he visited; and among the young ladies at the School where he conducted a class-meeting, some will be his "joy and crown of rejoicing in the day of the Lord Jesus."

About Midsummer of the year 1868, Mr. Wood was compelled to relinquish the care of his classes; and in September of that year came the last official service in which he ever engaged. It was the baptism of his little granddaughter at the Portland Street chapel. His son says of that service, "He was then very feeble, and only able to walk to and from the font with assistance; but, at the conclusion of the baptismal service, he knelt down at the communion rail, and prayed, with almost all his old vigour and earnestness, imploring the Divine blessing on the assembled congregation, and on the Church and the world at large."

With that prayer the public life of this man of God closed. Months of feebleness, overshadowed by the failure of his mental powers, followed; but, even in the wanderings of his mind, when he could not recognise his dearest relatives, he would talk of the preciousness of Jesus, and, as if engaged in his former beloved work, urge on his supposed congregation or class the present acceptance of salvation. During this time, almost to the very close of life, he himself conducted family-worship; and in his prayers there was no incoherence. In that exercise he seemed to rise above his feebleness, and to commune with God as he had been wont to do. It was with difficulty, also, that he could be persuaded to give up his pastoral work, even when the failure of his mind disqualified him for it.

At length the time of his departure came. There was a pleasing interval of perfect consciousness, and he gave utterance to the words of exulting hope, "I shall reign with HIM on His throne. Hallelujah." Soon after, he peacefully "slept through Jesus," on June 23rd, 1869, in the seventy-third year of his age.

His honoured remains were conveyed to his native village; and they repose under the shadow of yew-trees in the Banwell churchyard, in a spot which he had himself selected. They were followed to the grave by the members of his family, and by the Methodist Ministers of the Banwell Circuit; and the funeral procession included an aged man, a working mason of the village, who had known and loved him from his childhood. This man, George Wilcox, who was then in his ninety-first year, has since gone home to heaven; and it is pleasing to associate his name, in this Memoir, with that of the eminent Minister whose early piety he sought to foster.

Before closing this narrative, I gladly place on record the testimony of an esteemed relative of Mr. Wood, who, at various periods of his ministry, enjoyed intercourse with him, and who visited him frequently when his day of active service was over. The Rev. Benjamin Hellier, the Classical Tutor of the Headingley Branch of the Theological Institution, has favoured me with the following communication :—

"My acquaintance with the Rev. Joseph Wood began in 1842, when I was at school in Bristol. I remember hearing him preach at King Street chapel, in the May of that year, on the words: 'Thy will be done on earth, as it is in Heaven;' in expounding which he chiefly insisted on the possibility and duty of doing the will of God '*willingly*, *fervently*, *constantly*,' because thus it is done in heaven. After hearing this sermon, I could not help saying to myself,—'Now I know what *unction* means.' I had heard of men preaching with unction, but had not understood what it meant. Now the matter was explained. The sermon was logical in its arrangement; its language was clear and energetic; and by the principles of mental philosophy I could explain a part of the effect which it produced on my own mind; but not the whole. I felt that I was subject to a powerful influence which I could not regard as the mere result of the action of one human mind upon another. I thought then, and think still, that this influence superadded to the effect of human eloquence was the unction of the Holy Spirit, resting on the mind of the preacher, and powerfully affecting his hearers.

" From this time forward I regarded Mr. Wood with high esteem, which ever grew with increase of knowledge respecting him. I found that he was well versed in several branches of science; that he was remarkably familiar with the Hebrew Bible and Greek Testament, each of which he had read through several times, and that he had a quenchless thirst for knowledge. But I also observed that the pleasures of literary pursuits were largely sacrificed to what he regarded as the imperative claims of his pastoral work. How great was his diligence in this branch of service you well know; but I may here mention one illustration of it, in which I was personally deeply interested. During the time of his first appointment to the Bristol South Circuit, he came to preach the opening sermons of a small chapel at Yatton, near

Bristol. A dear sister of mine was present, who previously was 'not far from the kingdom of God,' but had not attained assured peace. In the interval between the afternoon and the evening service Mr. Wood engaged her in conversation; and the result was, that soon after she was able to rejoice in a sense of sins forgiven, became a Methodist, and for several years afterwards adorned her profession, until God took her home to Himself.

"Whilst Mr. Wood was a Supernumerary at Redland, I called upon him whenever I had opportunity, and felt constrained to glorify God in him. He still exerted himself to do good to the utmost limit of his strength, and his interest in every part of the work of God was as lively as ever. On the occasion of my latest visits, I found him in a truly shattered condition, which it would have been very distressing to witness, had not the soul risen superior to the body's infirmities. He told me, in answer to my inquiries, that one foot had been seriously injured,—'My hand,' he said, 'constantly trembles, and I cannot control it; my speech, as you perceive, is affected; my lapses of memory are often truly ludicrous; but all is right; I am in the Lord's hands; and I enjoy perfect peace.' Whilst he went through the list of his troubles, a pleasant smile played upon his countenance; and if he had been relating several instances of good fortune lately fallen to his lot, he could scarcely have appeared more cheerful.

"I shall ever think of Mr. Wood as one of the best specimens of an Englishman, and of a hard-working, useful Methodist Preacher that I have ever known. He had a frank, honest, generous soul. He hated all meanness and hypocrisy, and was ready to reprove and denounce sin when occasion required. But he loved all good men, and towards the afflicted, sorrowful, and penitent, he was tender and compassionate. I cannot doubt that his diligence, zeal, and usefulness in the great work of our blessed Lord entitle Joseph Wood to a place in that company which I believe to be noblest and most honourable of all, composed of those who 'turn many to righteousness.' "

Similar testimonies to the grace of God which was with this beloved and honoured Minister might easily have been accumulated. The letters of condolence which were addressed to Mrs. Wood, on the occasion of his departure, evinced the profound esteem and warm affection which his character inspired. And when his name was read in the Conference assembled in Hull in 1869, among those of Ministers who had died during the year, many of his brethren expressed, with deep emotion, their high sense of his Christian worth, and of the abundant usefulness with which it had pleased the Head of the Church to crown his labours.

CHAPTER XVII.

CONCLUDING REMARKS.

AFTER tracing the course of this eminently holy and successful Minister of Jesus Christ, it may not be improper to dwell, for awhile, on the special characteristics of his public teaching. I do not, indeed, propose him as a model for *all* preachers; for I wish devoutly to acknowledge the diversity of gifts which the Lord Jesus bestows on His different servants, for the accomplishment of the work in which He condescends to employ them. But there are *some features* of Mr. Wood's ministrations in which he was an example to us all; and just in proportion as the simplicity of purpose, and the holy earnestness, which distinguished him, are cherished by the ambassadors of Christ, and the grace of the Spirit is invoked by us in earnest prayer, may we hope for accessions to the Church of awakened and converted men.

The observations of Mr. Vasey given in the ninth chapter, and those of Mr. Hellier introduced at the close of the preceding one, afford a general view of the character of Mr. Wood's preaching, and of the impression which it was calculated to produce on a thoughtful mind. But the subject admits of further illustration.

There were some occasions, as the preceding

narrative shows, when Mr. Wood ventured to preach
on passages of Holy Scripture with very little previous
preparation: but these occasions were comparatively
rare; and he has recorded his decided conviction,
that careful study, combined with earnest prayer,
should precede every attempt, except under extraordinary circumstances, to unfold and apply the
truth of God. When he did venture to speak on a
text almost without premeditation, his intimate knowledge of the Scriptures, and of the general scheme of
truth which they unfold, derived from his constant
habit of studying them in the early morning, gave to
his addresses a pointed and earnest character, though
doubtless they were wanting in thoroughness of
exposition. But his ordinary Discourses were in a
high degree instructive as well as impressive; while
the unction of the Holy Ghost which attended them
often affected the hearts of multitudes.

It need not be said that Mr. Wood was *not* a
memoriter preacher. However frequently he might
preach from the same text, though the leading
sentiments and the plan of discourse might be the
same, the freshness and glow of his feelings led him
to clothe many of his thoughts in language which
occurred to him at the moment, and to combine with
his well-studied ideas others which rushed upon his
mind, as he surrendered himself to the constraining
power of the truth, and to his holy solicitude for the
salvation of his hearers. It will be a sad day for the
Church of God, if preachers generally should cease
to do this, and should either read carefully elaborated
discourses, or repeat verbatim sermons which they
have committed to memory. Most ministers, probably, have again and again been conscious of a

vividness of thought, and a power of utterance and appeal, given to them in the very act of preaching, the loss of which would be poorly compensated by precise accuracy and chastened beauty of style, or by the most fascinating imagery. The ambassador of Christ, entreating men, in His stead, to be reconciled to God,—the faithful pastor, unfolding the grand arrangements of the mediatorial scheme, inviting believers to the attainment of their high spiritual privileges, and urging upon them the duties of the Christian life,—may well utter glowing words, as the heart expands under the influence of the truth, and the Holy Ghost Himself imparts an unwonted power. "There are times," says the Rev. R. W. Dale, "when we are conscious of a strangely vivid and intense apprehension of the eternal and Divine. A power which is not our own takes possession of us. We cease to originate our own thoughts. We listen in silence to supernatural teaching. The people know when these visions have come to us: the words which we speak under the inspiration of the Holy Ghost move the very depths of their spiritual life." *

We have intimated that, usually, Mr. Wood did not apply himself to the deeper exposition of Holy Scripture. There are some Ministers whose minds have been specially formed for this, and who are enabled greatly to edify the Church by bringing out the profound meaning of the word of God, more especially as it bears on the economy of redemption, and the privileges and hopes of believers. We have seen that, during his ministry in Exeter, Mr. Wood expounded the Book of Psalms, on consecutive

* "The Holy Spirit in relation to the Ministry, the Worship, and the Work of the Church," p. 29.

Saturday evenings, in the smaller chapel; and that his teaching, on these occasions, was felt by many to be eminently profitable and edifying. But his preaching on the Lord's day was marked, not so much by variety and wealth of exposition, as by *the distinct and forcible presentation of great and leading truths.* It was eminently *intelligent.* It evinced a mind of clear and accurate perceptions, as well as of strong convictions. There was no mistiness about his method of declaring the truth. His language was well chosen, with no attempt at embellishment; and his utterance was fluent and distinct. In his earlier years, and perhaps during a considerable portion of his ministry, he occasionally strained his voice, as he pleaded with men, "crying aloud" and "sparing not," under the influence of his own deep emotions. But he always uttered truth,—solemn, momentous truth, and never talked wildly or incoherently.

Mr. Wood's preaching was marked by its *directness of aim.* He felt that he had to negotiate, on behalf of his Lord and Master, a great business with those whom he addressed. That business he was anxious to accomplish. He sought to produce conviction, and to lead men then and there to the Saviour. He grappled with the consciences of his hearers. He sought to take hold of them, and to bring home to them the fact of their sinfulness,—the overwhelming guilt of a course of transgression,—and the duty and blessedness of an *immediate* acceptance of the Saviour. And when he spoke to the tempted and sorrowful among Christ's people, of the abounding of His grace, his teaching went straight to the heart, and often contributed to the increase of spiritual comfort and strength.

But the great characteristic of his preaching was

its *intense earnestness,*— an earnestness prompted and
sustained by a lofty faith and an undying love to the
souls of men. This earnestness, too, was all the more
impressive, as his personal godliness, and his readiness for every service to his fellow-men, threw around
his affectionate pleadings and his faithful warnings
an inexpressible charm. His countenance was lighted
up with animation, and evinced the glow of his commingling emotions, as he pleaded with men to lead
them to Christ. Sometimes, indeed, his whole frame
seemed to speak, as he poured out his thrilling
appeals.

Above all, Joseph Wood *honoured the Holy Ghost.*
His habits of devotion doubtless contributed very
largely to his success in the pulpit. He sought in
earnest, continuous prayer, the unction of the Holy
One to attend his ministrations. He went forth
relying upon the Saviour's promise, "Lo, I am with
you alway, even unto the end of the world." He
looked for the presence of the Spirit of Christ, and
for His powerful movements on the minds of men,
whenever he stood up "to preach the word." Nor
was he disappointed. There were few, if any, occasions on which that "word" did not come with
power to some hearts, deepening the spiritual affections of believers, and guiding the penitent to the
Cross, even if careless sinners were not brought to
embrace the overtures of mercy. In this habit of
dependence upon the Holy Ghost, and firm expectation
of His presence and grace, Mr. Wood was an
example to us all who are engaged in the holy
ministry, whatever our special gifts, or our peculiar
constitution of mind.

The same directness of aim which marked the

public teaching of Mr. Wood characterised also his pastoral visits. These he ever made to bear on the spiritual welfare of the persons visited, and often addressed them pointedly respecting their state towards God. He was anxious, also, for the conversion of the children of his people. A friend of his in this city tells me, that on one of his visits to it, some years after his regular ministry in it had closed, he accompanied him in several of his pastoral calls. Mr. Wood had dined with him, and after dinner they had some conversation on geology,—a science in which, Mr. Wood stated, he had once taken a lively interest, and had indeed collected some valuable specimens, but the study of which he had given up, since all his energies were required in the direct work of Christ. Instead of sitting after dinner to enjoy the refreshment of social converse,—except, indeed, for a very short time,—Mr. Wood went forth to spend the afternoon in visits to some members of his former charge, and his friend went with him. They called at the house of an office-bearer, whose wife was at home, and received Mr. Wood with evident pleasure and gratitude. After some other kind inquiries and remarks, Mr. Wood asked, "How many children have you?" and when the number was stated, he immediately rejoined, "And how many of them are converted?" "None." "O, then," said Mr. Wood, "we must have recourse to prayer!" And he knelt down, and poured out a prayer of fervent intercession for the conversion of that family, which was accompanied with a powerful and melting influence. That visit was never forgotten; and that prayer has been answered from on high. Several of the younger members of that family are now devoted to God, and stand as witnesses of the Saviour's grace.

I will not, however, protract these notices of my honoured friend ; nor will I attempt in this place, formally to delineate his character. It is not necessary. They who have now followed his course, as well as they who knew and loved him when on earth, will be impressed with his Christian excellencies. But, as I close this work, I am affected with the thought of the *moral beauty* of such a life, and its *lasting power for good*. JOSEPH WOOD did not live in vain. Hundreds of his spiritual children rise up, to acknowledge that, through his instrumentality, the life-giving Spirit led them to the Lord Jesus, and created them anew in Him. But all the beauty and all the power of his life were derived from the grace of our Saviour Christ. It was that grace which restrained him from sin, and gave to his youth and manhood purity and nobleness. It was that grace which kindled in his soul spiritual affections, filling him with holy delight in God, an earnest longing after perfect conformity to His will, and an intense desire to save his fellow-men. It was that grace which sustained him amidst the cares, the temptations, and the sorrows, of his varied course, and which upheld him in his arduous and unceasing efforts to extend the Redeemer's kingdom. And in nothing was that grace more beautifully exemplified than in the meekness and resignation with which he bowed to the stroke which changed his life of activity to one of weakness and suffering, and in the unabated attachment to the ordinances of God's house and the fellowship of believers, which he evinced when his opportunities of public service in the Church were past. In the

T

strength of that inward life which he derived from Christ, and which was sustained by habitual fellowship with Him and with the Father, through the power of the Holy Ghost, he glorified his covenant-God in suffering, as well as in the toils of an active ministry. His bright example may well encourage us who are left to seek the richest supply of the Spirit of Jesus Christ, that, treading in the steps of his "faith and patience," we, too, may, at last, "inherit the promises." And while we are affected by the removal of one who toiled so zealously and faithfully for the souls of men, we are cheered by the assurance, that He who was the Source of all his purity, and zeal, and love, and power, still lives, the Head of His Church, and the Sovereign of all worlds. To HIM we look with confidence, to raise up a succession of devoted, holy, earnest Ministers. The Churches are called upon to remember with affection and gratitude those who led them onward in the path of truth and righteousness, and watched over them with tender affection and thoughtful fidelity; but the sorrow which their departure inspires is chastened by the thought, that "JESUS CHRIST IS THE SAME YESTERDAY, TO-DAY, AND FOR EVER."

HAYMAN BROTHERS AND LILLY, 19, CROSS-ST., HATTON-GARDEN, E.C.

www.ingramcontent.com/pod-product-compliance
Lightning Source LLC
Chambersburg PA
CBHW021043030726
47496CB00006B/1663